Descendants of Light

DESCENDANTS OF LIGHT SERIES, BOOK 1

Susan Alford Ashcraft
Lesley Alford Smith
Candy Alford Barnett

TRILOGY CHRISTIAN PUBLISHERS

Tustin, CA

Trilogy Christian Publishers
A Wholly Owned Subsidiary of Trinity Broadcasting Network
2442 Michelle Drive
Tustin, CA 92780

Descendants of Light

Cover design by: Candy Alford Barnett

Illustrated by: Candy Alford Barnett

Manufactured in the United States of America

10 9 8 7 6 5 4 3 2 1

Library of Congress Cataloging-in-Publication Data is available.

ISBN: 979-8-89041-003-0

E-ISBN: 979-8-89041-004-7 (ebook)

Dedication

For our grandparents, Homer and Pearl, who entertained angels unaware.

And the light shines in the darkness; and the darkness has not overcome it.

—John 1:5 (ESV)

From within or from behind, a light shines through us upon things, and makes us aware that we are nothing, but the light is all.

—Ralph Waldo Emerson

Contents

Chapter 1

Rocky Mountains, Colorado

The heavy snow blew across Lucas's face. It was cold, but he didn't mind. Even though his ten-year-old twin sister, Lily, was light on her feet, he passed her easily. Up ahead, his father turned down a path that led deeper into the forest. The twins followed and reached the small clearing, breathless from their run.

"Your old man has still got it! Beat ya fair and square!"

Elijah Quinn's wide mouth split into a smile.

His father's thick brown hair, dusted with falling snow, looked almost grey. His clear green eyes, a perfect match to his own, twinkled.

"But I beat Lily!" he shot back proudly.

"Betcha I can make a snow angel faster than you," Lily boasted.

Never one to back down from a challenge, he plopped down beside his sister and furiously waved his wiry arms and legs in the snow. He didn't like to lose. When he hopped up, he pointed proudly to his snow art and exclaimed, "I won!"

"It doesn't even look like an angel," Lily retorted. "It's just a big mess! Mine is perfect."

"I think that's enough snow time for today. I don't know about you two, but I'm starving," Eli interrupted. "Wanna head back for breakfast?"

"Yes!" the twins answered together.

"I hope Mom's making pancakes," Lily said, grabbing Eli's hand and pulling him toward the path.

"Hang on, little lady," Eli laughed and then called back over his shoulder. "Come on, Lucas! It's freezing out here."

His father was right. It was very cold, so much, in fact, he felt like his body was freezing in place. Something was wrong with him.

It was very strange.

"Lucas!" his father urged.

Lucas willed himself to move, but no matter how hard he tried, his body remained unmovable. He tried to open his mouth to call out, but his lips felt like they were superglued shut.

"Stop playing around, Luc," Lily said, walking back over to him.

When Lily pulled on his arm, his body didn't respond. His boot-covered feet were cemented to the snow. His heart started racing, and his vision turned blurry. Why couldn't he move?

Eli knelt in the snow in front of him and rubbed his motionless arms and legs.

"Son, what's wrong? Talk to me."

He could hear the desperation in his father's voice.

When a soul-shattering scream rent the air, Lucas felt as if the oxygen had been sucked from his lungs and his heart clamped tightly in a vise. His father and sister didn't react to the scream. Why did they not hear it? He needed to tell them. Focusing all his energy, Lucas tried to open his mouth, but no matter how hard he concentrated, his lips remained shut.

Suddenly, his whole world turned upside down. His hearing was so keen that the falling snow sounded like the beating of a snare drum. His mouth became dry. His throat and nostrils burned like fire as he breathed in the most foul and indescribable scent. Everything hurt but his eyes. They were wide-open, his vision acutely clear. The shadows in the forest around him took shape and became unearthly silver lights that wove gracefully through the trees.

"Turn around, Dad, please," his mind pleaded. "Can't you see the lights?"

His father and sister were oblivious to it all as they tried to wake him from his frozen stupor. When the haunting illuminations emerged from the forest, they took shape. Lucas had never been more frightened in his life.

The extraordinary, winged creatures were beautiful and faultless in their appearance. Clothed in incandescent garments, the commanding figures pulsed with a silvery white light. Each wore a breastplate of gleaming silver. Thick colorless hair flowed down their backs. Some wore lustrous diamond masks, while others displayed their stunningly perfect countenances. Their massive leather-like wings were translucent, with crimson blood pulsing through them. All had the same icy blue eyes.

Accompanying the beautiful creatures were great black beasts, their thick muscled bodies covered with short rough fur. The otherworldly animals growled and gnashed their razor-sharp teeth, barely restrained by their masters' hold on their resplendent silver collars. The creatures paused their advance and surrounded him and them in the clearing.

One of the terrifying creatures separated himself from the others. Lucas figured he was the leader of the horde because he was bigger and dressed differently than the rest. He was clad in black from head to foot. The creature's wings dragged the snow as he advanced toward them. His long-hooded cloak billowed behind him. An ornate ring of obsidian black was affixed to the man's middle finger on his right hand. As the creature drew close, Lucas gagged on the smell of death that swirled around the hooded figure. He wanted to vomit when a calculating smile spread across the formidable figure's full pale lips.

"Elijah, old friend," the hooded man called. "Let us greet one another."

His father whipped around, then finally aware of the danger that now surrounded them. He pushed a wide-eyed Lily behind him and took a defensive stance in front of his children.

With lightning force, the beautiful creature delivered a backhanded slap, sending his father to his knees. Lucas felt the ferocity of the blow as if he had been hit as well. He willed his father to get up. When he stood slowly and squared his shoulders, Lucas saw the bright red blood trickling from his father's mouth.

"You were never my friend, Cain!" Eli gritted out.

"Hmm, you disappoint me. And here I thought you might be happy to see me again," Cain laughed sarcastically.

"What do you want? My time is past."

"True, you no longer serve any purpose," Cain answered with a meaningful glance. "But your children, well, that's another matter entirely."

"If you try to touch them, I will kill you."

"Tsk, tsk, Elijah, you know as well as I do that if I want them, I shall have them."

"Your soul is as black as the pit you climbed up from," Eli swore. "I don't fear you."

"I would be sorely disappointed if you did," Cain smiled. "I'm not so sure, however, about your children! Look at the poor souls, Elijah. I believe they are much afraid."

Elijah jutted out his chin, and in a steely voice Lucas had never heard before, his father challenged the creature.

"You will not take my children."

"Hmm, have you ever heard the whimpers of a child when his bones are broken, one by one? Or when her flesh is gnawed and torn from her pathetic form? Children are very fragile, Eli, so easy to break. When they beg for the pain to stop, you will fear me then. Won't you?"

A roar ripped from Eli's chest, and he lunged. He landed heavily in the snow. His target had been too quick, disappearing and then materializing a short distance away. Lucas watched as the creature's smile was slowly replaced with a chilling look of hatred. In the blink of an eye, silver lights exploded all around them, and the bright figures that had been waiting along the tree line now encircled his father. Their unearthly blue eyes were icy flames. His ears burned with the hideous chant coming from the beautiful ones. Their words were beyond understanding, but Lucas knew it couldn't be good.

No longer restrained, the growling black beasts circled the twins. Separated from their father, Lily moved closer to him and took his frozen hand in hers. He knew his sister was scared to death. But he was powerless to protect her, still locked in his sensory prison. Across the clearing. Eli was still, his head bowed and eyes closed. The creatures shrieked; the palms of their long-fingered hands burned with cold blue flames.

"Daddy, please get up," Lily whispered.

With all his might, Lucas willed his father to obey his sister's plea. They had to escape. When Eli turned, he met his father's eyes across the clearing. Instead of fear, he found only confidence and resolve in his father's gaze. Lucas was shocked to the core by what happened next.

Eli scooped up a large amount of snow. His father's hands moved rapidly with a carpenter's precision to craft the icy powder into what he could only call a shield. When the beautiful ones flung their first fiery blue darts from the palms of their hands, Eli moved to a crouching position and deflected each one. Then, he leaped to his feet and ran toward his children, using the shield to bash the black beasts that stood in his way.

Lucas cringed inside when one of the beautiful ones pounced on Eli's back. A glittering diamond faceplate covered her face; her long-braided hair hung down her back. She wasn't like the others. She looked almost human. But her slight wingless form belied her incredible strength. She hoisted Eli into the air and flung him with great force across the clearing into a tree. She hissed in delight.

"Finish him," Cain ordered.

Helpless, Lucas watched the woman stalk toward Eli. Blood flowed freely from a wide gash across his father's forehead.

One of his arms now lay at an odd angle against his bruised body. His other arm twitched in the snow. Lowering herself into a crouch beside Eli, the woman placed her fiery hand over his heart.

"Your children will watch you die!" she jeered.

Before the blue pulse coming from her powerful hand could penetrate his chest. Eli drove a snow sword deeply into the creature's shoulder. Lying in the snow, he must have fashioned the weapon while the woman was approaching him. Shocked and momentarily thwarted, she fell back. Eli stood and brandished the sword. The beautiful ones writhed in anger.

A warm glowing light burst through the snow clouds above. The ground trembled like an earthquake, and a golden man with glittering wings embedded with deep grey eyes landed next to Eli, surrounding him in a rich, warm light. Lucas struggled to believe what he was seeing. This was no man; it was an angel.

The hideous beasts were paralyzed, whimpering like dogs. Their masters hissed in frustration at the arrival of the man from the sky. Lucas watched as the golden man whispered something in Eli's ear and then was gone as quickly as he had appeared. The warm glowing light that had enveloped Eli slowly faded away. Even from a distance, Lucas could see the whisper of a smile on his father's face.

Her shoulder bleeding from Eli's sword thrust, the woman pounced once again on his father's back, knocking him down. She grabbed Eli's hair and jerked his head from the snow, exposing his neck. Flaming blue darts sizzled through her hands. Eli's body shook violently. The air crackled with electricity.

Then, she released him to the frenzied attack of the scavenger beasts.

Suddenly, Lucas was free from his sensory prison. He reached for Lily, but she was already running toward Eli. He watched in horror as one of the beautiful ones astride one of the hideous beasts swept her up. Lucas started after his sister, but a strong, clear voice checked him.

"Not that way, Lucas; you must run."

He hesitated and looked around. Who was speaking to him?

The voice returned, "Run, Lucas."

"I can't leave them," he shouted, trying to find his sister in the melee.

"Trust me," the voice commanded. "Move your feet."

Instinctively, he ran, moving his feet as fast as they would carry him away from the clearing.

"Faster, boy," the voice urged.

Gasping for air, he pumped his wiry legs and arms. He stumbled over a tree root and fell hard. He struggled to his feet and sprinted through the forest with a speed only fear could induce. They were gaining. He could hear them, smell them. His legs felt so heavy. He could barely see through the hot tears streaming down his face. Still, he pressed on. Silver lights shot through the trees on either side of him. Ahead, two of the beautiful ones waited with triumphant smiles. He skidded to a halt. He was trapped. It was no use. There was nowhere else to run.

Not knowing what else to do, he screamed into the frigid wind, hoping the voice would somehow hear his, "Help me!"

The fear and desperation gripping his heart disappeared instantly when the golden angel swooped from the sky and picked him up, enveloping him in his glittering wings. They shot through the air like a rocket. Soaring above the death below, he stared in wonder at the myriad of sparkling colors shimmering all around his rescuer. The eyes embedded in the man's majestic wings gazed back at him. He felt as if they were looking straight into his soul, willing him to be calm.

When his protector set him down in the snow, Lucas was surprised to see that he was home in his backyard. Smoke curled from the chimney into the blue sky. His father's work boots sat at the door. A freshly fallen snow crunched under his feet. And he was alone. The golden angel was no longer there.

Lucas shook his head. Maybe it had all been a nightmare? Maybe he would run into the kitchen and find Eli drinking his morning cup of coffee? He would just close his eyes, and when he opened them again, it would be like nothing had ever happened.

"You are safe now, Lucas. Go inside."

Obeying the voice, he stumbled across the short distance of the yard and flung open the back door. His mother, Mia, was at the stove, flipping pancakes. When she saw him, her spatula clattered to the floor.

"Luc, what's wrong? Where's your father? Lily?"

He grabbed his pounding head, remembering, "The screams, they were chasing me."

"Who was chasing you, Luc?"

"I ran away," he whispered, brokenly collapsing on the floor. "I left them both."

"Take a breath, Son," Mia urged. "Tell me what happened, slowly."

"She killed him. I think she killed them both."

"Who, Lucas?" Mia said, fear lacing his mother's soft voice.

At a dead run, his eight-year-old little sister, Zoe, slid on sock-covered feet into the kitchen.

"Mom, what's wrong?" Zoe asked.

"Call the park ranger, tell them it's an emergency. They need to come now." Mia said quickly.

Zoe grabbed her mother's cell off the kitchen counter and did as she was told.

"I've gotta go back out there, Mom," he insisted urgently. "I have to find them."

"No one is going anywhere, not until the rangers get here to help us. The snow is really coming down now," Mia said, peering out the kitchen window. "It's too dangerous."

Lucas wasn't about to disobey his mother, but his heart felt like it was going to explode. He looked at the kitchen, hoping his father and sister would walk in. Surely, the angel went back to rescue them.

"Zoe, help me get your brother to the den," Mia asked.

They helped him into the den, and he sat in his father's worn leather chair. Zoe crawled up beside him and put her small hand in his.

"Where's Papa and Lily?" Zoe asked quietly.

Before he could answer, a sharp rap sounded at the door. Mia flung it open and shouted with relief.

"Lily!"

Standing on the front porch, a park ranger held a very dazed Lily in his arms. An egg-sized knot marred her forehead, and dried blood smeared her face.

"Come in quickly; just lay her on the couch, please," Mia beckoned.

"Of course, ma'am," the ranger answered, depositing Lily on the overstuffed plaid couch.

Fear etching his mother's soft face, Mia sat by her daughter and stroked her hair. "You're safe, now, little one."

Lily just stared into the distance, not saying a word. Lucas could only imagine the horror his sister had witnessed after he had run from the clearing.

"Mrs. Quinn, I found your daughter unconscious not far from here in the clearing off the Silverdoe Trail. I put her in my truck straightaway. On the way, she woke up. She doesn't remember anything. When I received your emergency call from dispatch, I figured it might have to do with the little girl, so here we are."

Mia nodded in thanks and then asked the one question Lucas had been dreading. "My husband?" Mia asked.

The ranger took off his hat and squeezed it between his large hands. "Yes, ma'am, your husband was with your little girl. I tried everything I could, Mrs. Quinn. But he was already gone."

Mia hung her head; her body racked with silent sobs. Zoe hid her face in his shoulder and whimpered. Lucas didn't want to believe what he was hearing.

"You're wrong. My dad just needs a doctor," he declared, jumping up from the chair. "I'm gonna get him, Mom, and bring him back home. You'll see, Dad is gonna be just fine—he's just cold, that's all."

When he tried to get to the door, the ranger stood in his way.

"Son, I can't let you do that. There's at least one angry bear out there, maybe more. I found tracks all over the clearing. It's not safe. I'm sorry, Son, but your father is gone."

"Bears don't come down the mountain this far, not this time of year," he argued with confusion.

"It is unusual, but it can happen," the ranger answered. "Mrs. Quinn, the EMTs have your husband, and they are transporting him to the hospital as we speak."

Lucas turned toward his grief-stricken mother and two sisters. Mia sat silently, tears streaming down her cheeks. Zoe had curled into a fetal position and buried her face in Eli's chair. And Lily just stared at him, betrayal burning in her eyes.

He deserved it. When his family had needed him most, he had just run away. It was his fault that his father was dead. He went to the bay window and stared at the darkening sky. His whole life, all that had made him feel safe and secure, had been ripped from him in an instant. Nothing made sense about today—nothing at all. He wasn't sure what to do in this new world he now found himself in—a world without his father. Eli would expect him to lead and take care of his family. But how could he? He was a coward.

"Let me take you and the children into town, Mrs. Quinn, to the hospital. Your daughter needs a doctor, and you'll want to see your husband," the ranger urged.

When his mother answered, she echoed Lucas' own dark thoughts. "Yes, you're right. I don't believe we are safe here anymore."

The pleasure was almost more than she could bear. Beautiful desire pulsed through her. Even now, she could feel her prey, the muscled strength of his body under hers, the moment he had breathed his last breath. And yet, her lust was not satisfied.

She supposed it never would be. It had only deepened, filling the darkest corners of her sadistic mind. It wasn't the power wrought from the killing itself but the insatiable thrill of the chase. Today, she had been awakened from a profound slumber. He was her first. The beginning.

Chapter 2

Cleveland, Tennessee
Present day

Lucas turned on the blinker of the battered white SUV and veered off the highway toward their destination. All night, mile after mile, from Florida to Tennessee, he had prayed for their safety. Their previous home had become too dangerous for the Quinn family. They all did sooner or later. He wasn't surprised any longer. It was just another place to add to the growing list of his family's failed attempts to put down roots. They had lived in five different states in the last seven years, struggling to adjust with each new place. When they fled Colorado that fateful day, he was ten years old. Now at seventeen, he wondered if he and his family would ever find a place they could call home. Would he ever close his eyes at night and know peace?

After his father died, he had retreated into his music. Alone, deep in his dark thoughts, playing his guitar was the only thing that soothed the ache in his soul. He missed Eli. He knew his twin sister did as well, but she had chosen to cope with her grief in a different way. He spared a glance for Lily in the passenger seat beside him.

She was zoned out. Her honey-blonde hair hung in long waves past her shoulders. Her sketchbook, which was never far from her, lay open on her lap. Her eyes were closed, and her face was a blank space. He was thankful. Whenever Lily turned her dark blue eyes on him, all he could see was resentment and anger. He missed his best friend. Even though she had no memory of the awful events in the clearing, he knew that day in the snow had forever changed his sister. Gone was the energetic, happy girl he had known—in her place was a rebellious and distant young woman.

Emotions were a two-edged sword, bringing great joy but also immeasurable pain. He knew his sister wanted neither—not any longer. It seemed that apathy had become her mood of choice. She had withdrawn from all of them, especially him. He struggled knowing that he would never be forgiven for leaving her behind when she had needed him most.

She was lost to her thoughts; Lily's left leg hadn't stopped its on-and-off rhythmic bouncing for the entire drive. She was petite, but her movements were strong enough to make him feel like the car was shaking. He reached over and placed his hand on her knee as he had often done during their childhood to still her leg. Lily jerked away from his touch. It broke his heart.

His mother, Mia, was quiet as well, staring out the window in the back seat. He had grown to deeply respect his mother. She was stronger than he had ever imagined. But living on the run was taking its toll. Plagued with fear and worry, his mother's beautiful face was too often pale and drawn. Only he and Mia knew the truth about the danger that always followed them. He hoped that moving to live with his mom's sister, Audrey, would bring his mother a safety she had not known since Eli died. Maybe, just maybe, his family could put the roots down here in Tennessee that had been torn from the icy ground of Colorado.

"Looks like we made it," he announced to no one in particular.

"I can't wait to see Aunt Audrey. I bet she won't even recognize me," Zoe responded.

His fourteen-year-old sister grinned at him in the rearview mirror. Always quick to smile, Zoe was tall, lanky even, with thick dark hair, caramel skin, and a spattering of dark freckles sprinkled across her nose. Her hazel eyes didn't miss a thing. To be so young, she was effortlessly comfortable in her own skin. On a visit to India, his parents had fallen in love with Zoe. Just a baby, with both parents deceased and no other living relative, Zoe had been placed in an orphanage. That's where Eli and Mia had found her. And the rest was history!

No matter the situation, he could always count on Zoe's positivity. The glass was always half full for her. Instead of withdrawing from the tension, his sister just dived into it. He often thought Zoe would truly wither and die if she ever lost her ability to talk. For their entire road trip, to buoy his mood, she had entertained him, singing every song that played on the radio, dishing up the latest Hollywood gossip, and discussing all the latest activities and places she had added to her bucket list.

"Got those directions, Zoe?" he asked brightly.

"Of course!" she replied, pulling out her phone to review the text Audrey had sent with directions to her house. "Turn left up here and go straight through downtown."

Small businesses and shops lined both sides of the quaint street. The summer sun was beaming in the clear blue sky.

Brightly colored flowers were blooming in big planters all along the way. Stopping at a traffic light, he watched the people, smiling and laughing, strolling down the sidewalks, and coming in and out of shops and restaurants. When they passed the ornate gates and grounds of Centenary Academy, the city's private high school, Mia sat up closer to the window.

She whispered, "I'm finally home."

"Wow, it's beautiful," Zoe commented. "How long has it been here?"

"Over two hundred years," Mia answered. "When it first opened, it was a school for girls. Fifty years later, Centenary accepted its first class of male students."

"Really?" Zoe remarked. "Now that's cool," Zoe returned.

Driving down the street that soon became shaded on both sides by majestic oak and magnolia trees, "We're going to be happy here, Mom," he promised.

"I think so, Luc," Mia answered with a smile. "I truly do."

"These houses are enormous," Zoe observed. "And absolutely gorgeous!"

Stately historic homes lined the quiet street. Passing each expertly crafted home, he knew they all had a unique story. His father had instilled in him from an early age an appreciation for building and crafting. He knew that Eli would have loved these old houses.

He sighed, "Yeah, they are."

"This is it, Lucas," Mia pointed.

The large three-story grey Victorian house sat on a cozy corner lot. A gingerbread house with its intricate lattice trim, green slate roof, round turreted second-story window, and wrap-around porch. Ceiling fans were spinning, lush green ferns were hanging, and white wicker furniture with bright yellow cushions looked inviting. A beautiful stained-glass window topped the front door. Everything about Audrey's house invited you in. His aunt had bought the house as a fixer-upper after her divorce. He could tell she had poured all her creative energy into it because it was truly amazing.

As soon as he parked the car, the door opened, and a woman ran across the lawn to greet them. It had been two years since he had seen his aunt, but she hadn't changed at all. Her chestnut hair was shorter than he remembered, but there was no mistaking those dancing green eyes and her merry laugh. She taught English Literature at Centenary Academy. Her students loved her for her wit and intellect. She had a way of making the words on the page of a poem or novel come to life. His aunt was passionate about life, and it showed in her every word and action.

"I thought y'all would never get here," Audrey McCant exclaimed in her thick East Tennessee accent.

Mia was the first to exit the car and ran to hug her sister. He knew that Audrey had been the constant in his mother's life before she had married Eli. He hoped that she would fill that gap once again.

"When are you going to learn? You can't put me on a schedule like I'm one of your students," Mia laughed.

"Probably never. But I don't give up easily," Audrey replied and then looked at him. "Lucas, come on over here and let me see you."

He unfolded his athletic frame from the driver's seat in one fluid movement and wrapped his arms around his aunt's petite frame.

"Hello, gorgeous," he drawled, trying to match her southern accent.

"Hello, yourself," Audrey laughed. "You haven't changed a smidge, young man. Still a charmer!"

She stepped back from him and looked at him up and down. "And that thick brown hair and those big green eyes, a killer combination. I bet all the girls are crazy for you."

"None of them are as pretty as you, Aunt Audrey," he grinned.

"Oh my, I can see your daddy all over you. Your smile lights up a room just like his did."

"Yeah, but I'm still your favorite," Zoe planted a kiss on Audrey's cheek.

"Zoe, my little miss, all grown up! And who is this beastie?"

The white German shepherd nuzzled Audrey's hand.

"This is Jack. He followed me home one day from school, and we've been inseparable ever since."

"Well, it's nice to meet you, Jack," Audrey replied, bending down and giving the shepherd a quick hug. She looked up then and remarked, "It's been too long, my precious family."

"I know, it has, but we are here now," Mia squeezed her sister's hand.

For the first time in a very long time, he felt the tight grip on his heart loosen. Maybe the nightmare would finally end for all of them, especially Lily. She was standing to the side, headphones dangling from her ears, looking as if she couldn't care less about seeing her aunt or her new home. He could feel her internal wrestling, despite the lack of emotion on her face. He had always believed it was just a twin thing, a connection of sorts. But over the last few years, he realized his ability to sense what was unseen was more powerful than he had imagined.

"Lily, gonna say hello?" he asked.

Lily frowned slightly at him and turned her attention toward her aunt. "Hi, Aunt Audrey."

"Hey, sweet girl," Audrey smiled and put her arm around her niece for a quick hug. "I can't wait for you to see your room, Lily."

"I'm sure it will be great," Lily replied noncommittedly.

Mia suggested, quickly hooking her arm in her sister's, "Why don't y'all unpack the car? My big sister is gonna show me around the place."

He and Zoe started unloading the sum of their lives from the back of the SUV. Lily just stood gazing at the house, making no attempt to help. After Zoe carried the first box into the house, Lucas cleared his throat.

"You just gonna stand there all day and stare at a hole in the house? How about some help?"

Lily turned to him and said, "This is the last time, Luc."

"I know you're tired, Lily. We all are. But I believe Cleveland is gonna stick."

"That's exactly what you said about every other place we've tried!"

"We can make this work. You just gotta give it a chance."

"You and I both know it's only a matter of time until Mom gets freaked out over something silly, and then all bets are off. We'll pack our bags in the middle of the night, leave our friends, and run away, just like always. I'm done moving from place to place on her paranoid whim."

"You don't mean that. You have no idea what Mom has sacrificed for us. If you did, you wouldn't be so selfish."

"Selfish? That's rich, coming from you."

"Lily, I know..."

"It doesn't matter," she interrupted. "As soon as I can, I'm going to live my own life somewhere far away from her—and you."

"Fine. Stay angry," he said shortly. "Shut out the people who love you. Leave us if you want. But you are fooling yourself if you think you will ever be happy if you do."

He picked up two big suitcases and stalked angrily into the house. He was beginning to think his sister really was lost to him.

Chapter 3

Lily refused to believe that her brother might be right. For as long as she could remember, she had felt it. At first, it had been a raw, burning anger. After only a few months, her anger had turned into a deep-seated resentment that was limitless and raw. Her father was dead. Her mother was crazy with fear and paranoia. And her brother, well, he was a liar, insisting Eli had been killed, not by a bear, but by a supernatural monster who leaped off the pages of a fantasy book. Worse than that, Lucas was a coward. He had betrayed both her and their father, leaving them behind to save himself. She would never forgive him for that.

She couldn't trust either of them, not anymore. She had made a vow to herself, not long after they had fled Colorado, that she would never allow herself to care deeply for anyone again, especially her family. Caring meant pain; it meant loss. She knew that she would break, lose herself, if anyone was taken from her again. She bid her time, counting the days until she could walk away from the family who loved her but who could also destroy her if she loved them in return.

She needed to run—to clear her mind. She bent down to pick up a bag, and when she straightened up, she was surprised to meet a pair of coffee-brown eyes staring at her from behind a pair of horn-rimmed glasses.

"I'm sorry. I didn't mean to scare you."

She studied the young man in front of her. He was bigger than Lucas, but his baggy jeans and ill-fitting T-shirt swallowed his wiry frame. He had a nice face but nothing out of the ordinary. He pushed his glasses up the bridge of his nose and offered her a shy smile. It was a nervous gesture that Lily immediately found to be endearing. She returned his smile.

"No worries, you just startled me. I'm Lily Quinn. And you are?"

"Jude Butler. I live next door. I guess that makes us neighbors."

Jude gestured toward the craftsman-style house to the right of Audrey's Victorian and then continued, "Dr. McCant told me you would be moving in today. My dad teaches with her at Centenary."

"Nice to meet you, Jude Butler."

She was surprised by the friendly ease of their exchange. She never felt comfortable around people, especially strangers.

"Would you like some help with your stuff?" Jude asked politely.

"Sure, that would be great."

When Jude hefted a large box from the trunk of the car, her running shoes fell to the ground.

"You like to run?"

She bent to pick up her shoes. "I love it! Can't get enough, it seems. I ran a half-marathon earlier this year. What about you?"

"Nah, never a real race, but I do it to clear my head from time to time."

"Me too; the world just slips away, you know?"

"Well, if you're up to it, we could go for a run in the morning. But, if you have something else to do, I totally understand..."

"Tomorrow morning would be perfect. Come on in and meet my crazy family."

When she and Jude entered the house, they passed Mia, who was propping open the front door for easy entry and exit.

"Mom, this is Jude Butler. He lives next door."

"It's nice to meet you, Mrs. Quinn," Jude announced, offering his hand to Mia for a quick handshake.

She grinned when she noticed Jude's glasses fogging up. The coolness of the interior of the house was in stark contrast to the hot June day outside.

"Nice to meet you too, Jude. Thanks so much for helping us move in."

"No problem—I'm glad to do it."

"Which room, Aunt Audrey?" she asked as her aunt walked through the foyer carrying a vase of fresh-cut flowers.

"First one on the right, top of the stairs," Audrey answered over her shoulder. "I see you've met our neighbor. Hey, Jude."

"Hey, Dr. McCant." Jude waved, balancing the heavy box in one hand.

"Follow me," she gestured to her new friend. "And be careful not to drop that box; I've got some breakables in there."

"Sure thing," Jude responded.

She climbed the stairs with Jude following close behind. When Jack bounded down the stairs chasing a tennis ball, Jude tripped and teetered but managed to keep the box and all its contents safe. Regaining his balance, Jude turned and then bumped into Lucas, who was on his way down to get another load.

"Sorry, my bad," Jude said sheepishly.

"Don't worry about it, man," Lucas waved his hand, continuing down the stairs and out the door.

"My twin brother, Lucas. Don't mind him," she offered before walking into the room that was to be hers.

"Where do you want this stuff?"

She pointed to the far side of the room without answering him. She was soaking it all in. The afternoon sun streamed through the double window casting the room in a golden light. The blue walls were the color of the ocean waves and sky in any season. The old-fashioned tongue and groove floor was worn but beautiful. The dark walnut hue reminded her of the floor in her childhood home. An antique brass bed with a fluffy white down comforter, mahogany dresser, and desk completed the space. It was perfect. She reminded herself to thank Audrey for putting so much effort into making her feel welcome.

"It's perfect," she sighed. "When I was a little girl, my dad painted my room this very shade of blue."

"Lily, who's your new friend?"

She turned around to see Zoe leaning against the doorframe with her canine shadow, Jack, by her side.

"Zoe, this is Jude Butler, our neighbor. Zoe is my little sister."

"Not so little," Zoe laughed.

When Jack sniffed suspiciously around Jude, Zoe laughed. "Don't worry; Jack is harmless," Zoe said brightly.

"I think he likes me," Jude grinned, rubbing behind Jack's ears.

"Jack doesn't usually take to strange men. He's very protective," Zoe agreed.

"Well, I think Jack is a good judge of character," she announced.

"And looks," Zoe teased. "Happy to meet you, neighbor! I gotta go help Lucas with his closet. He is a terrible organizer."

After Zoe left the room, she said, "Feel like another trip to the car? I think we can get it all up here in a couple of trips."

"I don't have anywhere else to be, so sure," Jude answered.

Later, when all her things had been unpacked and her room organized, she and Jude joined everyone else in the spacious yet cozy family room. If rooms truly did represent a person's personality, then this one was the embodiment of her Aunt Audrey.

Thoughtfully arranged and decorated with a traditional yet eclectic flair, the room was quintessentially English. The tall windows, framed by floral curtains, allowed the sun to bathe the room in bright light. Floor-to-ceiling mahogany bookcases, holding both new and vintage books, lined one entire wall. Two oversized upholstered chairs and a buttery soft grey leather couch anchored the neutral-colored space. Vintage lamps and antique furniture created the old-world ambiance her aunt was so fond of. The gentle aroma of the fresh hydrangeas and lavender in the ginger jar vase on the coffee table was sweet. Around the room, there were photos of family and Audrey's favorite places. A landscape painting hung over the wood-burning fireplace. Lily knew it had to be one of her Aunt Scarlett's creations.

"Your room all finished, Lily?" Mia inquired.

"Yes, ma'am. Everything unpacked and put up."

"Please tell me this is the last time we're going to move," Zoe pleaded.

"I second that," Lucas returned, sitting up from his prone position on the floor.

"I think this house feels like home already," Mia interjected.

"Mission accomplished then," Audrey smiled and then turned to Jude. "You were a big help today. Thank you so much."

Jude blushed and then said quickly, "No problem. But I better get home. My mom will send out a search party if I miss dinner."

"I'll walk you out."

She followed Jude into the foyer and opened the door for him. Jude loped down the porch steps and crossed the lawn toward his house. She was just about to close the door when he turned and shouted, "Still on for our run in the morning?"

"Absolutely; see you tomorrow!"

When she returned to the family room, Zoe announced to no one in particular, "I like him."

"I agree with Zoe. Jude is very sweet, cute even, in a nerdy sort of way," Mia teased. "Don't you think so, Lily?"

"Friends only, Mom," she said before plopping on the couch beside Zoe and Jack. "And I would appreciate it if you wouldn't try to make it into something more than that."

"Come on, Lily, would it hurt for you to loosen up a little?" Lucas asked. "We were just having a bit of fun. You've got to admit the guy is the poster child for awkward. Just your type."

"Is that the best you can do?" She tossed a pillow at her brother, hitting him square in the face. "You are such a pain in the..."

"Children," Mia interrupted. "Mind your words."

She caught herself smiling. It had been a long time since she and Lucas had teased one another. She was surprised at how much she missed it.

"Seriously, though, I like him. I've got a feeling he's a good guy."

"A feeling?"

Her light mood was gone in an instant, replaced by the ever-familiar resentment she felt toward her brother. Lucas was always feeling something—usually, it was bad—and when he did, it wasn't long before he had Mia stirred up with fear, and their lives turned upside down. Her dark thoughts were interrupted when the front doorbell chimed.

"Mia, kids, come here; I want you to meet someone," Audrey called from the foyer.

Mia and Lucas were the first ones up and out of the room. She wondered at the excitement that was clearly written all over them.

"Come on, Lily, Audrey called all of us," Zoe urged, grabbing her sister's arm and pulling her to her feet. They walked arm and arm into the foyer.

She was surprised to see Mia warmly embracing an older man, comfortably dressed in jeans and a black T-shirt. Deep soulful blue eyes accented his strong face. His short dark grey hair was streaked with white at the temples. He was tall and well-built for his age. Her mother and Lucas acted as if the man was an old friend. She had never seen this man before, and considering her family had a very short list of acquaintances, much less friends, Lily was dumbfounded.

Mia announced. "Lily, Zoe, this is Dr. Nolan Gable, my favorite history teacher from my days at Centenary Academy."

She offered the man a polite but cold hello. She knew both her parents had been students at Centenary, it's where they met, so it made sense that her mom knew this Dr. Gable. But what about Lucas? How was he acquainted with him?

"I am pleased to finally meet you girls," Nolan greeted. "Your mother and brother have spoken so highly of you. Please call me Nolan."

Before she could ask him how he knew Lucas, Audrey announced, "Dinner's ready. Please, stay and eat with us, Nolan."

"I would never pass on one of your meals, Audrey," Nolan returned warmly.

Everyone followed the tantalizing aroma of meatballs and marinara into the dining room. Bringing up the rear, she noticed the front door was wide open, and Lucas was standing on the front porch. He was staring at the dense copse of trees across the street. She joined him on the porch. It was not quite day but not quite night either. Shadows were falling—it was twilight. Her father had always called this time of day "the gloaming." It was an inconsequential yet meaningful detail from her memory that made her heart ache with grief.

"There's something out there," Lucas whispered.

She studied the trees but found nothing there out of the ordinary. And yet, a cold sense of dread slowly crawled along her spine. She shivered despite the warm humidity of the night.

She pulled her brother's arm, noting his pale countenance. "Luc, it's nothing."

"I haven't felt like this in a long time, Lily. And I'm telling you, something or someone is there in the trees watching us."

"Don't be ridiculous. I don't see anything, Luc. Let's go inside."

Reluctantly, Lucas took her arm and followed her into the house. Once the front door closed behind them, she felt the worry gnawing in the pit of her stomach subside. They were safe; of course, they were.

"I'm sure it was nothing. You're just tired and hungry, big brother," she offered with a lightness she didn't feel. "Let's get some food in you."

They were so close. She could smell them in the heavy damp air. She flexed her hands, releasing the tension. It had been too long since she had tasted the sublime satisfaction of a kill.

Too many times, this cursed family had escaped her. They were protected on all sides. But their time was running out. She would not be denied, not for much longer. The master's plan was unfolding.

She knelt and ran her hand over the soft grass.

"Soon, children, your blood will run sticky sweet on the ground just like your father's. I swear it will be so."

Chapter 4

Dinner was organized chaos. The Quinns were a lively group, laughing and teasing each other. Nolan smiled, enjoying the warmth of family.

"Aunt Audrey, this is fantastic," Zoe complimented. "You must teach Mom how to make this sauce."

"How about I teach you?" Audrey smiled. "Lucas, you inhaled your food. Would you like some more?"

"Yes, please." He handed his plate over for a refill. When he took a bite, he said, "It's like heaven in my mouth."

"You say that about everything you eat, Luc," Zoe teased.

The joyful mood around the table was contagious—except for Lily. He studied her closely. Withdrawn and just going through the motions, Lily ate little and talked even less. It was obvious to him that she would rather be anywhere else but here at this moment. He could see her growing irritation as the dinner progressed.

"Lily, you're just pushing your food around your plate," Audrey asked. "What's wrong, honey?"

"I'm not very hungry. It's been a long day, you know," Lily scooted her chair back from the table. "May I be excused?"

"Don't go just yet, Lily. I would love for you to hear some of Nolan's stories about your dad in his younger days. Wouldn't that be nice?" Mia suggested gently.

"Sure, whatever," Lily answered reluctantly.

"Nolan, will you tell them about Eli?" Mia asked brightly.

"Of course, from the first day I met Elijah, he impressed me. He had such a love for the past. He was full of questions and so eager to learn. When he wasn't studying history in the library, he was in my office wanting to talk about history. At least, that is, until he met your mother."

"We were inseparable, that's true," Mia laughed. "I was just your age, Lily, seventeen, when I met your dad in Nolan's Ancient World History class. It was our senior year at Centenary. He was the most handsome and kindest boy I had ever known. And he made me laugh."

"He had a dry sense of humor, to be sure," Audrey added.

"Everyone loved Eli, even Scarlett, and that's saying something. She was skeptical of most people," Mia shared.

"Your twin sister?" Zoe asked.

"Yes, she was very protective of me."

"Elijah and Scarlett were like oil and water," he teased. "However, they were able to find some common ground."

"What was that?" Zoe asked.

"Their artistry and appreciation for beauty—Scarlett as a painter and Elijah as a craftsman."

"They had a rough start, but Eli and Scarlett ended up being very close," Mia added. "She loved to tease us about being Barbie and Ken dolls. I only wish she could have seen the life we built. She would have loved being your aunt."

"Just like I do," Audrey said brightly.

"Mom, you don't ever talk about Scarlett. What happened to her?" Zoe asked.

"She disappeared the night of our graduation. We were all supposed to meet up at a bonfire in Chilhowee, but she never showed up. We searched for days. The police finally decided that she must have lost her footing somewhere along the trail and fallen to her death. We never found her body, which is the most difficult part. It happened so long ago, but there isn't a day that Audrey and I don't miss her. I even get that sixth sense sometimes that she's close," Mia recounted.

"Their twin telepathy," Audrey said.

Zoe offered gently. "I'm sorry about Aunt Scarlett."

"We are too, baby," Audrey said. "But tonight is not for sadness and grief. Tonight is for remembering the good times and the sweet things about the people we love and have lost."

"I loved your father; you all know that, and I always will," Mia pledged.

"This from the woman who fled in the middle of the night leaving her husband's body in the county morgue. Alone—no family to bury him—no one to mourn him. What kind of love is that?" Lily demanded angrily.

"Lily Amanda Quinn, you will not speak to your mother that way, not in my house," Audrey chided.

"She didn't love him. Not truly. She couldn't have," Lily accused. "She didn't even have the decency to honor our father with a funeral and proper burial!"

As Lily continued her tirade, he noted the pallor on Mia's face, the shock playing across Audrey and Zoe's features, and Lucas' grim countenance.

"Speechless, mother? You can't deny it, can you? Because it's the truth. You loved yourself more than you ever loved him," Lily raged. "You dragged us from our home with no explanation except for the delusions of a ten-year-old boy, who was obviously in shock."

"That's enough, Lily. Losing Dad has been difficult for you; it has been for all of us, but Mom was just trying to protect our family," Lucas responded vehemently.

"Always the faithful defender! Mom was protecting us from what exactly, Luc? And don't you dare tell me some scary story about demon monsters and things that go bump in the night! I want the truth. I deserve the truth."

"And you shall have it," he said forcefully. "Everything Lucas told you about that day in the clearing is the truth. Your father was murdered by demons. You've blocked the events from your memory because it was too painful for you to understand. I was there that day, Lily. Don't you remember me?"

He saw the recognition slowly materialize in her angry gaze.

"It was you. You were the park ranger that found me and brought me home. But that can't be."

Lily shook her head in confusion. He knew she was at war with her memories and her disbelief. Knee-deep in silence, he waited. All eyes were trained on Lily. The apprehension in the room was palpable.

"Unlock your mind and your heart to the truth, Lily," he encouraged softly.

The chime of the grandfather clock suspended the silence. One, two, three, it rang. No one moved. Four, five, six, and seven. At the last chime, Lily stood, knocking over her chair and slamming her hands on the table. He felt her burning gaze; so much anger for one so young, he thought.

Lily pointed at him, "You told me it was a bear that had killed my father, and now you are telling me it was a bunch of demons? I don't think you even know the truth. It doesn't matter—not anymore. You are all crazy," she shouted.

"It does matter, very much, because you are all still in great danger," he said.

"Lily, please," Mia sobbed. "Let me help you to see the truth."

"I don't care about your truth, Mother. Here's mine: demons do not exist. There is no evil trying to destroy our family. Dad was mauled by a bear, plain and simple. You've let Lucas convince you of something different with his nightmares of supernatural monsters. Your favorite child is lying to you—all of you. Lucas is a coward. He ran away and never even looked back. He left us. If he had stayed, maybe, Dad would still be alive," Lily ranted. "I guess that's why you made up this whole story, Lucas? It's because you can't handle the truth of what you did that day."

And with that final blow, Lily ran from the room. He knew Lily's accusations had devastated everyone around the table. Audrey was trying without success to console Mia, who was weeping. A shell-shocked Zoe was surely struggling with all that she had heard. And Lucas, well, he was expressionless, just staring at Lily's vacant seat at the dining table.

He hadn't been surprised in the least by Lily's reaction. Although it grieved him, he knew she would fight until the bitter end to resist acknowledging the truth. He also knew the road Lily would have to travel toward forgiving her mother and brother for the parts she believed they played on that fateful day would be long and fraught with adversity. He must find a way to help her come to terms with the reality of her family's current situation. The Quinns were living on borrowed time. The days would test them all in extraordinary ways.

Zoe was the first one to speak. "Will someone please explain what just happened?"

"Why don't we all go sit on the porch and talk?" Mia suggested tremulously, wiping tears from her face. "This room has become very warm."

"Yes, I think some fresh air would do us all some good," he agreed.

Mia and Zoe left the room. Before Lucas followed, he stopped him. He laid his hand on Lucas' shoulder and squeezed it lightly.

"It will be alright, Son, I promise. Lily just needs some more time."

"I know. It's just tough to hear the things she says and even worse to watch how her words hurt my mom."

"They hurt you as well. It would be easy to pull away from her because of it. But Lily needs you now more than ever, even if she can't recognize it."

"I know, and I promise I won't turn my back on her."

"Right, then, let's find your mother and sister."

He followed Lucas to the back porch. Mia and Zoe were swaying slowly on the cushioned porch swing. Lucas moved near them and perched on the porch railing. He chose one of the large wicker chairs. It was a beautiful space, old and inviting. The perfect place to pass a warm summer night. The air was fragrant with sweet honeysuckle. Fireflies flitted across the yard, and cicadas sang their evening song. He prayed the peacefulness surrounding them would help to calm the Quinns.

"What truly happened to my father?" Zoe asked softly.

Grief and confusion were written all over Zoe's face. He prayed that the youngest Quinn would be more open to the truth than her sister.

"Let's start at the beginning. Elohim, the Creator of all things, is the source of all light and life in our world. Everything you can see and that which you cannot, natural and supernatural, was created by Him. Elohim has a plan for all His creation, including all of us."

"Elohim? Isn't that one of God's names in the Bible?

"Indeed. He is known by many names. Elohim is God's first name at the creation of the world. It's Hebrew."

Lucas interjected. "Zoe, remember the stories Mom used to tell us about the great war of the angels?"

"I love those stories," she smiled. "There was a very beautiful angel named Lucifer. He was favored by God, but he was vain and selfish. He wanted to be like God."

"He was prideful," Lucas offered.

"Yes, Lucifer was impressed with his own beauty, intelligence, power, and position. He began to desire for himself the honor and glory that belonged to Elohim alone."

"Yes. And that pride fueled him to lead a rebellion against Elohim. However, Lucifer and his angel army were defeated. Elohim cast them all out of the heavens. Since that time, Lucifer and his fallen angels, the ones we call Scáths, walk the earth seeking to destroy everything considered pure and good—all that Elohim has created."

"But there's more to this story, isn't there?" Zoe continued. "God sent His Son, Jesus Christ, to save us from Lucifer and his evil."

"Just so! Elohim did send His only Son, Yeshua, the light of the world, to earth, to walk among His creation."

"Yeshua is the Hebrew name for Jesus Christ," Mia added. "Jesus taught everyone about God, to give them hope, to show them the way to live their lives for their Creator. He performed miracles. He stood up to the evil that was in this world."

"Christ had a special mission that only He could fulfill," Lucas said.

"Yeshua's singular purpose was found in His death," Nolan added. "He gave his life for yours, Zoe. And with his resurrection, all who place their faith in Him will receive the gift of salvation and eternal life."

"But Nolan, what does any of this have to do with how my father died?" Zoe asked.

"While he was on this earth, Yeshua chose twelve individuals to become His disciples, warriors of His light. These men were known in the supernatural world as the Sorcha. Each one possessed a unique and powerful supernatural gift that could be wielded against Lucifer's evil. And when their gifts were united, they could produce a force that was unstoppable. These gifts have been passed down throughout the centuries to the descendants of the Sorcha. They are heirs to the power of Yeshua's light. In each generation, twelve are chosen.

"My dad was a Sorcha, wasn't he?" Zoe asked incredulously.

He smiled, confident that the youngest Quinn sibling would embrace this significant truth.

"He was. And that is what led to what happened in the clearing that day."

"Lucifer fears the Sorcha, Zoe," Mia interjected. "He wants to destroy the light forever. He wants to erase all that is good, all that was created by God."

"Lucifer wants nothing more than to replace light with darkness. He hunts the Sorcha, each generation, and he takes great pleasure in killing them before they can unite their gifts," Lucas concluded.

"How does he kill them?" Zoe wondered.

"His army of demons do his bidding."

"Scáths, right?"

"Yep, and their commander is Lucifer's most trusted warrior. His name is Cain. He is evil itself. Ruthless, relentless, and shows no mercy. I saw him that day in the clearing. One of his minions murdered Dad."

"Wow!" Zoe mused, and then asked, "Nolan, you said at the table that we're still in danger. Why?"

"Two reasons. First, with your father's death, your mother is the last remaining member of the Sorcha of her generation."

"Mom?" Zoe said with surprise.

"Your father and I were members of the Sorcha. Nolan taught and trained us both at Centenary. But we were never able to unite with the rest of our generation. Cain made sure of that. He killed so many of us."

"I'm so sorry, Mom," Zoe countered sympathetically. "But, what's the second reason?"

"Dad's death was the catalyst for the next generation of Sorcha to rise up and fight," Lucas answered.

"What do you mean?" Zoe asked, turning her gaze to him.

"The day your father died was the day that your brother's gift of light was awakened. Lucas is the first of the twelve in this generation. His gift allows him to see what others cannot see, the supernatural. Lucas saw the demons that day, Zoe, before they revealed themselves to your father and sister."

"The day Dad died, my whole world turned upside down. I was so scared because I didn't understand what was happening to me. But, since then, Dr. Gable has helped me to accept my gift and use its power in preparation for the battle that's coming. Look," Lucas urged, pulling his earlobe forward.

Zoe leaned in to study the skin behind her brother's ear. "What's that? It looks like a star."

"The symbol of the Sorcha. I've had it since that day," Lucas said proudly. "So, what do you think, Zoe?"

"So much of our life since Dad died makes sense now. Mom took us away that night to protect you from Cain. We've been running ever since because you and mom are in danger. I totally get it. But how will we keep the Scáths from finding us? How can we ever be truly safe?"

"Tell her, Nolan," Lucas urged.

"Elohim created the Dìonadain for that very purpose, Zoe. They are warrior angels who can also take human form. They exist only to shield and protect the Sorcha. Always watching, ready to defend."

Zoe looked at him very closely. "Are you an angel, Nolan?"

"Indeed, I am."

Chapter 5

Thankful for the darkness and the accompanying cool it brought to the sultry night, Lucas wandered down the street, lost in thought. When he passed a series of grand brick buildings, some old, others new, but all majestic and filled with Southern charm, he stopped. A large sign illuminated the words: Centenary Academy. He exhaled sharply. His father had likely stood in this same spot years ago. He could imagine Eli full of life, ready to conquer the world. He could almost see him strolling through the quad, laughing, even holding Mia's hand. Not a care in the world.

Had he known the pain that would come? Did he realize the darkness that was already shadowing his path? Would he have tried to run away from it if he had known? He wished so badly that he could talk to Eli, ask him how he had prepared for what lay ahead. He needed his father now more than ever.

Lucas walked to a fountain sitting in the center of the front lawn and sat down. He propped his elbows on his knees and hung his head. He didn't often allow himself the luxury of mourning his father. He had to be strong for his mother and sisters. But he was alone now, no one to see his grief. His throat constricted thick with emotion. An unchecked tear slid down his cheek. He closed his eyes and remembered.

Running across the yard to his father's woodshop, his Saturday chores done, he couldn't wait to be with his dad. When he flung open the barn door, he inhaled the pungent scent of sawdust. And the afternoon sun gave his father's handcrafted furniture stacked against the walls a glow.

He loved this place! His father was a master craftsman. He had built the family home and almost everything contained within it as a labor of love. On a whim, his dad had even crafted the cuckoo clock that hung on the wall in his woodshop.

He watched his father in awe. Eli was standing in the center of the room, carving a piece of wood using a knife to concave and convex the wood into its perfect shape. He was singing as he always did when he was working with his hands—creating his masterpieces of wood. It was one of his father's favorites, "You Are My Sunshine."

He stepped over the piles of wood shavings scattered across the floor. "Hey, Dad, I finished my chores. Whatcha making?"

"Something for you, little man!"

"Is it what you promised? One of my very own?"

"What do you think?"

He ran his small hand down the neck of what would soon be his very own handcrafted guitar.

"It's amazing. Thank you, Dad." He wrapped his arms around Eli's neck.

"Well, I could use some help finishing her up. Why don't you hand me that small saw over there?"

He searched for the tool on and around the walls around the worktable. There were so many he wasn't sure which one his father wanted.

He finally chose one with a well-worn handle and long blade. Intricate designs were etched into the blade itself.

"Is this it?"

He held the saw out to his father. Eli took it from him and touched it reverently. "No, but this tool has been in our family for generations."

"Why is it so special?"

"It is a symbol of our family's commitment to our craft. My father passed it to me, and one day it will be yours."

"What are all those squiggles on the blade?"

"I asked my dad the very same question. He told me the squiggles are words. It's a very old language spoken by the tribe of people who were our ancestors. They were woodcrafters but also fierce warriors. The etchings on the blade are the words they would chant before battle. It's been passed down through our family tree to the firstborn child for over a thousand years. Pretty cool stuff, huh?"

"More than cool." He touched the leather hilt of the saw. "I promise when it's my turn, I'll take really good care of it.

"I know you will, Luc. I'm counting on that."

"I won't let you down, Dad. I mean it."

"That's a serious promise, Luc. When a man gives his word, he must keep it, honor it, no matter what; he is committed to it. Do you understand?"

He nodded his head solemnly. "Yes, sir, I do."

Eli looked at him for a long moment. His father's green eyes peered intently into his own. He figured his father was satisfied with what he saw when he grinned and said, "It's done then. Now let's get busy on your guitar."

Profound regret filled his heart. He hadn't kept his word. In the rush to leave his home the day his father had died, he left the saw behind. He had never forgiven himself for the broken promise. He opened his eyes and noticed the ring of bricks surrounding the fountain where he was seated. The bricks formed an intricate design. They were embossed with letters and an all too familiar symbol—the star-shaped sign of the Sorcha. He wasn't surprised when he saw his father's name, as well as his mother's, inscribed on a brick.

No one in Cleveland, not even the students who went to school here, had any idea that Centenary Academy served as the stronghold of the Dìonadain and home of the Sorcha. Nolan had told him long ago that Centenary was the perfect place for each Sorcha to be trained to use their gift. It was secret and safe. His parents had learned here, and now, so would he. The connection he felt with his father here at this moment was very strong. He would finish what his father had started. He would become a warrior. He would fulfill his purpose as a Sorcha.

"I've always wondered about those names and that strange symbol," a husky voice interrupted his thoughts.

He started at the bottom. Her red-polished toes peeped from bronze gladiator sandals. Long tanned legs graced her denim shorts. A thin white blouse skimmed her broad shoulders. Her jet-black hair hung in a blunt sweep. Ebony eyes glittered beneath thick lashes. Lucas was glad he was seated because the sight of her was knee-weakening. Recovering quickly, he flashed his most charming smile.

"You know this is my first day in town, and you are definitely the best thing I've seen all day."

"Well, aren't you a charmer?" she teased.

"Enough to get your name?"

She smiled when she sat beside him. "I'm Lysha. And you?"

"Lucas Quinn. Are you a student here?"

"No, I just graduated from the University of Tennessee. My family lives here in Cleveland, though. I don't think I've seen you around before. I would have remembered you."

"Nah, I'm the new guy. Just arrived today, in fact, with my family. We moved in with my aunt. Her house is down the street. But enough about me—I'm interested in you. Got a job in town?"

"Talbot Industries, do you know it?"

"Of course, I know it. Multi-billion-dollar internet company built from the ground up by Flynn Talbot, the media mogul. Wow, working at Talbot must be fantastic!"

"I love it so far. I work in their nonprofit sector as a marketing associate. My focus is raising global awareness for all of Talbot's charity projects via social media. I just got back from Southeast Asia yesterday."

"Impressive! I've always wanted to travel outside the States. Tell me about it."

"It was beautiful and very exotic. Time moves slowly there—like you're in a dream, you know? It was the most marvelous place."

"I bet it was."

He couldn't tear his eyes away from her striking face. This woman made it hard to think straight. Searching for something else to say, he was glad when she absentmindedly touched the necklace clasped around her throat. It was unusual. A small silver vial hung in the middle of a silver chain flanked on either side with intricately designed butterflies.

"Did you get that on one of your trips? It's very pretty."

"It is, isn't it? I got it on one of my family trips. I've always liked butterflies; I consider them my good luck charm. Now, it's my turn to ask a question. How old are you exactly, Lucas?"

"Old enough. I'll be a senior at Centenary. Don't break my heart just yet, Lysha. We're just getting started."

"I believe you just might be trouble for me."

"I hope so. Would you like to talk a walk?"

"I was on my way to meet my brother and some of his friends for dinner. Would you like to come?"

"Best invitation I've had all day. I accept."

"Great! It's just a few blocks down the street."

He and Lysha strolled companionably down the street, headed to the center of town. Their conversation had most definitely advanced to some serious flirtation. He knew once she figured out how old he was, she would probably shut things down. But until then, he was making the most of it.

Most of the storefronts were closed, so the streets were empty. It was almost eerie. Passing Courthouse Square, they came to a park. Massive trees, their branches heavy with foliage, surrounded the area. Providing cool shade in the day and shadowy seclusion in the evening, the grand oaks must have been a hundred years old. An outdoor amphitheater anchored one end, and at the center stood the giant head of a Native American carved from an oak tree rooted in the ground. The sober Cherokee kept a silent vigil over the deserted space.

"Sleepy town; the streets are empty."

"It certainly can be, but there's plenty of excitement around if you know where to look. Here we are," she announced. "You are going to love it!"

Chapter 6

Walking into Della's Diner, Lucas immediately felt like he was in the middle of a yard sale. Old and new album covers from the Rolling Stones to Coldplay and Dolly Parton to Taylor Swift decorated one wall. Polaroid pictures of customers, old and new, lined the opposite one. Intermingled between all the wall décor were athletic jerseys, sports memorabilia, old toys, and other vintage junk. The chairs, tables, and even the walls were like a high school yearbook covered with customer's signatures, words of wisdom, and funny jokes.

There was a dance floor at one end of the large room. Country music boomed from the jukebox in the corner. T-shirt- clad servers were weaving in and out through the packed space, delivering orders. It was loud, and it was friendly. Everyone seemed to know everyone else. Lucas loved everything about the quirky place.

He followed Lysha to a large private booth at the back of the diner. The occupants looked and acted as if they owned the place. He wasn't entirely surprised when Lysha planted a kiss on the cheek of a guy who had to be related to her.

"Hey, handsome. I've brought someone for you to meet," she said. "Lucas Quinn, this is my brother, Aiden Talbot."

"Talbot?" He looked pointedly at her. "As in Flynn Talbot?"

She winked slyly. "Guilty as charged."

"My sister loves a good surprise," Aiden replied with a grin.

Lysha's cell buzzed. "I need to take this." Before she walked away, she whispered in his ear, "Hope I see you later."

"Most definitely." He, along with every other male, watched her exit the diner.

"Have a seat, Quinn," Aiden invited. "I heard you were moving into town today. You know, small town, word travels fast."

Although Aiden appeared deceptively relaxed, he could feel his tightly leashed energy. Interesting, he thought. This guy was wound up. He also knew without a doubt that Aiden was the leader of the small group sitting around the table. No surprise there, considering who his father was. Lucas took the empty seat beside the brunette sitting next to Aiden.

"Hey, I'm Rachel Pooley." The slow cadence of her voice oozed sweetness. Thick platinum blonde hair fell straight past her shoulders. Eyes the color of molasses complemented her oval face. Rachel looked like the quintessential Southern belle. She probably acted like one too, all sugar and spice—heavy on the spice, if he was any judge of character.

"Will you be going to Centenary this fall?" she asked.

"Yeah, actually, I'll be a senior."

"You will love it."

"Rachel is right; Centenary is a great school," Aiden added. "Okay, everybody, introductions, please."

The guy leaning back in the chair across from him with an air of cool indifference said, "I'm Grayson Lee."

Lucas figured Gray didn't like new people much, especially the ones that weren't invited to hangout. Gray's feigned nonchalance couldn't hide the look of wariness about him.

"Gray is old money, and he throws the best parties," Rachel explained.

"You would know," Gray winked, taking a long sip of his drink.

"Hey, man, I'm Daryl Stuart."

Big, burly, and a little rough around the edges, Daryl Stuart was a human-sized tank. He had to admit he felt a little intimidated. Daryl's muscles had muscles. He wouldn't want to get on this guy's bad side; there might be pain involved. Rachel must have read his mind.

"I know he looks like a bulldog, but he's harmless as a fly," Rachel whispered.

"Shut up already! It's my turn," the guy sitting across from him jested. He was compact, with precise features, and a lot of curly brown hair. "Marshall Cooper, everybody's plus one, right, Rachel?"

He caught the longing expression in Marshall's brown eyes. It only lasted a split second, and then it was gone, replaced by an impish grin. Marshall had a thing for Rachel but was working hard to hide it.

"And you?" Lucas asked the girl sitting on his right.

"Jenna Mabry, Rachel's best friend."

He liked the way Jenna tossed her dark fringed bangs back from her heart-shaped face. Then, she scooted closer to him in the booth. She smelled like strawberries. He offered Jenna his most winsome smile. This town sure had its fair share of beautiful women.

"Well, y'all, what will it be tonight?"

He looked up at the rusty-sounding voice. She was dressed head to toe in the orange that most Tennesseans favored. Her platinum-blond hair was pinned in the back, but her bangs were something to behold. They made her at least an inch taller. Everything about her was loud but lovely just the same. Her friendly eyes crinkled when she smiled. It was easy to understand why everyone felt at home with a hostess like this.

"I think we'll go light tonight, Miss Della. Sweet tea all around, two orders of wings, some fried pickles, a couple of baskets of fries, and throw in a chicken-salad sandwich for my new friend here." Aiden continued, "You haven't lived till you've tried Della's homemade chicken salad."

Della nudged Aiden's shoulder, "That's my boy. Now, Lucas, you listen to Aiden. He won't steer you wrong."

"Yes, ma'am, I'll do that."

After the drama at home earlier, he was happy to push reality away for tonight. Some cool new friends, pretty girls, and melt-in-your-mouth food were a great recipe for forgetting who he was for a bit. Enjoying his extraordinary stroke of good luck, he ignored his cell vibrating in his pocket more than once.

"What do guys do for fun in this town?" he asked.

"Well, as you can imagine, the possibilities are just end less," Marshall drawled sarcastically.

"Besides eating at Della's and catching a movie every now and then with these guys, there's not much going on until school starts back," Rachel added.

"So says the party girl! If I remember correctly, you enjoyed getting pretty wasted last night," Gray interjected.

Rachel glared at Gray and then said to Lucas. "Ignore him; I always do. Why don't you come with us to the river tomorrow? It's gonna be hot, and the water will feel really nice."

"Rachel, give the guy a chance. He just got here," Aiden interrupted. "He may have other plans."

Before he could think twice, he said quickly, "I got nothing else to do. Count me in."

"Great, it will be fun," Aiden returned.

"Seriously, man, our town may be small, but we've got a drag-race track that's open every Friday and Saturday night. The most beautiful lake you've ever seen is just up the road. You can wakeboard on crystal blue water for miles. We got the mountains for climbing, hiking, and camping. But the best thing we have going for us is the Ocoee River," Daryl interjected enthusiastically. "Insane Class 4 rapids!"

"I'm down."

Conversation stopped when Della served up their order steaming hot from the kitchen. When he took the first bite of his chicken-salad sandwich, everyone around the table paused to watch, including Della.

"So?" they asked in unison.

"Honestly, Miss Della, this is the best!"

As the group enjoyed their dinner, he noticed a black and royal blue basketball jersey hanging on the wall above the booth. Talbot and number 5 were emblazoned on the back.

Marshall noticed his interest, "Yeah, that's Aiden's jersey. He is legendary at Centenary, you know, captain of the team and basket at the buzzer to win the state finals."

"Do you play, Quinn?" Aiden asked.

"Yeah, I do, actually."

"You should try out, man; we could use some people with some skill," Aiden encouraged.

When Rachel got up from the table and pulled Aiden with her to the dance floor, he noticed Marshall watching them closely.

"That guy is gold, man," Marshall said to no one in particular. "Everyone who knows him wants to be him."

"So, I guess they're a thing?"

"Obviously," Marshall answered.

"You want to dance with me, Lucas?" Jenna asked sweetly.

"Sure, why not?"

He followed Jenna to the dance floor. She was easy to look at and made him laugh. He had never really had time to pursue girls. Now two beautiful women had crossed his path in the very same evening. How much luckier could he get? Maybe this move to Cleveland was going to be better than he had thought.

An immediate change in the atmosphere made him shiver. Two guys strolled into the diner and sat at the bar. Each wore a baseball cap with the Centenary crest emblazoned on them. He felt the tension in Aiden from across the room.

"Party's over. It's late," Aiden announced. "Miss Della needs her beauty sleep."

Although it happened within the blink of an eye, he sensed a current of electricity pass between Aiden and the two guys when they passed by them on the way to the door.

"Bye, Della! I really enjoyed it," he called over his shoulder, following the others out.

"You come back soon, honey!" Della answered.

"Who were those guys?" he asked, joining the others on the sidewalk outside the diner.

"Trash," Gray scowled.

"Yes, the boys had a run-in with them this past semester," Jenna whispered to him.

"About?"

Aiden interrupted. "Don't worry about it, Quinn. It's all good."

He didn't buy it. Based on Aiden and Gray's reaction, he knew whatever had happened between them and the other guys from Centenary, it was not good, and it was most definitely not over. Before he could ask Jenna for more details, a midnight-black Bentley pulled up to the curb in front of them. A well-built man exited the driver's side door. He was a study in contradiction—intimidating in stature but graceful in movement. His ink-black skin was in stark contrast to his white linen suit. His kinky hair and piercings in both his nose and ears were set off by his strangely colored amber eyes. Everything about this guy was sketchy.

"He freaks me out," Jenna whispered nervously. "His name is Kayanga. But the family calls him Kay. Mr. Talbot adopted him from somewhere in Zimbabwe. He's a year younger than Lysha. Anyway, Mr. Talbot never goes anywhere without him."

When Kay opened the passenger door, Lucas experienced a rush of anticipation. He was about to meet Flynn Talbot. Not only was the man richer than Midas, owning companies and land that stretched across the globe, but he was also the chief executive of the most lucrative internet conglomerate in the world. Now he was about to meet the man he admired so much.

Dressed in a well-fitted dark suit and open-collar white shirt. Mr. Talbot was indeed larger than life. He was lean and muscled. His dark wavy hair was swept back from his angular face. He had a strong countenance, one that exuded power and control. The man radiated a magnetism that wasn't easy to ignore. He had to admit he was a little awestruck. He felt a pang of jealousy when Aiden and his father shared a quick embrace. He wondered how he and Eli would have greeted one another as father and grown son.

"Good evening, all," Flynn Talbot greeted. "I see you've added someone new to your group, Son."

"Dad, this is Lucas Quinn. He just moved into town today."

He extended his hand to Talbot in greeting. He felt the restrained strength in man's handshake. "It's an honor to meet you, sir. I researched Talbot Industries last year for a school project. Your company is doing life-changing things for people all over the world."

"Kind words, Lucas. Serving others has always been of value to me," Mr. Talbot responded kindly. "And welcome to our little city. It seems you have already made a good impression on my son and daughter."

The backseat window in the Bentley slid down to reveal Lysha. She waved her hand and winked slyly at him.

"I told you I would be seeing you again," she teased.

"You will find Cleveland has much to offer a young man such as yourself, Lucas. Drop by my office one day; I would be happy to give you a personal tour."

"Thank you, Mr. Talbot. That would be amazing."

Talbot walked back to the car. Before getting in, he turned back, "Aiden, see you at home?"

"Yes, sir. I'll be along soon," Aiden promised.

As the Talbot Bentley sped off, he acknowledged for the second time his good luck today.

"So, what's the plan?" Daryl asked.

"Lucas and I will meet you at your house at nine to load everything up. Then we can swing by, pick up everyone else, and head up to the river," Aiden responded. "That work for you, Quinn?"

"Yeah, man, sounds good."

He didn't miss the look of displeasure on Gray's face when Aiden extended his invitation. It was obvious that he didn't like the attention that Aiden and the others were giving him. He didn't care. He had plans. He never had plans, especially with friends. This night just kept getting better.

"You better be ready, Marshall," Aiden ordered good-naturedly. "Or you can walk to the Blue Hole."

"Okay, okay, you won't be waiting on me," Marshall complained.

"Jenna and I have cheer practice in the morning. We'll just meet you up there," Rachel explained, hooking her arm through Aiden's. "Will I be seeing you later?"

"What do you think?" Aiden said as he leaned in for a kiss. "Come on, Quinn, I'll give you a ride home."

Everyone dispersed and went their separate ways. He followed Aiden to his car parked down the street. When they stopped beside a sleek dark blue BMW M6 convertible, he whistled in admiration.

"Sweet ride, yeah?" Aiden asked with a grin. "It was a Christmas present from my dad."

Aiden climbed in behind the wheel, and Lucas settled in the plush leather passenger seat. When Aiden pushed the ignition button and the engine roared to life, he looked at Lucas and shrugged nonchalantly, "I like speed."

"Who doesn't?" Lucas countered.

They arrived at Audrey's house very quickly, too soon for him. He would have liked to cruise in Aiden's car a bit longer.

"Pick you up in the morning," Aiden asked.

"Yeah. Thanks for the ride home."

"No problem, man," Aiden said before speeding into the night.

He sighed; his fun night was quickly being replaced by his reality. He ambled slowly across the yard and up the porch steps. He knew a reckoning was waiting for him behind the front door. He had ignored Mia's texts, caught up with his new friends. In the past, he had always been so careful not to worry her, always following the rules. He had a lot of explaining to do.

"Here goes nothing," he muttered under his breath.

He opened the front door quietly and entered the house. Mia was sitting on the bottom step of the staircase. Her face was drawn, and the seriousness of her mood was clear all the way from her eyes to her mouth. Her face told him everything. He steeled himself for the words he knew would follow.

"Where have you been?" Mia scolded. "You know the danger we are in. You know the consequences, Lucas. I've sat here for the last few hours just imagining the worst. One call or text to let me know that you were okay; that's all you had to do."

"I'm sorry, Mom. I went for a walk to clear my head. I ended up at Centenary. I knew I was safe. Nolan is always watching over me. But then, I met this girl. She invited me to eat at a diner downtown. And then I met her brother and some other people. I was having so much fun. Time just got away from me."

"Yes, Nolan was with you. But you left the safety of Centenary's grounds and made yourself an easy target for the Scáths. You risked too much, Lucas."

"I know, I know. It won't happen again, I promise." He joined his mom on the stairs. "It's just been so long since I've been able to live a normal life. For a few hours tonight, I was just a regular guy. And it felt good."

"I know our crazy life hasn't been easy, Luc. You've had more than your fair share of heartache and change. But you know as well as anyone what we are facing. You must promise me you will be more careful?"

"Yes, ma'am. I promise." He embraced Mia and placed a light kiss on her forehead. He loved this woman with his whole heart. He hated disappointing her.

"You made friends? Tell me about them," Mia encouraged, her countenance growing brighter.

"They all grew up in Cleveland and go to Centenary. Seniors, so that's a plus. They are great, Mom. I think you would like them. And two of them are Flynn Talbot's kids!"

"Isn't that the man you wrote about in your paper last year?"

"One and the same. I even got to meet him tonight."

"That's wonderful, honey. Any of these new friends happen to be girls?"

"Yeah," he winked. "Pretty ones, too."

"Well, that explains your lack of caution."

"Am I forgiven?"

"Always. One more thing, Luc, before you go to bed, will you talk to Lily? She's shut up in her room and refuses to talk to any of us."

"Not sure she will listen, but I'll give it my best shot."

He climbed the stairs two at a time. Lily's light was on, so she was still awake. Praying for the right words, he tapped lightly on her door. "Hey, Sis, can we talk for a minute?"

"Not in the mood."

"Please, I hate this distance between us."

His plea was met with silence.

"I'm sorry, Lily. I know you're mad at me and missing Dad like crazy. I just want to help."

Lily flung open the door. He winced.

"Save it! I'm not the one who needs help. You're so delusional you don't even see it."

"It's the truth, all of it, whether you choose to believe it or not. Just because you didn't see what I saw, doesn't mean it didn't happen."

"I'm tired, Lucas; tired of all of it. For the life of me, I can't figure out why you've created this crazy fantasy. I mean, come on, demons? And the worst part is, you've convinced Mom it's all real! Zoe is probably on your side too. You are the ones that need help, Lucas. Tonight, I realized just how much."

"Lily, please..."

"We've lost seven years of our lives, Lucas, seven years! Instead of living our life, we've been running from it instead." Lily's dark blue eyes were welled with tears. "I didn't even get to say goodbye to Dad. I'll never forgive her for that."

"She did what she had to."

Lily's face shifted from sorrow to anger in a split second. "And that's exactly what I'm doing."

"I know you, Lily, better than anyone else. You're pushing me away because you're angry that Mom believes me and not you. But most of all, you're afraid deep down that you could be wrong about all this."

"Good night, Lucas."

She slammed the door in his face. Lucas sagged against the doorframe, his hand on the closed door. His heavy heart ached for his sister.

Chapter 7

Nolan knelt in the shadow of the magnolia tree, contemplating the enormity of the task set before him. As commander of the Dìonadain, he was charged with the guardianship of the Sorcha. For thousands of years, he and his brothers had fought many battles to secure the Sorcha and their powerful gifts of light. They had come close, several times, to uniting the twelve. However, Cain had thwarted their attempts at every turn. So many had been lost. This time would be different. No quarter would be given. He and his brothers would succeed. They must. The darkness was growing in strength, and only the Sorcha could stop its advance.

"Elohim, strengthen the Dìonadain for what lies ahead," he prayed. "Whatever is required, whatever the cost, guide us, quick and sure, to the others." Rising, he spoke into the deep shadows. "What news, Asher?"

The dark figure of a man emerged soundlessly from the gloom. Asher was Nolan's second. They had fought side by side for a millennium, and their bond was strong. Asher was tall but more powerfully built than he was. His friend's dark hair and full beard were short and neat; his deep-set hooded eyes were always somber. Asher favored the austere; his attire was simple and functional. His time spent defending the Knights Templar during the Crusades long ago had forever changed and decided Asher's choice for his human form.

"The council is waiting. A messenger has arrived from Spain."

"And Centenary?"

"Secure. Our boundaries are unbreakable."

"The Scáths will be cautious because of our great number; nevertheless, we must stay alert. Cain will be vigilant. He will not hesitate to strike, especially when he senses that the uniting is close at hand."

"We will do what we must, as we always do," Asher agreed grimly.

"There is no margin for error, Asher. This generation must see the Sorcha unite their gifts."

"As Elohim wills it," Asher returned.

"As Elohim wills it," Nolan repeated.

"I confess I have wondered at times throughout the long years if all that has been foretold will ever occur."

"Patience, my friend, with each battle we have fought throughout the ages, every win and loss, we have moved one step closer to the uniting of the Sorcha and our promised victory. We must continue down the path that Elohim has laid before us. We will complete our task."

"Forgive my doubt, brother."

"Your apology is misplaced. Your desire, Asher, to see this finished is as strong as my own."

Asher extended his hand and arm. Nolan clasped it. Their bond of brotherhood was absolute and unwavering. Nolan trusted Asher and knew that his friend would do whatever was needed to win the battle before them and, ultimately, the war that would destroy Lucifer's evil forever.

"Let us go. The council awaits," he said.

Nolan and Asher shed their human forms, becoming invisible to the natural eye. Spreading their massive topaz wings, they flew across the starless sky to a small marble mausoleum, that stood adjacent to the old Centenary chapel. For the Dìonadain, the tomb served as a sober reminder of the urgency of their mission.

Inside was a single sarcophagus, the final resting place of Nina Craigmiles. Only seven, she had been tragically killed when the horse and buggy she was riding in was hit by an oncoming train over a hundred years ago.

The day after Nina was laid to rest, blood-red stains appeared on the white stones of her crypt. For years, people tried to remove them, but the stains always returned. No one had ever solved the mystery of the mausoleum, so most considered the place to be haunted and stayed clear. It provided the perfect cover for the entrance to the Dìonadain Council chamber.

He and Asher slipped easily through the mausoleum's great iron door. He passed his hand over the great marble sarcophagus. It slid away, revealing a set of stone stairs. The ground beneath Centenary Academy had served as a base of operations for the Dìonadain guard since its inception.

Down they went, deep underground, gliding effortlessly through a series of dark tunnels. The glowing light from their spectral bodies illuminated their path. A natural rock archway signaled the entrance into the chamber itself. A great stone table with four ornately carved stone chairs stood in the center of the cavernous space. Suspended above the table was an iridescent globe. It rotated slowly, marking the exact movements of the earth.

Around the walls, radiant in their battle armor of purest gold, Dìonadain warriors kept vigil. Their glorious topaz wings, full and thick, were folded behind them. All members of the order were charged with different responsibilities. Around the world, Watchers observed the movements of the Scáths, monitoring their location and activity. Messengers were appointed to relay all communication regarding the Sorcha to the Dìonadain Council. Warriors went to battle, fending off the Scáths in defense of the Sorcha.

Guardians trained and protected the Sorcha, even fighting alongside them if needed. Once a Dìonadain guardian was assigned a Sorcha to protect, the guardian would remain with the Sorcha until death. Whether in angel or human form, the Dìonadain were a mighty force to be reckoned with.

Nolan joined the other three members of the Dìonadain Council at the stone table. As commander of the Guardians, he served as the leader of the group. Before speaking, he respectfully regarded the others around the table. Each one was fiercely beautiful and brilliant to behold.

Othiel, commander of the Watchers, studied the globe intently. His timeless patience and acute analytical mind made him an exceptional observer of everything around him. Hila, commander of the Messengers, was anxious to begin. Her mercury-red hair tumbled over her shoulder, a match to her fiery spirit. The massive Andreas, commander of the Warriors, rubbed his thick blond beard thoughtfully. Nolan knew his brother's mind, never at rest, was surely weaving strategies of defense in preparation for what was to come.

"Come forward," he commanded in a melodic language unknown to man.

The Dìonadain messenger approached the council table. He was dressed in the traditional uniform of his station, a leather jerkin with golden buckles, long fitted pants, high leather boots, and a golden shortsword strapped to his waist. Nolan knew the messenger's rigid stance and bowed head were a respectful response to the epic proportion and appearance of the council members as well as their positions of authority.

"Speak, Samuel."

"We have located a Sorcha in Algeciras, Spain," the messenger announced.

"You are certain?" Othiel asked sharply.

"The globe shows an emerging," Hila returned sharply. "Samuel would not be here if he was not sure."

"Doubt does not become you, brother," Andreas said to Othiel before addressing the messenger. "And the mark, Samuel? Did you see it?"

"It is visible," he confirmed. "I have seen it myself."

"Then, we must be swift; timing is critical," Andreas implored.

"I concur," Hila offered. "We would be foolish to underestimate the speed or the cunning of the Scáths. Their network of informants will have already relayed this same information to Cain."

"Yes, commander, the Scáths are already en route and gaining ground by the minute," Samuel reported.

"We must pray we are not too late," Nolan declared.

As commander, the responsibility of choosing the guardian for each Sorcha when they were found rested on him. The choice was simple. He turned to his trusted friend, "Asher, the task is yours."

"Recite the Dìonadain oath, brother," Hila commanded.

"Pure of heart and mind, I will protect and defend the Sorcha with all my strength. I will never leave his side. I will not intervene unless called upon. This is my solemn oath," Asher said reverently.

"Elohim has made our path clear but not without obstacle," Nolan said. "Asher, it's up to you now; bring the Sorcha home."

Chapter 8

Hanging out late with friends last night had not been his best idea, Álvaro Díaz decided. Desperate to block the sound of the blaring car horn and the bright morning sun streaming through his window, he burrowed deeper into his pillow. He had a monster headache. Why did he tell his little brother he would take him to see the whales this morning? Benicio, fourteen and eager for adventure, would not let him renege on his promise. The precocious boy, who was his constant shadow, was tenacious and committed to a fault. Trying to go back to sleep at this point was a futile endeavor. He knew his little brother wouldn't give up.

He groaned, rolled out of bed, and managed to make it to the bathroom without injury. Squinting at his blurry reflection in the mirror, he ran a hand through his thick brown hair. This morning, he looked much older than his twenty-two years. He swallowed two aspirins, pulled on a pair of worn jeans and a T-shirt, and headed to the kitchen. If he was going to make it through this day, he needed to start it with one of his mama's homemade magdalenas. He grabbed the lemony muffin, savoring the first bite, before leaving the house.

"*Vamos*, Álvaro," his little brother waved impatiently.

"*Bueno*, I'm coming!"

He loped across the yard. He hopped up into the cab of the dilapidated truck and cranked the engine.

"I think it's too early even for the whales today, Beni."

His brother grinned, part love and part mischief.

"Oh no, they are waiting for us. You look awful! You should really think about getting more sleep, brother."

"I'll sleep when I'm dead!"

He drove toward the city. The industrial port city was situated on the eastern end of Algeciras Bay in southern Spain, across from Gibraltar. Although Álvaro would never describe it as pretty, Algeciras did have its fair share of attractions. As the main transportation hub between Spain and Tangier and other ports in Morocco, the Port of Algeciras was one of the busiest in the Mediterranean, with its international shipping vessels, passenger ships, fishing boats, and transport ferries.

And more recently, the port had become a popular tourist stop for those who wanted to visit the Rock of Gibraltar or enjoy one of the many whale-watching excursions in the Strait of Gibraltar. The strait was a migration route and natural habitat for several distinct species of whales. Today, Álvaro and Beni would join the many tourists who traveled by boat from the Port of Algeciras out into the bay to watch the mammoth giants of the sea.

The closer they got to the docks, the more the sounds and smells around him reminded Álvaro again just how much he hated his job. The Díaz brothers were fishermen, spending their days helping their father to cast and pull in nets from the tuna-rich waters of the Strait of Gibraltar. He didn't want to end up like his father, tired, weathered, old before his time, with no more ambition in life than to bring in the next catch. He had bigger dreams. He wanted people to know him when he walked down the street.

Parking the truck at the pier, he said, "All right, little brother. I'm your captain for the morning."

"Let's go see some whales," Beni cheered.

Álvaro followed Beni to the boat. He often wondered how he and his brother could have come from the same parents. They couldn't be more different. Where he was never satisfied and always looking out for his best interests, Beni was bighearted and unassuming, never asking for anything for himself. When his brother wasn't helping his father with the nets or his mother with the vegetable garden, he was helping neighborhood families with odd jobs or tutoring younger kids in school. Beni was everything Álvaro was not. He smiled ruefully. He knew Beni thought he hung the moon. It was displaced hero worship, to be sure, but Álvaro was thankful for it today.

Working together, it didn't take the Díaz brothers long to ready the boat for departure. The early morning sun was already hot. Álvaro pulled a hat on as he maneuvered the boat out into the smooth waters of the bay.

Beni pointed to a passing boat, "Whale watchers!"

Álvaro grinned. Beni's energy and curiosity were contagious. He was glad he had kept his promise. Out on the water on this beautiful day, enjoying time with his brother, Álvaro almost felt content. The frustrations and unmet desires that continuously plagued him disappeared as he steered the boat toward the horizon. It felt good.

Álvaro dropped anchor a few yards from one of the larger safari boats. Pulling his hat low, he settled back in his seat and watched Beni check the water in every direction for the whales he loved so much. Smiling to himself, he took joy in the small role he had played this morning in making his brother happy.

"Look, Álvaro, there he is," Beni shouted.

A magnificent orca whale emerged about sixty meters off the port side. As Álvaro watched as this giant of the sea left the depths of the bay, a tall geyser of water erupted from its blowhole. Rolling over in the water, it dove quickly out of sight, only to rocket out of the water a few meters farther away. Beni cheered with delight. It wasn't long before another whale a greater distance away from them rocketed out of the water. And then another.

Álvaro scanned the dark blue waters. There was a lot of traffic, both human and amphibian, on the strait today. He hoped Beni had thought to pack them some lunch. It was a long time till dinner, and he was sure Beni would want to stay out until dark. After a time, lulled by the warm sun and rhythmic rocking of the boat, Álvaro closed his eyes and drifted off.

When a loud boom sounded across the water, he was instantly alert and surveying the space around the boat, "What was that?"

Clouds of black smoke billowed from a safari boat just three hundred yards away. Flames engulfed her stern. People were jumping from the boat in a panic. Álvaro didn't hesitate. He transmitted a distress call, weighed anchor, fired the engine, and headed straight for the safari boat.

Beni choked out, "Closer, Álvaro." He pointed. "The people in the water are swimming the wrong way."

He could just make out the small group thrashing in the water. Unable to see in the thick smoke, they were swimming back toward the sinking boat that they needed to avoid. If they didn't turn around, Álvaro knew they would surely be sucked under, judging the rate at which the boat was faltering.

"Get their attention, or they're not going to make it!" Álvaro shouted.

Cupping his hands around his mouth, Beni yelled across the water, "Aquí! Aquí!" ("Here!")

In the chaos around them, the frantic people gave no indication that they had heard his brother.

"It's not working, Álvaro. They can't hear me. Use the loudspeaker."

"Deténganse! Se están alejando. ¡Aquí, aquí!" ("Stop! You are moving away. Here, here!")

The desperate people turned toward his voice, but the confusion on their faces confirmed his worst fear. They didn't understand Spanish. Álvaro wiped his arm across his face to clear the soot clouding his vision.

"They don't speak Spanish. I don't know how to make them understand. Think of something, Beni."

When his brother didn't respond, Álvaro turned around to find Beni staring intently across the churning water. He shouted, "Beni, snap out of it. I need you to help me."

Beni turned his head back toward his brother; his face was pale but confident. "Repeat the words exactly as I say them, okay? Use the loudspeaker and repeat after me."

Álvaro was puzzled, Beni never acted this confidently, but he nodded his head in agreement anyway. Now wasn't the time to question the change in his brother's behavior. He turned up the volume on the loudspeaker and shouted, "Okay, ready!"

"*Hier! Schwimmen zu mir.*" ("Here! Swim this way.")

"What does that even mean? Is that German?"

"Trust me, Álvaro. Just say it."

Beni repeated the German command again for Álvaro. He had no idea where Beni had learned German, but he bellowed the phrase into the loudspeaker nonetheless. The effect of the command was immediate. Three of the people in the water turned and began swimming toward the boat.

"Again, Álvaro," Beni pressed.

He repeated the command over and over until the three people were close enough for Beni to pull them from the water. They fell to the deck, sputtering and coughing up water. Only two more are still out there.

"Now say it this way," Beni directed.

Álvaro awkwardly repeated the words as Beni gave them to him. His best guess was that he was speaking Russian and then Korean. Recognizing their native tongue, the people in the water responded, swimming toward their rescuers. Once Beni had them safe on deck, Álvaro tried to steer the boat away. It was difficult work. The churning water around the sinking safari ship was creating a forceful whirlpool. When the engine sputtered and died, Álvaro feared the worst.

"We're not going to make it, Beni, if we don't get that engine started!"

His brother rushed below deck to restart the engine. With each passing second, the Díaz boat was pulled closer to the swirling whirlpool. They were trapped.

"Try it now," Beni shouted.

Álvaro cranked the engine, and miraculously, it roared to life. Whatever his brother had done below, it had worked. Álvaro sped away from the danger zone and headed back to port. They passed the rescue boats, sirens blaring, that were moving out toward the wreck.

Arriving back at the port, Álvaro, Beni, and their bedraggled but grateful passengers were surrounded by a flood of anxious bystanders. When officials for the port authority realized the six tourists pulled from the water were from different countries and spoke no Spanish, interpreters were found so their stories could be told. Soon, everyone knew the rescue was, in fact, due to Álvaro's ability to communicate with the survivors in their own languages. Álvaro opened his mouth to correct this faulty assumption but was stopped short.

"My brother, Álvaro, is a hero," Beni announced proudly.

The gathering crowd cheered. Friends and strangers were congratulating him on his bravery. Only in his wildest dreams had he ever imagined a moment like this. Álvaro gestured to Beni to join him, but his little brother just shook his head slightly and stepped back from the crowd.

When the local news crew broadcasting the explosion and the rescue focused on him, he fully embraced the heroic narrative that everyone else already believed to be true.

"Mr. Díaz, how many different languages do you speak?" a reporter asked.

"I don't know any language except Spanish."

"Then how did you do it? Tell us what happened out there."

"The words just came to me, like someone was whispering them into my ear. I can't explain it. It was a miracle."

"Thank you for your courage, Mr. Díaz. Today was a tragedy. But, because of you, five people still have their lives ahead of them."

"I'm just glad I was there and that I could help," he offered humbly.

The crowd began to chant his name. For the first time in his life, he felt significant. And it felt good! Álvaro laughed as they hoisted him on their shoulders and carried him into the city for a celebration.

She smiled as the perfectly wicked plan evolved in her mind. It was almost too easy. She only had to feed his pathetic ego, compliment his form and his deeds. She would make him believe she desired him. This one was greedy for attention. It would be his downfall.

She would take her time. Savor the chase. She would not offer him death quickly. She would make him beg for it. She smiled wickedly and followed the crowd.

Chapter 9

As the day progressed, stories of the miraculous rescue at sea filtered across the world's television stations and internet sites. Álvaro's ability to understand and speak multiple languages he was unfamiliar with was touted as miraculous. The world celebrated with Álvaro, but none more than the city of Algeciras. Joaquín Díaz boasted of his son's deeds to all who would listen. Sophia Díaz cried tears of joy, thankful her son had saved not only those desperate people in the water but her sweet Benicio as well. People who had never noticed Álvaro before were seeing him for the first time.

Beni enjoyed his brother's fame and fortune from the sidelines. Álvaro was happier than Beni had ever seen him. Watching the festivities, he couldn't ignore the gnawing in the pit of his stomach. He was frightened. He had replayed the rescue repeatedly in his mind, but he still couldn't explain what had happened to him. How was he able to speak the correct words in a language unknown to him? He rubbed his throbbing temples. As the crowd dispersed, he realized he hadn't eaten anything since breakfast, and fading sunlight indicated it was way past dinnertime. No wonder he felt out of sorts.

"It's time to get the real party started," one of Álvaro's buddies suggested. "La Ballena is the perfect place to continue the celebration!"

"You read my mind," Álvaro answered eagerly.

"Álvaro, may I go with you?" Beni urged.

"Of course, little brother, you're my good luck charm," Álvaro said, then he leaned in and whispered, "How did you do it, by the way?"

"I have no idea, and that scares me."

"Don't be scared. How it happened doesn't matter. People's lives were saved. Don't sweat the details."

Beni nodded his head, even though he didn't agree with Álvaro. It did matter a lot, at least to him. But there would be plenty of time to figure things out tomorrow after Álvaro's celebration was done.

Loud cheers greeted them when they walked into the main room of the bar. Beni figured it would be weeks, maybe even months, before people stopped congratulating his brother. For Álvaro's sake, he hoped the people of Algeciras never forgot his brother's heroic deeds. He knew his brother well enough to understand that Álvaro needed attention, lots of it. He didn't get the fanfare he craved as an ordinary fisherman. But now, things would be different. The city of Algeciras knew his brother's name. He hoped that Álvaro would be happier with his life now.

The smoke-filled bar, which combined loud music and a raucous crowd, had taken Beni's headache from manageable to nauseating. He sat at a small table in the back corner as far away from the dance floor as possible. From his vantage point, he could just enjoy watching Álvaro celebrate with his friends.

"You must be proud, eh?" Tomás, the proprietor, said. "Your brother saved the day."

"He's a hero," Benicio agreed. He looked longingly at the plate of steaming paella Tomás held in his hand.

"Hungry?" Tomás laughed, setting the plate in front of him. "Enjoy, it's on the house."

He dug into the paella. The warm spicy food filled his empty stomach and dulled the ache in his head. When he pushed the empty plate away, he was satisfied and felt much better. Thinking he would just rest a bit until Álvaro was ready to go home, he laid his head on the table. Just before he gave in to sleep, he noticed his brother being led to the dance floor by a dark-haired woman in a red skirt.

"He always gets the pretty ones," he mused and closed his eyes.

When he woke, the bar was quiet. He scratched the tingling itch behind his ear, wondering how long he had been asleep. It must have been a couple of hours because the bar was almost empty. He didn't see Álvaro.

"He just left a few minutes ago, Benicio. And I don't think he wants any company if you know what I mean," Tomás snickered.

"Thanks for the paella, Tomás," Beni offered before exiting the bar.

He started toward home, wishing that he had the keys to the truck. Even though home was just three miles away, he would much rather drive the distance than walk. When he passed a narrow side street, he noticed Álvaro and the pretty woman from the bar going into a tiny hotel. He wasn't surprised. His brother had always been popular with the ladies. Now that he knew where Álvaro was, he decided to wait for his brother to give him a ride home. He went around the side of the building and sank down against the wall in the alley to wait. It was almost dawn. It shouldn't be too long. He yawned. Maybe, he would just close his eyes for a moment, just until Álvaro was done.

He must have dozed off because he jumped when he heard the front door of the building slam open. Peering around the corner, he saw the pretty woman walk out. She was talking on her cell. And whatever she was saying, he bet the person on the other end wasn't enjoying it if her tone was any clue. When she turned toward him, he was glad he was hidden from her view. He gasped when he saw the knotted rope bracelet around her wrist. It belonged to his brother. He had given it to him for his birthday.

"Why would Álvaro have given the bracelet to this woman," he wondered.

When a silver car with tinted windows pulled up to the curb, the woman got in and sped away. Something wasn't right. Álvaro had not come out of the building. What was he waiting on? Beni left the alley quickly and entered the hotel to search for his brother. The small lobby was dingy and dimly lit. There was no one working at the front desk. The place looked deserted.

"Hello, is anyone here?" he called out.

He rang the front desk bell. The shrill sound echoed in the silent lobby. Something was very wrong. But he climbed the stairs to the upper level anyway.

"Álvaro, where are you?"

Down a long hallway with several doors, he tried each one, but all the rooms were empty.

"Álvaro, stop playing around. I want to go home."

When he reached the last door and peered behind the door, his brother's name froze on his lips. Álvaro was lying face down across a dirty mattress, shirtless and shoeless, in the center of the gloomy room. He went to his brother and turned his brother's body over, and inhaled sharply.

"No, Álvaro, wake up," Beni wailed. "You can't leave me."

Álvaro's vacant eyes stared back at him. His face was ragged; deep bloodless gashes ran from his temple down to his neck. Dark purple bruises mottled his chest and his forearms. His brother's neck was distended and twisted at an awkward angle. Beni struggled to make sense of what was happening. Just a few hours ago, Álvaro had been alive, laughing, dancing, and enjoying his party.

Beni's entire body began shaking; his heart was beating like a freight train. He was struggling to catch his breath. Hundreds of questions flashed through his mind. "Who did this to my brother? Did he suffer, or was it quick? Was it the woman? If so, why would she want to kill him? What should he do now? He needed to get help, but he didn't want to leave Álvaro.

When he heard a car door slam, his panic increased. He crawled to the window and peered out the grimy glass. It was a silver car. She had returned—the woman in the red skirt. And she wasn't alone; two sizeable men dressed in tactical gear stood on either side of her. He moved quickly away from the window, hoping that she hadn't seen him. There was nothing for it. He had to move, or he would end up like his brother. He crawled back to Álvaro and kissed his cold cheeks in farewell.

"I'll come back for you," he promised.

He scooted toward the door to listen. He could hear the voices of men below. Just as he had feared, they were already in the hotel. He opened the door quietly and sprinted across the hall to the exit door that he hoped led to the roof. He had no idea what he would do after that. He prayed it would be easy to figure out. He was running on adrenalin now. Reaching the roof, he realized quickly he only had one option. He would have to jump across to the roof of the next building. He judged it to be a short distance; he prayed that he was right. He got a running start and hurled himself into the air. His feet landed with a thud. He had cleared the distance.

Back over his shoulder, he saw a man charge out onto the hotel roof. Flattening himself immediately to the ground, he held his breath, watching the man scan the surrounding rooftops. When the man turned his head and walked back toward the rooftop door, Beni jumped up to run. Too late, he realized his mistake. The man had only been waiting on him to move. Dumbfounded, he watched the man shape-shift into a fearsome black bird with cold blue eyes. As the creature spread its wings to take flight, Beni took off. From the roof, down the stairs, and onto the narrow street, he fled. All thoughts vanished from his mind, save one. He had to escape. He ran in the direction of the port.

As he zigzagged through the narrow streets of the historic district, the black bird exploded into a dozen screeching feathered creatures all barreling toward him. He ducked into the mercado, an open-air market. Weaving in and out of booths filled with ripe fruit, smelly fish, and colorful baskets, he ran. He jumped into a cart full of oranges. Unfortunately, he knocked it over, and the angry shouts of the vendor drew the birds closer.

Leaving the market, he skidded to a stop when a small child riding a bicycle crossed his path. Barely keeping his balance, he turned, veering down a smaller alley. Still, the birds followed.

He had to move faster. They were gaining on him. His lungs were bursting. Rounding the corner, he found himself at the Plaza Alta, the city's oldest square. He skidded to an abrupt stop. Four choices, four different paths leading away from the square, but which path should he take? Which one would lead him to safety, far from the evil that was closing in?

He closed his eyes and asked for help from the only one who could give it. "God, I don't know which way to go. Please show me."

When he opened his eyes, he could have shouted for joy. He hadn't noticed it before. But, in the southeastern corner of the square, rising majestically into the morning sky, the *Iglesia de Nuestra Señora de la Palma* was a beacon of hope, an answer to his prayer.

"Thank You, God."

Past the massive fountain, the poplar trees, and the colorful ceramic-tiled benches, Beni ran toward the church. He darted into the cool darkness of the sanctuary. The silence within comforted him. Seeing no one around, he made his way quickly down the aisle toward the confessionals that lined the west wall. He jerked open one of the stalls and shut himself inside. Afraid to move, Beni tried to control his heavy breathing. If they found him, there was nowhere else for him to run.

"God, save me; please don't let them find me," he implored.

Beni was startled when the wooden panel inside the confessional slid open, revealing a small window covered with metal mesh.

"My son, what are you here?" a soothing voice said from the shadows on the other side.

"Padre, I'm in big trouble. They killed my brother, and now they're after me. I need your help."

"Do not be afraid. You are safe here, my son."

"But, padre, if you could see the things I have seen; you must believe me, there is an evil out there."

"I do believe you, Benicio."

"You do?"

"Yes, my son, I know the evil that hunts you. I need you to do as exactly as I tell you. I know you are frightened, but will you trust me?"

He wondered how the padre had known his name but pushed this thought immediately from his mind. It didn't matter. For the first time this morning, he thought he might be safe.

"Yes, sir, I can."

"There is a small latch on the wall behind your seat. I want you to unhook it and then open the panel. I will meet you on the other side."

Counting his blessings that he had thought to run into the church, he found the latch and slid the back panel of the confessional aside. The kindest and warmest eyes he had ever seen greeted him.

"No fear?" the padre asked softly but with great authority.

Benicio was surprised to realize that, at that moment, he wasn't afraid. He couldn't tear his gaze away from the man's gentle countenance.

"Good. My name is Asher, and I have been sent here to help you. Come along."

He felt an incredible sense of peace as he followed Asher through a series of pathways that were hidden behind the sliding door of the confessional. The longer they walked, the more confident Beni became, which was unusual for him. When Asher opened the door at the end of the passage, Beni found himself outside in an empty alley. Then right before his eyes, the padre transformed into another being. He was a golden angel with spectacular wings that sounded like ocean waves rolling in at tide when they moved.

"Padre?" Beni was awestruck. He struggled to accept the incredible and yet undeniable truth right in front of him. He was sure Asher could see his uncertainty.

"It's a lot to take in all at once, but we don't have much time. I need you to be bold, Beni."

He swallowed hard. He didn't understand what was happening, but he knew he didn't have another option. So, he squared his shoulders and said, "Tell me what to do."

Asher smiled faintly and wrapped his strong arms around him. "Hold on."

Chapter 10

Standing on the front steps of her new home, Lily enjoyed the coolness of the morning on her skin. Sleep had eluded her; her thoughts focused on the past. Last night at dinner, she had wanted to hear stories about her father, hoping they would make her feel warm inside again. But they hadn't. Talking about him, remembering him, only shredded her heart into tinier pieces. And then her fight with Lucas had only made it worse. She couldn't wait to run. She was desperate to clear her head.

Anxious to get going, she pulled her hair back into a ponytail and texted Jude that she was on her way. The Butler house was a charming, two-story, Colonial-style brick structure with a gabled roof. Before she could knock on the front door, it was opened by a beautiful woman with a friendly smile and a flaming red updo dressed in an emerald-green housecoat.

"You must be Lily. Aren't you just pretty as a peach?" she gushed in a distinctly Southern twang. "I'm Pearl Butler. Jude will be right down."

"It's nice to meet you, Mrs. Butler."

"Why don't you come in, honey, and have some breakfast? Homer, Jude's daddy, is fixin' his famous homemade buttermilk biscuits and sausage gravy."

"Can't, Mom," Jude interrupted, scooting past his mom to join Lily. "We're going for a run."

"Well then, you two have fun. It was nice meetin' you, Lily. I hope to see you again real soon."

"Bye, Mrs. Butler," Lily said.

"Bye, Mom," Jude waved. Once they were out of earshot, Jude said sheepishly, "I know my mom's a lot."

"I think she's perfect."

Jude looked relieved, "Then you will love my dad! Come on, this way."

Lily followed Jude to the end of their street to the entrance to the greenway, the city's shaded running trail.

"How far does the trail go?" she asked.

"About six miles, give or take. You ready?"

"Let's just see if you can keep up," she challenged smugly.

Lily set the pace for the first two miles. Running along the bubbling creek that ran beside the trail was peaceful. Birds sang in the low-hanging trees, and the sounds of the waking city echoed around her. Despite Lily's challenge, Jude kept pace with her easily.

"Halfway. Need a break?" Jude asked.

She stopped to check her watch, calculating her pulse and elapsed time. She felt good. She was finally relaxing a bit. Wiping the sweat from her brow, she glanced at Jude. He looked as cool as a cucumber.

"You aren't even breathing hard! You didn't tell me you were a machine."

"What can I say? If the running shoe fits..."

"That's not even funny!"

"Yeah, but you're laughing!"

"Yeah, I am. And I don't do that very often."

Lily was surprised a little at how comfortable she felt with Jude.

"Wanna walk for a bit?" he suggested.

"Sure. You know, yesterday, I thought you were shy and kinda awkward if I'm being truthful."

"Awkward, that hurts!" Jude feigned an injured heart.

"I was completely wrong. I'm glad I met you, Jude Butler. You are easy to be around, unlike most people in my life."

"I'll take that as a compliment," he grinned sheepishly. "I like you too, Lily Quinn."

"Let's run every day, at least every day that we can. Deal?"

"Sure, I'm game. Running helps me put things in perspective."

"Me too! It's like my own little therapy session."

"What could you possibly need therapy for, Lily?"

She didn't know what to say, so she didn't say anything.

"Look, I know we just met, but Lily, I get the feeling that something is going on with you. Can I help?"

"Let's keep things simple, okay? The past is not something I like to talk about."

"Got it. But if you ever change your mind. I'll be a friend to you."

She searched Jude's face for some sign of insincerity. But all she saw was genuine concern.

"You really mean that, don't you?"

"Yeah, I do. And I'm a good listener."

"Well, that's definitely a plus," she smiled.

She could use a friend right now. She had been alone with her thoughts and feelings for too long. Lucas had been her best friend, but the separation between them now was impossible to mend at this point. She wanted to trust someone—she needed to trust someone. It was an easy decision.

"Okay, here goes," Lily said, mustering some courage. "When I was ten, Lucas and I were playing in the woods with my dad. A bear came out of the trees and attacked."

"Wow, that's awful. You must have been so scared."

"My dad tried to protect us. But the bear was too strong. He mauled my dad. I watched it all happen. I watched him die."

"Aww, Lily, I can't even imagine how hard that must have been for you."

"Nothing has ever been the same since."

She stopped walking, lost in her memories. Jude reached for her hand.

"You must miss him something awful."

"Every day. I've tried, I truly have, to be okay, to move on. But it's so hard without him."

Jude said nothing. He just rubbed her hand gently. Lily loved that he wasn't trying to offer advice or wisdom. He was just listening. He was being a friend. She had missed being this close with someone.

"I've locked so many parts of myself away. It's just too hard; It hurts too much. And I'm afraid I've lost some pieces of me because of it.

Again, Jude said nothing. He just waited for her to continue.

"But when I run, I feel like I get a little closer to the girl I was before my world was torn apart. Crazy, right?"

"Not crazy at all. You're much stronger than you think, Lily Quinn."

"I want that to be true."

She had never shared this much of her grief with anyone. She had always been so careful to keep people at bay, hiding her true emotions behind the only one that made her feel strong, her anger. But because of Jude, his easiness, his lack of expectation, and his kindness, she had allowed herself to experience something she had almost forgotten. Vulnerability.

"You've trusted me, Lily, with something very precious to you, your feelings. I won't take that for granted. I promise I won't let you down."

"Weirdly enough, I believe you. I think I've found my very first true friend in you."

Pushing his glasses, which never seemed to stay put, higher on the bridge of his nose, Jude beamed. He looked quite pleased with himself. She was growing quite fond of this awkward little tic of his. Eager to embrace this newfound sense of lightness she felt in her heart, she took off running.

"Hey, wait up," Jude shouted, taking off after her.

"I'm famished. Race you back?"

"You're on!"

Sprinting toward the end of the greenway, she just edged past him for the win.

"Now, who's the machine?" Jude said, panting with exertion. "Rematch in the morning?"

"Most definitely! Want to come to my house for some breakfast?"

"Will there be juice involved? I love orange juice," Jude declared.

She laughed, "I'm sure Aunt Audrey can make that happen."

Rounding the corner of Ocoee Street, Jude stumbled and fell hard to the pavement.

"Are you alright?"

His face winced in pain. "Yeah, sorry. I can be a real klutz sometimes. It's my knee."

She helped him to his feet. "I bet some orange would do the trick. Let's get you inside."

"You don't have to ask me twice."

With a slight limp, Jude followed Lily into the house. They were greeted by the sound of Audrey's favorite classic Southern rock.

"Be prepared. My aunt loves to dance while she cooks," Lily warned as they headed to the kitchen.

"Hey, Lily, Jude," Audrey greeted. "Just in time for my famous bacon and waffles."

"Amazing! It smells wonderful, Aunt Audrey."

"How was your run?"

"Best one I've had in a long time," Lily answered, exchanging a knowing glance with Jude.

"Great, y'all take a seat. I'll get your plates served up."

"Do we have any orange juice, Aunt Audrey?"

"Coming right up!" Audrey answered, dancing toward the refrigerator.

"Morning, everyone," Zoe greeted brightly, joining Lily and Jude at the big farmhouse table.

"Service with a smile," Audrey announced, serving up plates of warm waffles oozing with maple syrup and sizzling bacon. "Lily, you pour the juice."

"Sure thing!"

Audrey joined them at the table with a steaming mug of coffee.

"Where's Luc this morning?"

"Don't think he's up yet. You know how he loves his beauty sleep," Zoe answered while feeding a piece of bacon to Jack, who was sprawled under the table.

"That dog loves to eat," Audrey commented. Picking up the crossword puzzle from the morning newspaper, she asked, "Seven-letter word for an eighties hair band?"

"Bon Jovi," Zoe and Lily answered in unison.

Audrey laughed. "That's my girls. I have trained you well."

"She has a thing for rock bands and crossword puzzles," Lily whispered to Jude. "It's a daily ritual."

"My mom does too."

"Can you imagine them back then?"

"I try not to," Jude remarked dryly and then drained his third glass of juice. "I better get going, Lily. My mom is planting her garden today, and she gave me strict orders to be home to help."

"Sure, okay."

Jude stood, still favoring his knee a little. "Thank you for breakfast, Dr. McCant."

"You are always welcome at my table, Jude," Audrey answered kindly.

"See you later, Zoe. Jack."

"Bye, Jude," Zoe returned.

"And thanks for the run, Lily. I had fun."

"Me too. I'll text you later, okay?"

"Sounds good."

Leaving the kitchen, Jude ran into Lucas. Lily's light mood disappeared instantly.

"Hey man, hope you left some food for me," Lucas joked.

"Mornin, Lucas," Jude said on his way out the door.

"Waffles, my favorite," Lucas mused, taking a seat at the table. Serving himself a full plate, he continued. "How was your run, Lily?"

"Fine," she said curtly.

"That's good. I know how much you like to run. Zoe, what are you and Jack doing today?"

"Jack needs some exercise. So, I think we're going for a walk later. I want to explore. How 'bout you?"

"I met some people from town last night when I went on a walk of my own. They invited me to the river today."

"That sounds like fun," Audrey commented. "Students at Centenary? Maybe I know them."

"Aiden Talbot and some of his friends. They were super cool."

"Aiden was in my English class last year. He's a good one. But he doesn't always hang out with the best people."

"Gray Ramsey?"

"Bingo! Be careful around him, Luc. Based on my observation, he's got a big ego and doesn't mind treating people badly."

"Yeah, I kinda figured that out last night. I'm pretty sure he hates me already. But I'll be careful."

"I know you will."

"Where's mom, Zoe?" Lucas asked while pouring more syrup on his waffles.

"I don't know," Zoe answered. "I haven't seen her."

"I'll give you both one guess," Audrey offered.

"Hmm...back porch reading a boring romance novel?" Lucas answered.

"And don't forget the coffee," Zoe added.

Audrey laughed. "My sister is a creature of habit."

The three of them continued talking, enjoying each other's company. Watching Lucas' easy exchange and friendly banter with Audrey and Zoe stirred up conflicting emotions in Lily. She dearly loved her aunt and her sister. She wished she could join in the fun. But her resentment for Lucas made it impossible. Whenever her brother was around, she withdrew.

"I'm gonna find Mom," Lucas announced, carrying his dishes to the sink. "Thanks for the waffles, Aunt Audrey."

"Of course," Audrey answered, returning to the kitchen to straighten up.

"Lucas, will you tell Mom I'll be back in a bit? I've got a date with Jack and his leash. This boy is getting fat," Zoe said on her way out the door.

"Will do," Lucas replied and headed for the back porch.

Left alone at the table, Lily watched Lucas and Mia through the window. The familiar pangs of jealousy filled her heart. Her mother had always loved her brother best.

Chapter 11

Zoe strolled down the shady street. Jack was pulling at his leash, wanting to quicken their pace.

"Not yet, Jack, I'm thinking."

She was still trying to wrap her head around all the information she had learned about her family last night. It's not that she doubted the things that Dr. Gable had told her about God and the supernatural; she knew all of it was true. It was the fact that her brother had a supernatural power. How in the world was she going to keep that a secret?

But keeping the secret kept Lucas safe. He was her constant. Helping her with math homework, hugging her when she was sad, teaching her to play the guitar, encouraging her on the basketball court, playing Clue with her for the umpteenth time, cheering her on when she was in the school play; every time she had needed Lucas, he had always been there for her. Now, the tables were turned—he needed her. Not just to keep his secret but also to help him to heal his relationship with Lily. Zoe had been the peacemaker between her siblings for as long as she could remember. She didn't like conflict or seeing people hurt, especially the ones she loved. But after last night, hearing them fight with each other, her desire to bridge the gap in their relationship was easier said than done. She knew she had her work cut out for her.

A sharp bark from Jack brought her back to the present.

"I'm sorry, boy," she said, scratching her dog's favorite itch behind his ear, "You've got my attention. What do you see over there, boy?"

Following Jack's lead, Zoe jogged across the street toward a garden of wildflowers in a kaleidoscope of colors.

"Ahh, you heard the bees, didn't you, Jack?"

The white shepherd loved to chase and play with the insects. Their lazy buzzing was an irresistible temptation.

"Good morning, young lady," a female voice greeted. She hadn't noticed the woman on her knees in the flower bed. "You must be one of Audrey's nieces."

"Yes, ma'am. I'm Zoe, and this is my dog, Jack. He loves to play with bees."

"I can see that; I'm Dorothea Martin."

The woman stood less than five feet tall. Her close-cropped dark hair was speckled with grey, and her merry eyes sparkled. Her wide-brimmed straw hat flopped around her cherub face. Zoe liked her instantly.

"I've lived on this street going on thirty years now. I was tickled pink when Audrey bought the old Sweezy place. She's poured herself into remodeling that house."

"Yeah, the house is really pretty."

"What do you think of our little town, Zoe?"

"It's great, but very different from where I used to live in Florida."

"It will grow on you. I was born and raised here. Know almost everyone too. Not much goes on without me getting wind of it, to be sure."

"I can't imagine being in one place for so long. My family has moved around a lot."

"Well, I've always said it doesn't matter where you live if you are surrounded by the love of family. Love is a powerful thing."

"Yes, ma'am, it sure is."

"My two boys are grown and moved away. Since Mr. Martin and I retired, we just sit around twiddling our thumbs, waiting to be blessed with some grandchildren. Unfortunately, my boys are not in any hurry to settle down. Anyway, when Dr. Gable—he's that nice professor who works with your aunt at Centenary Academy—asked us if we would like to sponsor an exchange student from abroad, we jumped at the chance of having a young person in the house again."

"I met Dr. Gable last night."

"Well, that's just wonderful. Can you imagine our surprise when Dr. Gable called us last night to tell us he needed to place a student right away? Of course, we said yes! The poor thing arrived late last night. Poor thing, I don't know if he needed food or sleep more."

"That's great, Mrs. Martin; maybe I can meet him sometime."

"How 'bout right now? I'm sure he would love to make a friend before school starts. He's just your age."

"Sure, I'd like to make a new friend too."

"Oh look, here he comes now."

Zoe studied the young man in question as he approached. He sported a soccer jersey and shorts. His brown skin, round dark eyes, and jet-black hair, cut close, complemented an ordinary but friendly face. When he stopped in front of her, she realized they were just the same height.

"Zoe Quinn, this Beni Díaz. All the way from Spain, can you believe it?"

Zoe thought Beni looked tired, but there was also a hint of sadness around his eyes. She figured he must miss his family and home so far away. Her heart went out to him.

After he greeted her shyly, Beni asked, "Mrs. Martin, would you like some help in the garden?"

"Aren't you sweet?" Mrs. Martin cooed, picking up a basket of freshly cut colorful blooms. "But I'm done for the morning. I've got to change clothes and get these flowers to the church for a wedding. I imagine I am a sight!"

Zoe bent down and ruffled her dog's neck. "I was just taking Jack for a walk. Wanna come with me, Beni?"

"I would like that," Beni answered politely. "Is this okay, Mrs. Martin?"

"Of course, my boy! You two have fun," Mrs. Martin waved enthusiastically and hurried toward her house.

"Mrs. Martin seems really nice," Zoe remarked as she and Beni walked down the tree-lined street.

"Yes, she is, and her husband too. They were great, considering my unexpected arrival. My coming here sort of last-minute thing."

Zoe laughed. "Well, you could say, last-minute totally defines my life lately."

"You know we have a lot in common. My family just moved here yesterday to live with my aunt. I'll be a freshman at Centenary Academy in the fall. What about you?"

"Same. That's great luck, isn't it?"

"Yes, for sure. All the way from Spain, wow! I would love to go there someday."

"My home is in the southern part of Spain, near the Mediterranean Sea. It is very beautiful," he said wistfully.

"I bet it's hard to be away. You must miss your family too?"

Beni stiffened slightly, and his face clouded with sadness.

"It hasn't really sunk in yet. What about your family?"

Before she could answer, Jack stopped suddenly and started barking.

"Hey, it's a snow cone truck," Zoe said with excitement. "I'd recognize that annoying music anywhere. I haven't had one in forever."

"I don't think I've ever had a snow cone from a truck."

"Fabulous! It will be your first all-American dessert. My treat!"

Zoe waved as the truck passed, and the driver slowed to a stop. Others had heard the music, too, because they were soon joined by a couple of little boys on their bikes. All four of them gathered around the truck. There was a big chest of shaved ice and a colorful array of big plastic bottles with dispensers for the different syrup flavors set up in the flatbed.

"What'll it be?"

"I'll have cherry, please," the freckle-faced boy answered. "And what about your friend?"

"Noah can't talk, mister. I'll order it for him. He wants blueberry."

Zoe couldn't help but smile at the two boys. They couldn't have been more than eight years old, but the bond between the two was unmistakable. They walked back toward their bikes with their cones already dripping in the hot summer heat.

"How 'bout you, girly? I've got five different flavors," the man smiled. He removed his baseball cap and wiped the perspiration from his forehead. "Wanna try a kamikaze?"

Jack growled and pulled on his leash.

"Shh, Jack," Zoe commanded.

"What's a kamikaze?" Beni asked.

"All the flavors mixed together!" Zoe answered. "That sounds good. Two, please?"

"Sure, coming right up."

"Business has been slow this morning," he remarked while making their cones. "You got some friends around? Or is it just you two?"

"No, just us," Zoe replied, taking the snow cones from the man.

"Whew! It's a hot one today. Those cones are gonna melt before you know it."

"How much?" Zoe asked, digging in the pocket of her jean shorts for money.

"No charge, girly. You neither, boy. Consider it a gift."

"Thanks. Have a good day," Zoe said, anxious to be away from the man that was getting creepier by the minute. "Let's go, Beni."

"Wait a minute! How 'bout I give you two a ride back to your house? You could help me spot some kids who might want a snow cone along the way."

When Jack stiffened and growled again, Zoe instinctively retreated a few steps back from the truck. "Sorry, I don't know why he's so upset."

Jack's growl became a snarl and then a short, low-pitched bark. The shepherd was very upset, and Zoe's attempts to calm him weren't working. Beni stepped in front of her and took Jack's leash from her hand.

"We'll walk, thank you," Beni insisted, taking Zoe's arm and leading her back to the sidewalk.

"Let's walk fast. He gives me the creeps," Zoe said.

"I'm trying, but your dog is not cooperating. Something has got him spooked."

Beni tried to pull Jack without much luck.

"Here, give me the leash," she said. "Jack, come on, boy, let's go home."

Jack responded and stopped pulling against his leash. Zoe was a bundle of nerves. The whole situation was getting stranger and scarier by the minute. The snow cone man was still standing by his truck watching them. She knew they needed to find some other people real fast. When she heard the truck engine roar to life and the silly music play, she felt herself relax a little. But when the truck turned around and started coming toward them, her mother's warning about strangers rang in her ears.

"I've got a bad feeling about this guy," Beni said urgently.

Jack stopped abruptly; his barking intensified. When he jerked against his leash, Zoe was caught off guard. She lost her hold. Jack tore across the street toward the snow cone truck. Out of nowhere, a car driving way too fast roared down the street. At the same time, the little boy named Noah was crossing the street on his bike. By the time the driver saw the boy and slammed on the brakes, it was too late. At impact, Noah was catapulted into the air and landed with an awful thud on the hot asphalt street.

Chapter 12

Zoe ran to Noah. Beni, who had managed to catch Jack, followed close behind. She fell to her knees beside the boy, taking his small hand in hers. Noah's contorted body was motionless, and he labored to breathe. Beni, his face pale and drawn, was kneeling on the other side of Noah. Jack whimpered and nudged the boy's feet with his nose.

"You're okay, little man. Just hang on," Zoe soothed while stroking his brow. "Don't give up, Noah. We need you to stay with us, you hear?"

The driver of the car walked up and whispered, "I didn't see him. I'm sorry. I didn't see him."

When Zoe looked up at her, she could see that the woman was remorseful. When the faint sound of sirens echoed in the distance, the woman's countenance changed to one of fright. She was frightened, too, but not for the same reason.

"Do you hear that, little man? Help is on the way," she murmured to Noah.

"Please help him," the freckle-faced boy sobbed. "He's my best friend."

Zoe laid both hands on Noah's chest and prayed. "Please, God, let this sweet little boy be okay. Help me to help him."

She was startled by the warm tingle in her hands. In moments, her fingers were burning as if a bee had stung each one. Noah moaned, and his legs twitched.

"What's happening, Zoe?" Beni asked urgently.

Zoe looked up in painful confusion. "I'm not sure, but I can't move my hands."

It was like a magnet held her hand to the boy's chest. The searing heat coursing through her hands was almost unbearable. Then as quickly as it had come, the heat diminished, and her hands cooled. Noah's body was still, his breathing even and peaceful. She lifted her hands and stared at them in wonder. No burns.

When Noah's eyes fluttered open and he slowly sat up, Zoe whispered, "Impossible."

"Apparently not," Beni replied with a slight smile. "Here comes the ambulance now."

"Noah, are you okay? How do you feel?" Zoe asked.

Noah rubbed his head and then reached out to Jack, who immediately nuzzled him and licked his face. The boy giggled happily.

Zoe took Beni's hand and squeezed, communicating without words her joy as well as her wonder at what had just happened to Noah.

"Thank you for making Noah all better," the freckle-faced boy sniffled. He buried his face in Zoe's shirt and hugged her tightly. He let go abruptly and said, "Noah wants a hug too."

Zoe helped Noah stand. His body had been broken and bruised only minutes ago. Now, here he was, smiling and holding out his arms for a hug. It was the best hug Zoe had ever had!

When the paramedics arrived, Zoe stepped back with Noah's friend to watch. One examined Noah while the other spoke with Beni about the details of the accident.

"Only a few minor scrapes and bruises," the paramedic announced, then ruffled Noah's blond hair. "You are one lucky boy, Noah."

Noah returned the favor and patted the paramedic's hair, which was a match for his own. Then, he laughed. It was the sweetest sound Zoe had ever heard.

"We're all done here," the paramedic that was talking to Beni declared. "You boys want to take a ride in the ambulance? Your parents are going to meet us at the hospital."

"Yes, sir," the freckle-faced boy answered. He was beaming ear to ear. "Come on, Noah, let's go."

Noah followed his friend to the ambulance but stopped midway and ran back to her. Zoe crouched down so that she was at eye-level with him.

"You are such a brave boy," she whispered.

Noah put his chubby hand on the side of her face and leaned toward her. He touched her forehead with his own. And then he ran back to his friend, who was already climbing into the ambulance.

Pure happiness coursed through her body and soul. Zoe felt her heart would burst. Noah was alive. She didn't understand what had happened, but she was going to go with it. She waved goodbye to the boys and then noticed the skin behind her ear was tingling. She touched it gingerly and then walked over to Beni, who was waiting on the sidewalk with Jack.

"Where's the lady who was driving the car?"

Beni shrugged his shoulders. "I have no idea. She called 911, but she then must have driven away after that. I was so focused on you and Noah that I didn't notice."

Zoe stiffened when she heard a familiar voice behind her.

"My goodness," the snow cone man whistled. "I ain't never seen anything quite like it. I could've sworn that boy was a goner."

"Yeah, we were lucky," Zoe said abruptly.

Although the man was leaning against his car several yards away, she swore she could feel his hot breath on her neck.

"I don't know if I'd call it luck, girly; I'm thinking it's much more than that," he said, leaving his truck to walk slowly toward her. "I'm guessing you two will be wanting that ride now."

"Leave us alone," Beni warned, taking Zoe's hand in his.

The man's face darkened with anger, and he made a move toward Beni, "Listen to me, boy! I don't take kindly to rudeness."

The snow cone man's nostrils flared, and a feral countenance fell like a shade over his face.

"They said, leave them alone," a voice commanded.

"And I would listen if I were you," another voice added.

Zoe whipped her head around and breathed a sigh of relief. The paramedics who had treated Noah were behind them.

She thought they had left the scene already. Thank you, God; four against one put the odds in their favor. These guys were twice the size of the snow cone man. They were saved!

"Hey, just trying to help," the snow cone man whined. "No harm done."

He sauntered back to his truck and fired the engine. The silly melody echoed in the air long after the truck disappeared from her sight. It was then that Zoe realized she had been holding her breath. She exhaled in a whoosh.

"I'm so glad you guys showed up," she exclaimed. "I was worried we were in some big trouble."

"Are you alright?" the blonde paramedic asked.

"I think so, just a little freaked out," she replied. "It's gonna be a long time before I want another snow cone. Right, Beni?"

But Beni didn't answer. Her new friend was standing close to the dark-haired paramedic, deep in conversation. Their body language, the way they were talking, and the smile on Beni's face made her think they knew one another.

"Maybe I'm just paranoid, but I think that guy would have hurt us if he got the chance," she said, her attention once more on the blonde paramedic.

"Not paranoid; you are intuitive, Zoe. That man did intend you and Beni harm," Tov explained.

"Wait a minute," Zoe took a step back from him. "How do you know our names?"

The paramedic didn't answer.

"And you," she pointed at Beni. "You act like you know this guy! How is that possible if you only got here last night, Beni?"

"They're the good guys, Zoe," Beni encouraged. "They'll protect us.

"Protect us from what?"

Zoe's mind was racing through a hundred different scenarios, trying to find one that might explain what was happening to her. In the end, only one made sense.

"You're both like Dr. Gable, aren't you?"

"He is our brother," Tov answered simply.

"You're an angel?"

"I am your angel," Tov stressed. "Your guardian."

When Tov placed his hand lightly on her shoulder, her confusion and anxiety dissipated immediately.

"But why would I need a guardian?"

"You must know, Zoe," Tov assured with a gentle smile.

She touched the tingling skin behind her ear again. She did know. She had tried to explain it away, but she could no longer deny the truth of the power that had flowed through her when she touched Noah. She was only fourteen, but she knew the direction of her life had just shifted in an unsuspected and incredible way.

"I'm a Sorcha," Zoe announced with wonder.

"Yes, you are," Tov answered.

"I'll get Beni home," Asher said. "You have much to discuss with Zoe."

Tov gave a slight nod.

"If you want, I'll take Jack with me. You can come get him later?" Beni asked.

"Yes, thank you," Zoe responded and then bent down to give Jack a big hug. "See you in a little while, I promise."

"*Lehitraot*, brother," Asher said to Tov.

"*Lehitraot*," Tov returned.

Beni took Jack by the leash and waved goodbye before following Asher back home.

"What does that word mean? The one you said to Asher?" Zoe asked.

"It is the word my brothers and I use to say farewell," Tov replied. "It's Hebrew. The Dìonadain don't like to say 'goodbye,' it sounds so final. Rather, we say, 'lehitraot,' or see you again."

"It's a beautiful word."

"Yes, it is. Come, Zoe, let us walk, and you can tell me everything that happened," Tov invited.

Zoe walked alongside her guardian, and the words just rushed out.

"The little boy, Noah, was crossing the street on his bike. Then, out of nowhere, this car came barreling down the street and hit him. I ran over to him. He was barely breathing. I could only imagine the pain he must have been feeling. I wanted to help him. I didn't know what else to do but pray. So, I put my hands on his chest, and I asked God to heal him."

"What happened next?"

"My hands started to tingle, and then it was like they were on fire. I can't explain it but the heat from my hands when into Noah's body. When my hands cooled, Noah opened his eyes and smiled at me. It was unbelievable, and I don't understand it. Will you explain it to me?"

"We find it difficult to believe in the impossible because it doesn't make sense to us, or we are afraid. But what happened to you and to Noah was real. You asked God for Noah's healing. He used the light that lives within you to heal that little boy and make him whole again. God has gifted you, Zoe, with the power of healing."

For the first time in her life, Zoe was at a loss for words. She knew that Tov was speaking the truth. She couldn't deny that a miracle had happened when Noah was healed. It was just a little difficult to accept the reality of her role in the miracle.

"You are a Sorcha, my child."

"Just like Lucas," she whispered.

"Yes, and Beni as well; that is why he was brought here. He needed our protection, just like you do."

"The snow cone man? He knew what Beni and I were, didn't he? That's why he tried to get us in his truck?"

"Yes, he is a Scáth; therefore, you are both dangerous to him and those like him."

"I have so much I want to ask you, Tov."

"And I will try to answer them all. But first, we must reacquire a certain dog and get you both back home."

Questions, ideas, possibilities, dozens of them, were exploding in her brain. Whatever the path ahead, she was confident it would be the grandest adventure.

"I am very glad that you're my guardian, Tov."

Her angel smiled, "I as well, dear Zoe."

Chapter 13

A car engine rumbled outside her window. Lucas must be home from the river. Lily pulled the curtain back from the window. A black sports car was sitting in the driveway. She had to admit she was curious about who her brother might be with. Down the stairs and out the back door she went.

Unobserved on the back porch, she watched Lucas and his new friend, who could only be described as gorgeous, shooting basketball. His wavy black hair was cut short. Although clean-shaven, a grain of whiskers lying just beneath his tanned skin darkened his square jaw. Moving with the ease of an athlete, he was tall, lean, and well-built. She placed her hand over her stomach to still the flutter.

"What's up, Lily?" Lucas shouted, dribbling the basketball in the driveway.

As she crossed the lawn, she deliberately kept her gaze on her brother, ignoring the stranger that made her heart beat a little faster. She didn't like that feeling.

"Nothing really," she offered in a friendly tone. "Where have you been?"

"Swimming," he answered, taking a jump shot.

"Sounds like fun!"

"Heads up!" Lucas passed the ball to his friend. "Lily, this is Aiden Talbot."

Aiden caught the pass, shifted the ball under his arm, and offered his hand. "It's a pleasure to meet you, Lily."

"Yeah, you too." She moistened her lips nervously, trying to appear more confident than she felt. When her hand touched his, she felt a spark of electricity unlike anything she had ever known. It startled her. She dropped her hand quickly.

"Quinn, you didn't tell me you had a sister."

"Maybe there's a reason I didn't tell you."

Suddenly, she felt very awkward. Looking down at her flip-flops, she missed the glance the young men exchanged.

"Thanks for the swim today, Aiden. I'll catch up with you tomorrow." Lucas said abruptly.

"Glad you could hang out." Turning back to Lily, he added, "Next time, Lily will join us. Yes?"

She smiled noncommittally. She felt the flutter again in her stomach, only stronger this time, when Aiden gave her a slight wink.

As soon as his friend drove away, Lucas said quietly, "Be careful, Lily. He has a reputation for breaking hearts. Don't encourage him."

"Seriously? I can make my own decisions, thank you! Besides, I'm not interested."

Her words sounded hollow. She was interested in Aiden. She hoped her brother hadn't noticed.

"I'm just watching out for you, Sis."

"Well, I don't need your watching."

And with that, she spun around and stalked back toward the house.

"Hey, we're not finished!"

"Well, I'm finished with you," she shouted back over her shoulder.

"What's going on?" Audrey called.

Her aunt was standing on the porch steps and must have seen a bit of her exchange with Lucas.

"Nothing, Just Lucas sticking his nose in where it doesn't belong," she answered with an exasperated shrug.

"Well, that's why we love him, isn't it, sweetheart?"

When Lucas joined them, Audrey asked, "You two won't ever stop, will you?"

"Wouldn't be as much fun, would it?" Lucas flashed a quick grin.

"I guess not," Audrey agreed good-naturedly, hooking her arms with Lucas and Lily. "Come with me; I've got something to show you both."

She walked with her aunt and brother across the lawn away from the house.

"You know, Aunt Audrey, I think I'm gonna like living here," Lucas continued.

"I hope you both will. Cleveland is a special town. I've always thought there was a little bit of magic here."

When she rolled her eyes at her aunt's comment, Lucas teased, "I'm not so sure Lily is sold on this place yet."

"Give her time. We'll win her over," Audrey winked at her. "I think I may know what would help convince her."

Audrey stopped in front of the small garage at the back of her property. Lily had no idea what was behind the garage door, but she was curious.

"Your dad was like my brother. After you both were born, he gave me something to keep for you, something he wanted you both to have when you got old enough. I think the time has finally arrived."

When Audrey lifted the creaky door, Lucas whistled appreciatively, "Wow! Now, that's a car!"

She ducked into the garage and ran her hand gently across the hood of a vintage 1973 metallic blue Ford Mustang. Keystone chain wheels gleamed in the afternoon sunlight streaming through the big windows on either side of the garage. Her brother didn't waste any time. He opened the driver's side door and plopped behind the wheel on the cream leather seat.

"What do you think, Lily?"

"She's beautiful."

"This was really Dad's?" he mused, touching the steering wheel.

"Eli knew what he was doing. He spent a ton of hours restoring this beauty," Audrey explained, handing the keys to Lucas.

Her brother turned the key in the ignition, and the motor roared to life.

"Can I?" he asked hopefully.

"Of course," Audrey answered.

"Want to take her for a ride, Lily?"

"You don't have to ask me twice!"

She hopped in the passenger seat and grinned, "Don't get too comfortable in that seat, Luc."

"I know, I know," he laughed. "You never did like to share!"

For a few minutes, Lily wanted to forget she was supposed to be mad at her brother. She wanted it to feel easy and fun again. She decided to put her trouble with Lucas in the rear-view mirror, at least for this afternoon. As they sped down the shady street, music blaring on the radio, and the summer wind in her hair, she was truly happy. It felt good. Just for a time, she would let her heart roam free.

Live images streamed from across the globe danced on the screens lining the walls of the circular room. Any reference to unexplained events, miraculous happenings, or people performing impossible tasks would be seen and investigated.

At the center of the room, standing on a raised dais, her master studied her.

He was Lucifer's chosen one, Cain, the legendary commander of the Scáths.

She knew Lucifer had chosen him for his extraordinary intellect and lethal skill. Well-versed in all realms of warfare, Cain's sole purpose, throughout the centuries, was to hunt and kill the Sorcha. If they were ever allowed to unite their gifts, the power created would usher in the eradication of evil. Her master would not rest until all light was extinguished.

For as long as she could remember, she had aided her master in his hunt.

Killing Sorcha capitalized on her particular skill set. Yet, despite her careful planning and quick action, the Dìonadain had been able to secure three of the twelve. The Quinn siblings had slipped through her fingers, and now with her misstep in Spain, her master was displeased with her.

She had never failed him. She swore that she would not this time.

She was afraid the consequence would be beyond even her dark and twisted imagination.

"He is the one," she recounted. "I am sure of it."

"I will determine if he has the gift of light," he spat. "I believe I will come with you this time to oversee. The Dìonadain will be close."

"As you wish, master."

"Is your team ready?" Cain barked, his eyes flaming blue.

"Awaiting orders," she answered submissively.

"If this one is indeed a Sorcha, you will crush him," Cain ordered. "Do you understand?"

Her eyes flamed blue—the only answer her master needed.

Chapter 14

Atlanta, Georgia

Rafe Johnson closed the door to the small apartment he shared with his grandmother in one of the many low-income housing projects dotting the south side of Atlanta. Leaning his dark, sturdy frame against the door, he shook his head. The pounding pain was his constant companion. He had stayed out late again, not because he wanted to, but because he had no other choice. Unfortunately, in his short eighteen years, he had been forced to do many things he didn't want to do.

But two days ago, he had scored a job working for a man he knew only as Cyrus. His latest assignment would require him to hack into the computer mainframes of the largest bank in Georgia. Cyrus would then have access to multiple accounts with substantial amounts of money. He knew he was the key. He would give Cyrus a fortune, and Cyrus, well, he would be the answer to a better life for Rafe and his grandmother.

He pushed away from the door frame. He wanted the quiet darkness of his room. He needed to rest, even for just a little, in preparation for the job tomorrow.

"Where have you been, young man?"

"I've been working; remember, I told you I would be coming home late tonight."

Lying to his seventy-two-year-old grandmother twisted his insides into a knot. He knew his late nights and unexplained disappearances for days at a time were causing his grandmother a lot of grief lately. It couldn't be helped. Nana Rose was sick—very sick. To get her the medical care she needed, he had been forced to offer his special skill set to some very unsavory characters to earn the money. He had no other choice.

His nana had raised him and given him a loving home when his parents had deserted him. When he was three, his father had left the house one night after fighting with his mom and had never come back. After that, his mother had sunk into a deep depression, eventually turning to drugs to ease her pain. She had overdosed when he was only seven. His grandmother was the only decent person he had ever had in this world.

"Nana Rose, you should be in bed," he said, crouching beside her ratty old recliner.

"Not until you tell me where you've been. And don't lie to me 'cause I saw you, from my bedroom window, talking to that boy, Terrence."

"You worry too much, Nana. I did talk to Terrence yesterday, but it was just about a part-time job. We need the money. You know it's tough for us right now."

"What kind of job?"

"Terrence knows I'm pretty good with numbers, so he told me the director of the community center is looking for someone to tutor the kids in math."

"I know you're a good boy, Rafe. I just worry about you. I just want you to have a better life than the one your momma and daddy gave you.

"I've got everything I need right here with you, Nana."

"Rafe, you're special, you always have been, and you need more than a sick old woman to take care of and a minimum-wage job."

"The money I'm making at the computer store plus what I'll get for tutoring is our ticket out of this place and to a better life for both of us."

"For both of us," she repeated softly.

"You just need to concentrate on getting better. You hear me?"

He would not sacrifice this woman for anything, no matter the cost to himself. He needed her more than she had ever needed him. He lifted her small frame easily into his arms and carried her to her bed. He pulled the yellow crocheted blanket over her and kissed her wrinkled brow.

"Night, Nana Rose. I love you."

Nana reached both hands up to hold his face close to hers. "I love you, too, my sweet boy. There is so much good inside you. Don't you ever forget it!"

"No, ma'am, I won't."

"And Rafe?"

"Yes, ma'am."

"I like that new haircut. You look just like Grandpa Sam did when I married him."

"Yes, ma'am, I'll remember that."

He left Nana's room and went across the hall into his own. He laid down, willing the throbbing pain in his head to stop. He rubbed his head carefully, avoiding the tender place behind his ear. The barber must have nicked him. He closed his eyes, willing himself to relax. He had to be at his best tomorrow. There were no second chances if he failed. Just one more job, and he could make a new start for them both. Soon, he drifted off into a troubled sleep. His phone rang and woke him up a few hours later. He looked at the number and answered immediately.

"You ready?" Terrence asked.

"Pick me up at the corner in ten."

He rose quickly and dressed. When he looked in on Nana Rose, she was sleeping peacefully. Tossing his backpack over his shoulder, he left the apartment. Terrence was already waiting for him at the corner.

"Get in, man," Terrence urged, revving the car engine.

"Relax, nothing can happen without me."

"I'd get rid of that attitude before we get there if I were you," Terrence warned.

He was silent during the twenty-minute ride to the Ritz Carlton Hotel located in the center of Buckhead. They left the car with the valet and entered the posh hotel. Well-dressed men and women were milling about the beautiful lobby looking like they had just stepped out of a magazine. He felt out of place. It was surreal to think just minutes ago he had been riding down the street in one of the toughest and poorest neighborhoods in Atlanta, and now here he was in the lap of luxury. Heading toward the back elevators, he took a deep breath to steady his nerves, and the fragrant flowers adorning every corner of the lobby filled his nostrils. Nana loved flowers. One day, he promised himself, he would bring her to a place like this.

Reaching the twentieth floor, he and Terrence were met by two men in dark suits. After a thorough search, the men led them down the hall to a set of double doors. The doors were opened by another man dressed the same as the ones at the elevator. Terrance strolled into the hotel suite with a swagger. He followed behind, taking in every detail of the room.

Although he had never seen Cyrus before, he knew the man reclining on the gold upholstered couch in the center of the suite's living area could be no one else. His black hair was slicked back from his head and curled around his neck. He wore a navy pinstripe suit with a crisp white shirt. Lights from the crystal chandelier suspended from the ceiling glinted on his expensive gold cufflinks.

"Is this the kid?" Cyrus asked.

Terrance smiled like he was very proud of himself, "Yeah, this is him."

Cyrus motioned for him to take a seat in the chair across from him.

"Rafe, isn't it? Terrance tells me you have skill and that you can do the job. But I need more than that. I need an expert. I need someone who can get in and out clean with no one the wiser. Are you the man I'm looking for?"

"Yeah. I am. And I want the 50K you promised me before I open my computer."

"Do what I ask, then you get your money."

"Money first or no deal," he replied with a bravado that didn't go beyond skin deep.

"Give the young man his money," another voice commanded.

He hadn't noticed the other man standing at the window on the far side of the room. He had shoulder-length auburn hair and was dressed in a grey suit. He never turned his face from the glass.

The stranger threatened softly, "You are wasting my time, Cyrus."

"You would challenge me in front of my men!"

In the whisper of a second, the stranger was across the room, towering above Cyrus. This man was beyond dangerous, he thought. The stranger kept his back to him. He was glad; he didn't want to know who he was; it was safer that way. He couldn't wait to be far from this place and the imposing stranger.

"You forget your place," the stranger admonished, his powerful hand clenched around Cyrus' neck.

"Please, I meant no disrespect," Cyrus pleaded.

The stranger loosened his grip and moved back to the window.

Cyrus loosened the collar of his shirt and ordered, "Give the kid his money."

A woman dressed in black leather with long braided hair dropped a leather duffle bag on the dining table in front of him. It landed with a thud. He could almost see his new life with Nana Rose just ahead.

"Count it if you want, but do it quickly," the woman ordered.

He unzipped the bag and attempted to school his features. Inside the bag was more money than he had ever seen in his life. He closed it quickly and tossed it over his shoulder. He was anxious to get this job done and to never look back.

"Good luck, Mr. Johnson," the man at the window said softly.

As he was leaving the hotel suite, a chill slid down Rafe's spine. However dangerous Cyrus might be, somehow, the man at the window was much worse.

Chapter 15

Easy in—easy out. Rafe finished the last sequence of commands. Freedom waited for him and Nana Rose just outside this dark room. He pulled off his headphones, his favorite jazz music still playing, closed his laptop, and reached for the black duffle bag by his feet. He stopped cold when he felt the unforgiving barrel of a 9mm pressed to the back of his head. His eyes darted to the only exit. Too far—he would never make it.

"I did the job, man. Just let me walk away."

"Can't do that, Rafe. I gotta job to do, same as you did. On your knees."

Desperate situations called for equally desperate measures.

He had no weapon but himself. He slammed his entire body weight backward into Terrence, knocking them both to the concrete floor. The force knocked the gun from Terrence's hand, and it skidded across the concrete floor. Because he had been in his fair share of fights, he knew his agility and quickness would be the game-changer. He knocked Terrence back against the table and to the floor with a right hook. He struggled with the would-be assassin, grabbed his collar with one hand, and pummeled his face with the other. His fist stopped midair when a gunshot echoed in the warehouse.

"Police! Hold it right there!"

He looked up from Terrence's bloody face into the faces of the three large men surrounding him with guns drawn. Obviously, he hadn't heard them kick in the door. He sat back on his heels and held up his hands in compliance. The men weren't dressed in uniform, so that could only mean one thing: undercover cops. He shook his head in exasperation. The cops had probably been on to him for days. He should have been more careful. Now everything he had planned for Nana was ruined.

"On your knees, both of you, hands behind your back," the biggest of the four commanded.

It was obvious to him that this guy was in charge. Towering over the rest, the cop was ripped. His muscles had muscles! His long black hair was parted down the middle and hung straight past his shoulders. His brown skin, dark eyes, and sharp nose gave away his Cherokee descent. There was no way he was getting away from this guy.

"Got the computer?" the cop asked.

"Yes, sir, it's all here," one of the other cops answered.

He watched miserably as one of the cops grabbed his computer while another tossed the duffle bag with his and Nana Rose's future inside over his shoulder.

The guy in charge pulled Rafe to his feet and asked, "Which one of you losers is the computer genius?"

"It ain't me. Look, man, he's the one," Terrence cried. "He stole all that money, not me!"

"You going to deny it?"

He knew it wouldn't take long for the cops to figure out it was his computer. The best thing he could do was to tell the truth, and maybe they would give him a break.

"No, sir, it's mine."

"Well then, we've got a lot to talk about, don't we? Let's go, genius!"

Outside the warehouse, he was a little surprised to see only one car in the deserted parking lot.

"Get in," the cop in charge ordered.

He settled into the back of the car and then cringed when the cop in charge sat beside him. Things could always be worse, he thought. At least he wasn't lying in a pool of his own blood, dead from a gunshot to the head. Looking out the window, already trying to figure out his best plan of action, when he arrived at the police station, he watched the other two cops exit the building. After dumping his computer and duffle bag in the trunk, the cops got in the front seat of the car.

"Hey, where's Terrence? Tell me you didn't just let him go, come on, man!"

"They're coming," the cop in charge said with a faint smile.

"Who's coming?" he asked, very confused by the whole situation.

The cop in the driver seat revved the engine and peeled out of the parking lot into the street. His body slammed into the big man beside him. When multiple bolts of white-hot lightning hit the ground around the car, the driver swerved, barely missing the electric charges from the sky.

"Hang on," the driver shouted.

When two sleek silver cars appeared from a side street and gave chase, he yelled, "What's going on? Who chases a cop car?"

The men in the car with him didn't bother to answer. Leaving the deserted streets around the warehouse behind, the car reached the busy streets downtown.

When he saw a red light ahead, he begged, "Turn green, turn green."

The driver didn't slow down; he accelerated and shot like a bullet through the red light. Cars coming from opposite directions swerved and slammed into one another. Still, the driver was driving the car at top speed. He was scared. Whatever was happening wasn't good, and it wasn't normal. He did the only thing he could think. He squeezed his eyes shut and prayed for the first time in his life.

"Okay, big guy, if you're really up there, I promise I won't steal anymore. Just get me outta this, please."

A hearty laugh from the cop in charge surprised him. The man acted as if he was having the time of his life. This whole experience was becoming surreal. When an oncoming car swerved to miss them and hit one of the silver cars pursuing them instead, the cop in charge laughed again. But before he could ask him what was so funny, three motorcycles roared from a side street to join the chase. Swerving dangerously, the driver kept their car on the road somehow.

"We're gonna die," Rafe wailed.

"Not on my watch," the cop in charge grinned. "Relax."

"Relax? You're crazy!"

When the cop in charge laid his big hand on his shoulder, the soothing calm that flowed through him was undeniable. Just a few moments ago, he had been scared witless. Now, he felt safe, safer than he had in a long while.

Deciding he would join in the spirit of the chase, he roared, "Bring it on!"

The cop car jumped the curb and barreled down the sidewalk. Frightened people were running in every direction, trying to avoid getting hit. When the car swerved back onto the street, the last silver pursuit car followed and was broadsided by a Coca-Cola truck. The three motorcycles dodged the chaos and managed to stay right behind them.

"Hold on, not out of the woods yet," the cop in charge assured him.

"Just get me out of this alive, okay?" he shouted.

Looking through the rear window, he was surprised when one rider lost control of his bike, crossed the median, and slid under an oncoming car.

"One down, two to go," he yelled.

One of the two closed in and was almost beside them. Then, in a flash, the bike stopped dead, and its rider flipped head over heels over the handlebars into the street. The last rider, smaller than the other two, gave up the chase and sped away.

"It's over. They gave up," Rafe exclaimed.

He couldn't decide if he was surprised or relieved.

"For now," the cop in charge said with a big smile.

The driver slowed down the car and turned onto a quiet residential street. He took a deep breath when they rolled to a stop. The chase was over. Reality returned. He had broken the law, and he had been caught. The question was, by whom? He was certain these guys were not ordinary cops. He was worried they might be something even worse.

"What just happened back there? I want to know what's really going on. 'Cause I think it's pretty obvious you're not just undercover cops. Are you FBI? CIA?"

He replied easily, "Something like that."

"I'm no one special. But I can get you to someone who is. His name is Cyrus. He's the guy who planned the job. Maybe we could work a deal?"

"I don't think so, kid."

All bets were off then! He jumped out of the car and took off running at full speed. He hoped the element of surprise would give him a head start. He was caught almost immediately in a steely embrace.

"Slow down, kid," the cop in charge said kindly. "You have nothing to fear."

The same overwhelming unexplainable calm welled up within him again. His body relaxed, and his breathing was even. The cop in charge loosened his grip.

"Please tell me what's going on."

"Close your eyes, Rafe," the cop in charge requested softly.

He did as he was told. When the cop rested his hands lightly on either side of his face, he gasped when the last few minutes of his life replayed like a movie on the screen. He saw himself in the back seat of the patrol car. But this time, he saw what he had not seen before. Outside the racing car, warrior angels catapulted through the air in an explosion of colors. Men and women, garbed in dazzling gold armor and carrying broadswords, radiated light. He looked at the cop in charge next to him. He, too, was filling the space with warm golden light.

Bright silver lights shot by the window and transformed into creatures whose skin and armor pulsed with cold silver light. Frozen blue eyes, like shards of glass, shown through the slits in their glittering masks. They were terrifyingly beautiful. Intense blue flames shot from their hands, burning everything they touched. He knew what he was seeing was real but like nothing he could have ever imagined.

In positions of defense, the golden warriors formed an impregnable shield around the car. Their swords and shields sizzled when deflecting the blue flames of the silver sentinels. It was an intricate dance of hand-to-hand combat, a clash of massive proportions. When the three motorcycles started their pursuit, the warrior angels swooped from their perch atop the car. They challenged the three riders, causing them to lose control of their bikes.

He opened his eyes, dumbfounded. He couldn't explain what he had seen, but he knew beyond a shadow of doubt it had been real.

"I don't understand any of it, but I want to know more."

"I thought you might feel that way, Rafe."

"You know my name, but I don't know yours."

"Yona will do."

Chapter 16

Mia marveled at her good fortune as she drove outside the city. Two weeks ago, she had been unemployed and dependent on her sister for almost everything. But yesterday, while she was running errands for Audrey, her luck changed. She had noticed an advertisement for a job opening in the window of a magnificent historic home. The building served as the main office for the city's historical society. On impulse, she had applied. Gemma Bradley, the director, had hired her on the spot, starting immediately. She guessed her degree in history made up for her lack of experience in event planning because she was now the coordinator of events for the society.

The fact that the society was holding a fundraising gala at the local museum in just four weeks should have made her nervous. But it had done the opposite. It had energized her. Thus far, her first day had been a whirlwind of activity. She spent the morning creating a preliminary design for the event and was now headed to Talbot Industries to present her plan to the principal donor of the museum, Flynn Talbot.

Driving through the front gate, her first look at the company's home base was awe-inspiring. Nestled deep in a forested area a few miles outside of the city, the office complex was modern in style yet natural and organic in presentation. It had obviously been designed to fit into its natural surroundings. The exterior of the pristine glass building reflected the green of the forest and featured luscious hanging gardens from top to bottom.

She couldn't wait to see the interior of the remarkable building, considering the absolute beauty of the exterior. And she wasn't disappointed. The lobby's high glass walls and ceilings allowed the natural light in and provided a panoramic view of the surrounding woods and mountains. Indoor gardens with flowing waterways, trees and rocks, and walls, stairs, and handrails made of reclaimed timber added to a tranquil esthetic. Dark teak floors and the neutral décor completed the space. The faint scent of lemongrass clung to the air. It was an immersive experience with nature that gave Mia a great sense of calm.

A gorgeous mural spanning the entire east wall of the building drew her in; it depicted a variety of the charity endeavors of the company. Medical supplies to South America, orphanages in Rwanda, houses built in New Orleans after Katrina, and so many more. She marveled at the sheer enormity of good works Flynn Talbot conducted around the world. Intent on the mural, she didn't notice the man standing by the glass elevator on the left side of the lobby. Nor did she notice his admiring gaze when he entered the elevator and disappeared above.

Eager to present her gala plan and to see the floors above, she walked over to the reception desk and introduced herself.

"Good afternoon, I'm Mia Quinn from the historical society."

"Mrs. Quinn, we've been expecting you," the young man replied warmly. Picking up the phone to take a call, he continued, "Take the elevator to the top floor. Ms. Yamada will meet you."

In the elevator, she prayed her first meeting in her new role would be a success. When the doors slid open, a striking woman greeted her. The woman's perfectly coiffed black hair and well-tailored power suit were in stark contrast to her own floral summer dress. She was obviously underdressed for her meeting with the media mogul. A sharp pang of nervousness fired her belly, but she pushed it aside and offered the woman a warm smile.

"Good afternoon, Mrs. Quinn. Welcome to Talbot Industries. I am Kimiko Yamada, Mr. Talbot's assistant."

"It's a pleasure to meet you, Ms. Yamada."

"Please, it's Kimiko. Gemma called this morning to let me know you would be taking over the last-minute details for the event."

The biophilic theme and sensory experience of the building exterior and lobby continued in the design of the executive office on the top floor with one distinct difference, the art. Exquisite paintings of rich and startling colors adorned the walls. She had never been impressed with money or the things it could buy. But history and its natural companion, fine art, did capture her attention. She and Audrey had spent many happy Saturdays traipsing through art museums with their bohemian sister, Scarlet. These marvelous works of art made her feel as if her twin were close.

"These pieces are remarkable," she mused.

"Quite so. Mr. Talbot's collection of modern art is extensive. Klimt, Chagall, Kandinsky. He has an eye for the unusual."

"Our meeting is on the terrace. Right this way."

The glass-roofed terrace and lush Japanese gardens created an idyllic atmosphere, once again blurring the boundary between indoor and outdoor. And the view of the surrounding woodland and rolling mountains in the distance was fabulous. In the center of the space were a beautiful teak table and chairs perfect for alfresco dining or business meetings. Already seated at the table, a young woman stood and greeted her. She was struck by her exotic beauty.

"Good afternoon, Mrs. Quinn. I'm Lysha Talbot. I've been looking forward to meeting you."

"Please call me Mia."

"Your son speaks very highly of you and all your family."

"I didn't realize you knew my son."

"Lucas and I met a few weeks ago. I think he and my brother have really hit it off. Please have a seat. May I offer you something to drink?"

"No, thank you, I'm fine. This building and everything in it is, well, I've never seen anything quite like it."

Lysha smiled, "That's the response my father was going for when he had this building designed. He wanted to provide a multi-sensory experience for our team. Bringing nature into our workspace has not only created a clean, calm environment but it's also boosted the energy and well-being of the people who work at Talbot Industries."

"I can imagine that your employees love it here."

"My father will join us when he can, but why don't we begin with the preliminaries?" Lysha asked politely. "Mia, what are your ideas for the gala?"

"Right," she said, pulling her notes from her bag. "Because the money raised at the event will fund the museum's new *Artisans of Glass* exhibit, I would like to suggest a Venetian masquerade ball for the gala theme. Period costumes and masks, Italian finger food and desserts, candlelight, classical music, and of course, dancing would create the perfect atmosphere to celebrate the new exhibit."

"Isn't that a bit extravagant for an event like this? Not to mention the gala is scheduled in less than three weeks," Kimiko suggested.

"On the contrary, I think a masquerade is a perfect idea."

The deep baritone voice could only belong to Flynn Talbot.

As he approached, she couldn't help but admire him. His face was a series of chiseled planes like an ancient marble statue on display in the Louvre; his thick wavy hair only added to the effect. The crisp white open-collar shirt he wore with his navy suit fit his six-foot-two powerful frame like a glove.

She stood and offered her hand, "Mr. Talbot, I'm Mia Quinn. It's a pleasure to meet you." When his hand touched hers, she felt a jolt of electricity. She was so surprised by her reaction; she withdrew her hand quickly from his. She was flustered by her obvious reaction to the man.

He flashed a dazzling smile. "Please, it's Flynn. May I call you Mia?"

"Yes, of course."

He sat in the seat across from her and said, "Please continue with your proposal, Mia."

As she presented a detailed plan for the gala, her earlier discomfiture was soon replaced with a quiet confidence and an infectious energy. She believed in her event design; it was fresh, exciting, and creative. When she finished, Flynn nodded his head in approval.

"I like it very much! What funds will you require, Mia, to produce the event?" Flynn asked.

She slid a copy of the proposed budget across the table, "It's a rather large sum. But considering the time crunch and leaving room for the unexpected, I believe it's a fair estimate."

Flynn gave the budget sheet a cursory glance. "Agreed. Kimiko, release the funds for the society to move ahead with the project."

Mia exhaled a breath she hadn't realized she had been holding. It had been almost too easy. She had asked for more funding in her proposal, thinking she would probably get less.

Flynn laughed. "Mia, money should never be an obstacle when pursuing something for the greater good; we are blessed here at Talbot Industries, and we give back unconditionally."

"Thank you so much. The society is committed to doing everything possible to make it a grand event."

"I have no doubt you will succeed," he said.

When he came around the table to pull out her chair for her, she stood and met his steady gaze. He was close enough to her now that she could see that his eyes were not blue as she had first thought. They were a mesmerizing grey with tiny flecks of gold. She had never seen eyes like his before.

"It was lovely to have met you, Mia."

When he left the terrace, the magic of the moment for her faded away.

"I'll see you out, Mia," Lysha offered.

She collected her bag and followed Lysha back to the elevator, still a little flustered from her encounter with Flynn Talbot.

Lysha must have noticed her distraction because she asked, "Are you feeling all right?"

"Oh yes, I guess I'm just a little out of sorts," she explained lightly. "The meeting went very well, didn't it?"

Lysha didn't take the bait. She just smiled slightly and said, "My father often has that effect on people."

Obviously, she was not very adept at covering her surprised attraction to Flynn Talbot. Changing the subject, Mia remarked, "I look forward to working with you on the plans for the gala, Lysha."

When the elevator opened, she entered the small space quickly, eager to put some distance between herself and the thoughts of Flynn Talbot.

"Why don't we have lunch tomorrow? We can work and get to know each other better," Lysha suggested.

Before the doors closed, she responded, "Perfect! It's a date, then."

On her drive home, she replayed the meeting in her mind. She was ecstatic about the outcome, the gala would be spectacular, but she was quite unsettled by her strong response to Flynn Talbot. Back at Audrey's, she parked the car, turned off the engine, and just sat there.

"Wow, just wow. Mia Quinn, what are you doing?" she whispered. When she entered the house a few minutes later, she was still asking herself the same question.

"How was your first day?"

Audrey's voice brought her back to the here and now. Her sister was in the living room, lounging in on the couch and reading a book, with Jack snoring loudly at her feet. Vivaldi's Four Seasons played softly in the background.

"You would not believe my day."

"Well, come on," Audrey patted the space beside her. "I want to hear every detail."

She joined her sister on the couch and laid her head in Audrey's lap. She sighed with a mixture of exhaustion and wonder. She wasn't quite sure where to start.

"Okay, this is about more than just your new job if you are at a loss for words. Start at the beginning."

"I hate that I'm always so obvious."

"Mia, you have never been good at keeping secrets or hiding your feelings. Now, out with it!"

"My job is wonderful. I already love it. Mrs. Bradley, the director, didn't waste any time giving me an incredible assignment." She paused for effect, enjoying the anticipation on her sister's face, then squealed gleefully, "I'm doing all the planning for the huge museum fundraising gala that's being sponsored by Talbot Industries. Can you believe it?"

"Oh, my goodness, what an opportunity! That's one of the biggest events of the year in this town. Isn't it just a few weeks away?"

"Yes, but you know I work well under pressure. I've already come up with a wonderful plan...a masquerade."

"Fantastic," Audrey said. "I'm proud of you. But I know you're still holding out on me. Spit it out."

"Okay, okay. Something happened, something I wasn't expecting when I went to Talbot Industries this afternoon for a planning meeting."

"Something?"

"Someone, actually."

"Who?"

"Flynn Talbot."

"The Flynn Talbot? Oh, do tell."

She sat up suddenly, full of nervous energy. Now that she had started talking about him, she couldn't wait to tell Audrey everything.

"I had just started my presentation when he walked into the room. He is so handsome and charming, but he also has this energy about him. And when he touched my hand..."

"Go on..."

"Oh, I don't know. It was electric! I haven't felt like this in such a long time. I'm not sure what to think or feel. Crazy, right?"

"No, honey, you're not crazy. You're a woman responding naturally to a man. And Flynn Talbot is a very attractive man."

"I didn't think I was going to make it through my presentation because I was so out of sorts. When he looked at me, I felt like I was the only one in the room."

"No one would fault you for moving on with your life, Mia. Eli would have wanted you to be happy."

"I know. My head understands that, but my heart is a different thing altogether. It feels like I'm betraying his memory."

"I know it must be scary to think about moving on with your life and finding love with someone again. I felt the same after Ryan left me. I believed there would never be another chance for me to love and be loved. It's taken me some time and a whole lot of prayer. Not gonna lie. But, I've learned that if we allow ourselves to heal and to hope, God will bring beauty from ashes and love from loss."

"You're right; I know you are. I'm just afraid, Audrey. Maybe the relationship I had with Eli was a once-in-a-lifetime kind of love."

"It will definitely be different with someone else, but that doesn't mean it can't be wonderful." Audrey squeezed her hand. "You deserve happiness, Mia."

"We both do."

She hugged her sister tightly, thankful that Audrey was not only her best friend but that she was the one person who could say the tough things when it really mattered. For the first time, she allowed herself to contemplate what life may be like if she moved forward into a new future. The thought filled her heart with anticipation and joy. She had loved Eli; she always would, and nothing could change that. But there was still room in her heart for love. She wasn't sure of the path ahead, and yet she was hopeful of where it might lead.

She settled back into the soft leather cushion and curled her legs underneath her. It was very quiet in the house, too quiet.

"Where are the kids, by the way?"

"Zoe went to the Martin's house for dinner with Beni. And Lily went to the movies with Jude. Those two are becoming fast friends."

"I like Jude. I'm thankful she has found someone like him to hang out with. Lily has been drawn to the wrong crowd in the past."

"I couldn't agree more."

"What about Luc?"

"He left a couple of hours ago to visit a friend," Audrey said with a wink.

"A friend? Did he mention who this friend was?"

"Yep, he sure did."

Her sister was grinning ear to ear.

"Seriously, Audrey, just tell me who he's with."

"Hmm, I believe he said Aiden Talbot. Isn't it a small world?"

"Too small if you ask me," Mia laughed.

"On a serious note, Nolan came by earlier. Another Sorcha has arrived."

"Another one? So soon?"

"They found him in Atlanta. I met him, and let's just say he's got lots of personality. His name is Rafe."

"Maybe the uniting will happen, and our fight will be over."

Audrey's reply confirmed her unspoken fear. "I'm afraid, dearest sister, the fight has just begun."

Chapter 17

Driving through the ornamental iron gates at the entrance to Magnolia Park, Lucas couldn't help but appreciate the grand architectural details of the Talbot estate. Aiden told him that the mansion had been built in the early 1800s by one of the founding families in Cleveland. It sat at the end of a long drive lined with majestic magnolia trees. Typical of the Greek-revival style homes of the South, an expansive wrap-around porch and spacious balconies resting on massive white columns accented the grandeur of the house. Completing the picture, colorful roses and hydrangeas grew beneath the tall French windows.

Although he and Aiden had been hanging out for several weeks, this was his first visit to his friend's home. After parking his car, he climbed the porch steps to the oversized mahogany front door and rang the bell. It was opened by an older man dressed in a dark suit, crisp white shirt, grey waistcoat, dark tie, and shiny black shoes. Of course, the Talbots had a butler; he shouldn't have been surprised by that fact.

"Good afternoon, Master Quinn," the butler greeted. "Please come in."

On the other side of the front door, Lucas found the foyer impressive yet refined. The warm cream-colored walls were topped with richly carved crown molding. An extravagant sparkling crystal chandelier was suspended from the high ceiling. A grand staircase leading to the floors above anchored the opulent Italian marble floor. And in the center of the floor, an emblazoned crest with a roaring lion was fashioned with colorful silver and red tiles. He wondered if it was the Talbot family crest. Before he could study it further, Aiden descended the grand staircase.

"Quinn, it's about time you made it to my place," Aiden said and then nodded at the butler. "Thanks, Thomas."

"Of course, sir," the butler replied before leaving the room.

"Incredible house, man."

"Want the grand tour?"

"Yeah, that would be great."

He tagged along with Aiden, marveling at the extravagance of the home. When they passed by a dark paneled room set with a roaring fire, he stopped dead in his tracks. Broadswords, longbows, spears, maces, and battleaxes, all appearing ancient and showing use, lined the room from ceiling to floor. Gleaming suits of battle armor stood guard on either side of the fireplace. Faded tapestries depicting knights waging battle against foes and dragons hung along one wall. Intricate miniature models of castles were displayed in glass cases in the center of the room. Lucas felt like he had just walked on the set of a *Lord of the Rings* movie.

"Fantastic, right? This is my dad's collection of weapons and artifacts from all around the world. When I was a kid, I would play for hours in this room."

"Of course you did! Who wouldn't love this? I mean, look at this sword."

He picked up a wicked sickle-shaped blade from its resting place on a table. The hilt of the sword was smooth ivory, and the bronze blade lay heavy in his grip.

"It's a khopesh," Aiden explained. "Ramses III carried a blade like that in ancient Egypt thousands of years ago."

"Seriously? Wicked cool!"

"Your dad must have been collecting this stuff for years."

"Yeah, he acquired a lot of his collection at different auctions around the world. But his most prized possessions are the ones he found himself."

"Found? What do you mean?" he asked.

"Not many people know this, but Dad majored in Archeology. After college, and before he started Talbot Industries, he spent some years working at the British Museum in London."

"I would never have guessed that."

"I think he likes keeping at least one part of himself a secret."

"When I was researching him and Talbot Industries for a paper, I wondered. But I figured he majored in International Business or maybe Computer Science."

"Everyone thinks the same thing as you. Dad doesn't bother to correct them. He lets people assume what they want. He's never really cared much for what other people say or think about him."

"Why should he? Your dad has made Talbot a household name. He's successful and respected. But it must be tough on your family to be in the spotlight all the time."

"You mean everyone knowing who you are and watching what you do? Yeah, it's hard, but I've never known anything else."

"Where is your dad, by the way?"

"He and Lysha are on their way to New York City on business. They left before I got home from the gym. So, I've got the house to myself."

"Excellent."

He continued to wander around the room in continuing awe. His eye was caught by a worn leather-bound copy of *Morte D'Arthur* lying on the table in the center of the room.

"The absolute best book that was ever written," he declared, taking the book in his hand.

"Agreed. I wanted to be King Arthur and draw the mighty Excalibur from the stone," Aiden announced, pretending to draw a sword. "What about you?"

"Galahad was my favorite when I was a kid."

"The pure-hearted warrior, that's a lot to live up to, man!"

"When we were kids, Lily and I would pretend to be knights. I was Galahad, and she was Perceval, searching for the Holy Grail."

"For to die with honor is far better..." Aiden quoted.

"...than to live disgraced," he finished with bravado.

"I knew we had a lot in common, Quinn; I just didn't know how much. You hungry?" Aiden asked. "I've got some leftover pizza in the fridge calling my name."

"You read my mind. Lead the way."

He followed Aiden to the home's state-of-the-art kitchen. Bobby Flay would have been jealous of this elaborate setup. There was even a wood-burning brick oven!

"I thought you meant delivery pizza, not homemade."

"My father is a foodie! He raised us to be serious and thoughtful about what we eat. He says, and I quote, 'One cannot think well, love well, sleep well if one has not dined well.'"

"The Talbots don't do halfway, do they?"

Aiden smirked, "What would be the fun in that? Or the taste?"

"Touché!"

Brick-oven pizza and sodas in hand, they settled in Aiden's game room. High ceilings and hardwood floors created a space ready for play. A large billiard table stood in the center of the room. A huge LED screen was mounted on the wall, perfect for gaming. Oversized leather chairs fronted the screen. A basketball goal was located at the opposite end of the room, with an indoor court floor ready for some one-on-one. Large black-and-white framed family photos of the Talbots visiting vacation spots around the world covered the walls.

"Dude, you have been keeping this room a secret!"

"Sorry, man. I just had to be sure about you," Aiden said sincerely. "My father taught us to be guarded about sharing too much with people before we knew we could trust them. Not everyone is like you, you know."

"What do you mean?"

"Some people just want to get close to us because of what they think they can get. Having money is great, I guess, but it really makes it difficult to know who your real friends are. Like Gray and Marshall, I sometimes wonder what they're truly after."

"Well, if they're anything like me, they're after your Beemer," he teased. "Seriously, I've never had money, and I don't think I ever will. Simple is better. Money just complicates things."

"Sounds like my dad, except for the money part," Aiden scoffed. "No ties, no burdens, no problems! Kind of like his philosophy of women. There's been a revolving door of girlfriends for as long as I can remember. If it gets too complicated, he walks."

He noted the derision in Aiden's tone. He guessed the relationship between father and son wasn't so perfect after all.

"Has he always been that way?" he asked. "What about your mom?"

"No, my mom was special. After Lysha's mother left him, he met my mom. Thought it was his second chance at love, ya know? She was the love of his life. But then she got sick, and she died."

"I'm so sorry, man. Losing a parent is tough, I know."

"Yeah, you do understand. You know, I don't think my dad has ever gotten over losing my mom," Aiden said, no trace of his earlier disdain for this father.

"If she was anything like my mom, I understand why it's hard for him to move on."

Aiden smiled sadly. "Every day, my memories of her fade, except her long dark hair. I remember how soft it was. When I was a baby, I liked to twirl it with my fingers. That's really the only memory I have of her."

Aiden's eyes had a faraway look that he knew very well. He figured he looked just the same when he was reminiscing about Eli. Thinking about the people you loved that are now lost to you is a pain that can't be described. You only know it if you have experienced it.

"I'm scared one day I won't remember her at all," Aiden said quietly.

"It's the same with me. My memories of my dad are getting cloudier. It's like I lose him a little bit more every day."

"I know exactly what you mean. Sometimes, I close my eyes and imagine my mom's still with me. But then I open them, and it's the real world again. Weird?"

"Not weird at all, man."

"What about Lily and your little sister, Zoe, right? Do they remember more about your dad than you? Most of my memories are ones I've created for myself based on what my dad and sister have told me about my mom."

"No, Lily doesn't talk to anyone about Dad or anything else for that matter."

"Pretty private person, huh?"

"Hmm, not private, just closed-off, I guess. She really shut down after Dad died. Honestly, I'm worried about her."

"That's tough.

"I keep telling myself that everyone handles death in his or her own way and that she will come around eventually."

"Could I help? I mean, do you think she would talk to me?" Aiden asked. "Sometimes it's easier to talk to a stranger than to someone in your own family."

"I wish you could, but Lily is a hard nut to crack."

"Well, she seems like a great girl."

"She is really special," he said wistfully. "She doesn't know it, but she is. I hope being in Cleveland with family and going to Centenary in the fall will help her to finally heal. I miss the old Lily, you know, the girl she was before Dad died."

"I'm sorry, man. If there is anything I can ever do for you or your family, I hope you'll ask. Friends help friends."

"I know you've got my back."

"Well, let's just see if you feel the same way after I kick your butt at Fortnite," Aiden challenged with a smile.

Chapter 18

Crouching low, Daniel Sharon peered around the corner of the crumbling wall. There were three of them, lean and hungry, headed straight for him. Daniel had no doubt about their intentions. After generations of fighting, these men's hearts were fueled only by righteous anger and deep-seated hatred for the people that occupied their land. They wanted vengeance, and an Israeli soldier was the perfect target for their wrath.

His father's last words to him before he had left home for basic training echoed in his mind. "A soldier must always be prepared for an attack, the expected and unexpected. He must be ready for anything." Sure, every time Daniel left his post, he knew an attack could happen at any moment. Whenever the enemy wanted, they could attack. Operational readiness was a part of his training. But knowing this truth had not prepared him for living it.

For as long as Daniel Sharon could remember, he had dreamed of becoming a soldier. He had marked the years, one by one, until his eighteenth birthday because that was the day he would join the Israeli Defense Forces. Happy and expectant for a great future spent in service to his country, he left his family and home in Tel Aviv. After seven months of extensive combat training, Daniel had been stationed in the West Bank. He was finally living his dream. He proudly wore the camouflage beret and red combat boots that identified him as a soldier in the Kfir Brigade, the largest infantry group in the IDF.

Over the last four years, his platoon's mission of counterterror operations, and the escalating tensions between his country and Palestine, had placed his team in many precarious situations. Despite being shot at multiple times, avoiding their fair share of Molotov cocktails and IEDs, quelling rioting crowds, manning checkpoints, and conducting daily patrols, they had managed to remain unscathed. Considering his present position and situation, Daniel knew his good fortune had run out.

Today, his squad's routine patrol had taken a turn for the worse. As the team leader, he had made the decision to investigate the abandoned bus. Ordering the other three members of his squad to sit tight and keep eyes on the perimeter, he had exited their armored vehicle along with his second, Isaac Liev. Keen and cool-headed, Isaac was the kind of soldier a team leader wanted on his six. They had been tight since basic training, more like brothers than friends. The rigors of a soldier's life had brought them together, bonded them. Once they left the IDF, Daniel knew their bond was one that would not be easily broken. Just that morning, Isaac had asked Daniel to stand up with him as his best man when he married his childhood sweetheart.

Approaching the bus cautiously, he and Isaac had covered about half the distance when, out of nowhere, a rocket-propelled grenade hit the bus. The force of the blast had knocked him hard into the dirt. Disoriented, he had managed to lift his head just in time to watch the next RPG find its target dead on. The armored vehicle, with his squad inside, exploded in a fiery cloud of ash and debris. Coughing on the thick smoke, his ears ringing from the blast, he had looked for Isaac. When he found him, his gut twisted painfully. Motionless, Isaac lay a few yards away. Staying low to the ground, Daniel crawled the short distance to reach him. A wicked piece of shrapnel was lodged in Isaac's chest, and both his legs were missing. His friend was gone.

Before he had time to process the horror around him, a shot rang out. He had run for cover quickly to the demolished remains of a school looming eerily in the rising sun. When another bullet whizzed past his head, he dove behind one of the few walls still standing, hoping it would be strong enough to shield him from the sniper's bullets.

"You've got nowhere to go; come quietly, and we may let you live," the enemy's voice boasted from twenty yards away.

He was in trouble. The upper left side of his body was badly burned, embedded with small bits of shrapnel. The searing pain in his arm and shoulder was making it difficult to focus. Unable to use his hand, he couldn't hold his assault rifle. He would need to be creative in defending himself because the fight of his life was coming straight for him. Considering his options and deciding none was too good, he decided the best he could hope for was to take two of them out before they reached his position. At least it would even the odds a bit more. He withdrew his handgun from its holster.

"I wouldn't if I were you."

Daniel turned to find himself in the fixed sight of an enemy rifle. Intent on the three men coming toward him, Daniel had failed to identify the approach of the fourth. He was soon surrounded. Strong arms clamped down on his shoulders, hauling him to his feet. Disregarding the pain that flashed through his shoulder and arm, Daniel tried to unsuccessfully scramble away from the angry men. While the fourth man maintained his position, the other three went to work. One held him from behind while the other two delivered gut-wrenching blows. Daniel's knees buckled.

"Leave him," the man with the rifle ordered.

The others obeyed instantly. The leader closed the distance between himself and his captive. He grabbed the front of Daniel's vest and hauled him unceremoniously back to his feet.

Daniel met the man's murderous gaze. "Go ahead. Finish it! No matter what you do to me, a thousand more will take my place."

The man's response to his challenge was to offer more violence. He slammed Daniel's wiry frame into what was left of a concrete wall. Praying for strength and refusing to give up, Daniel fought to gain his footing. With a guttural yell resonating deep in his belly, he charged the leader, knocking him to the ground. He landed a couple of quick body punches before the others pulled him off. His courageous attempt to fight back only fueled the enemy's savagery. They shoved him into the dirt. Daniel was tough, hardened by years of training, but a boot kick to the gut was excruciating all the same. When the blows ceased, Daniel fought the waves of nausea wracking his body.

The leader spat contemptuously, "Get up!"

Daniel, bent, bleeding, and burned, stood slowly. He faced his tormentor, who once again had his rifle trained on Daniel.

"Today, you will meet your God."

Rifle shots rent the air dropping two of his attackers instantly.

"Put it down and back away," Daniel's rescuer commanded.

Daniel had never been so happy to see camouflage berets and red boots in his life. Busy with Daniel, his four assailants had missed the stealthy advance of another Kfir squad. Daniel breathed a ragged sigh of relief. When his assailants were escorted from the area, a medic moved to his side. It was Moshi Hoffman, another friend from basic training.

"How goes it, Sharon?"

"Well, I've had better days."

"You've got guts, man. Four against one—not the best odds. And I'm sorry about Isaac and the rest of your squad. They were good men."

"The best."

While Moshi was patching him up, Daniel watched a couple of soldiers preparing Isaac's body with great care for transfer. When they loaded him into a helicopter for transfer back to the base, Daniel's heart ached. Isaac had had so much life yet to live. He didn't understand why it had been his friend instead of him. As the copter lifted into the sky and sped away, he whispered, "Shalom. Until we meet again, brother."

After spending a month in the base hospital, Daniel received an early discharge. When he first arrived home, Daniel had battled both physical and psychological pain as he fought to heal from the blast damage to his body and the loss of his best friend. Where it would have hardened or broken many, Daniel's journey had only strengthened his resolve to live a life focused on peace and forgiveness. Now, almost a year later, he had a newfound sense of purpose—a deepening desire for relationship with Christ. Because the modern state of Israel had one of the lowest populations of Christ followers in the world, Daniel was accustomed to living life as a religious minority in his country. He and his family had attended a Messianic church since he was a boy. It was a small congregation, but since his return, Daniel had committed himself to the church's effort to grow their numbers.

Leaving his small apartment, Daniel drove the short distance to his family home, which was situated in a neighborhood on the outskirts of Tel Aviv. When he pulled up to the house, his parents were waiting outside for him. He greeted them with a bright smile as they got in the car.

"Shalom, my family."

"Shalom, my son," his father and mother returned.

"I've felt all morning as if I would burst," Daniel offered as he navigated the busy road. "I am anxious to be in God's presence."

His father smiled. "My son, all your life, you have spent more time in the church than anywhere else. When you are not home, I always know where to find you. There is safety in God's house, a sanctuary for our prayers."

The Sharon family made their way to the simple stone building that served as their place of worship. His father was right. He had always been at peace here, spending countless hours talking with the church elders, exploring the Scriptures, and praying for his family, his people, and his country. Since his return to Tel Aviv, he had been burdened to pray more and more, but he didn't know for what, specifically. Often, he had no words, running through his prayer list long before the desire to pray had left him. In those times, he had just been still, focusing on God and nothing else at all.

Entering the sanctuary, Daniel felt a familiar sense of peace fill his spirit. Taking their seats, his family joined the congregation as they lifted their voices in song. Surrounding him were the faces of those he had learned from, those he had laughed and cried with, those he had grown up with, and those he had prayed with. They were the most important people in his life, his church family. As the pastor shared the Scripture, a sudden noise at the back of the church drew Daniel's attention. It was a man with wild eyes and a black vest affixed to his chest. Once again, the unexpected had become his reality.

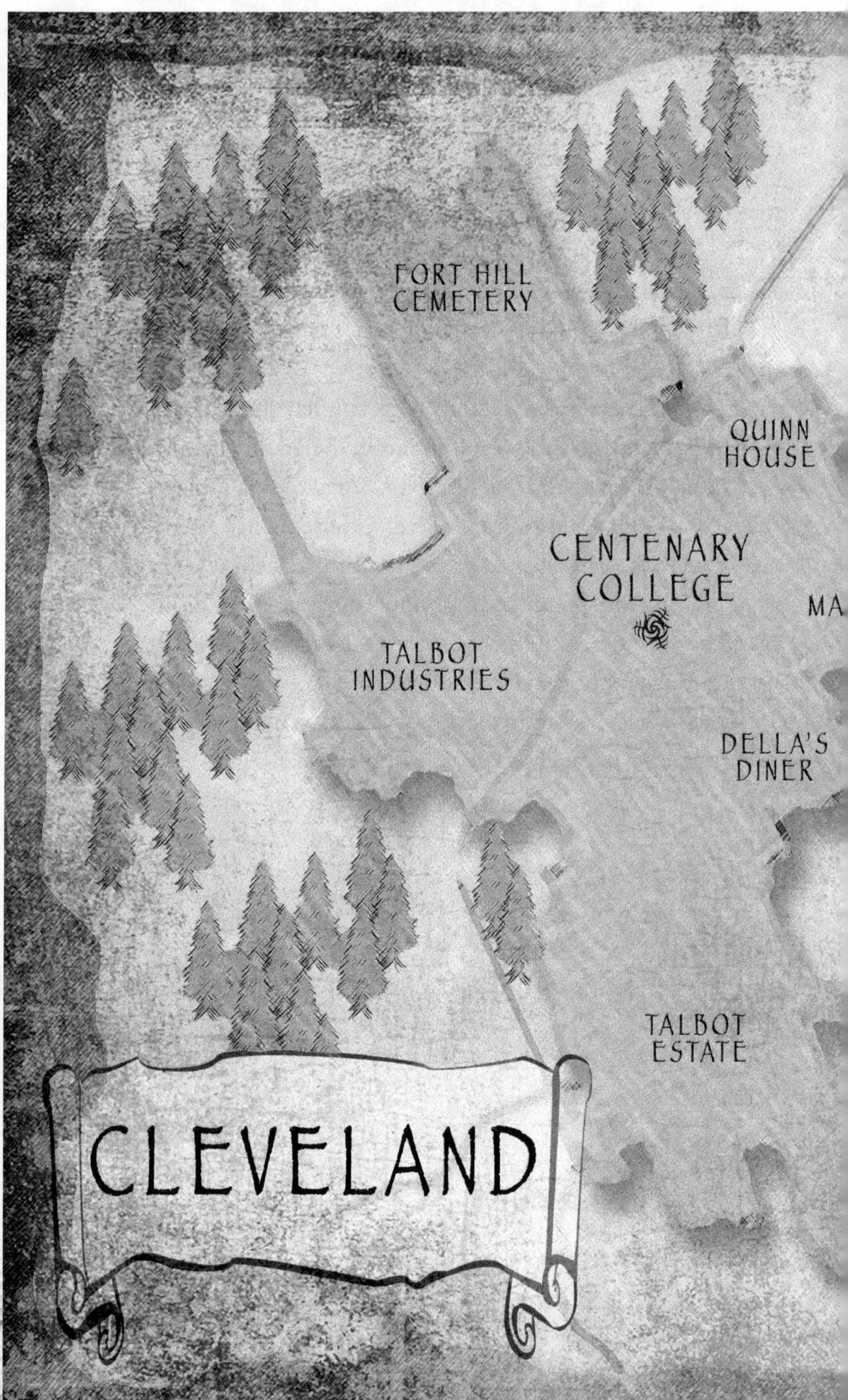
FORT HILL
CEMETERY
QUINN
HOUSE
CENTENARY
COLLEGE
TALBOT
INDUSTRIES
DELLA'S
DINER
TALBOT
ESTATE
CLEVELAND

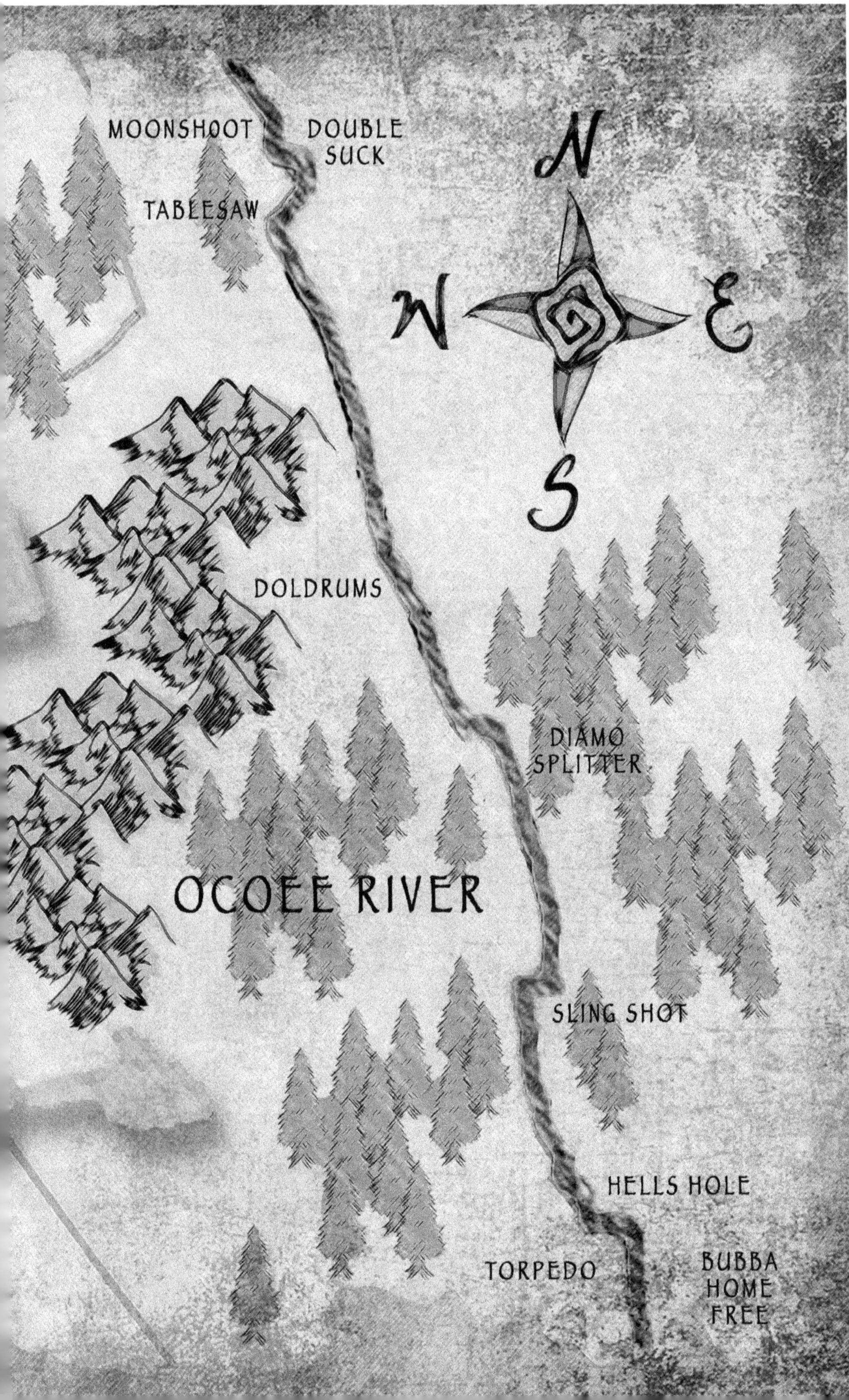

MOONSHOOT

DOUBLE
SUCK

TABLESAW

N

W

E

S

DOLDRUMS

DIAMO
SPLITTER

OCOEE RIVER

SLING SHOT

HELLS HOLE

TORPEDO

BUBBA
HOME
FREE

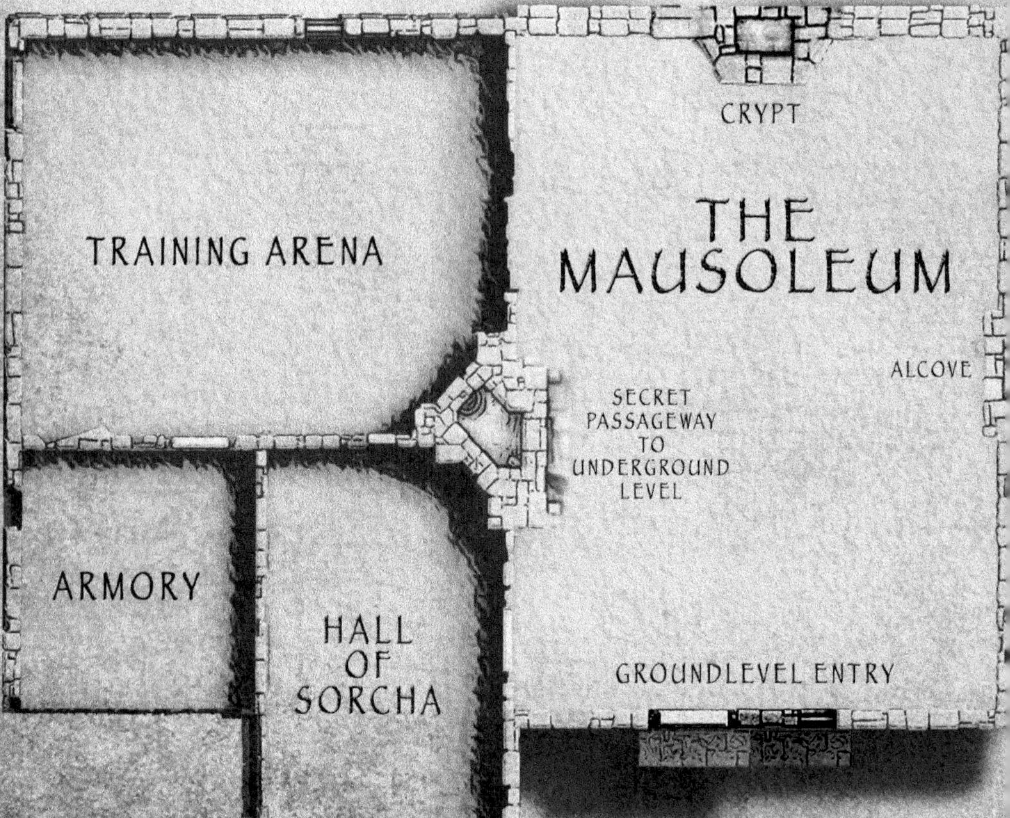

CRYPT

THE MAUSOLEUM

TRAINING ARENA

ALCOVE

SECRET PASSAGEWAY TO UNDERGROUND LEVEL

ARMORY

HALL OF SORCHA

GROUNDLEVEL ENTRY

Chapter 19

"You will pay for what you have done," the crazed martyr spat.

There was no doubt the man was serious. Daniel could see the stony resolve in the man's sunken eyes. If he detonated that bomb, Daniel would lose everyone he loved most in the world in the blast.

"Sir, we have no quarrel with you," Daniel insisted. "Think about your family, the ones you will leave behind. If you detonate that bomb, you die too."

"What family? Your bombs killed my wife and my son. My life was spared so I could deliver judgment upon you on this day. My body will be the instrument of your death."

"There are women and children here! Please, let them go."

"They are no better than you," he spat. "No more talk.

Everyone against the wall!"

Daniel joined his church family—men, women, and children, old and young. They lined themselves along the four walls of the sanctuary. Some were crying, others praying, in various states of shock and dismay.

"Silence! Your noise is making my head hurt," the bomber shouted. "Face the wall!"

Daniel looked at his father and mother on either side of him. His faith was strengthened by seeing the unwavering courage in their eyes. They had always taught him that when it was difficult to stand in this life, one only needed to kneel. It was at that moment he knew what he must do. He turned from the wall and lay face down on the hard floor. Prostrate, he extended his arms and began to pray aloud.

"I said face the wall!" the bomber screamed.

Daniel lifted his baritone voice. It filled the sanctuary. He was driven toward a singular purpose. He focused his heart, mind, and spirit on one thing only, an appeal to God. He asked for protection and deliverance, not for himself, but for everyone against the wall. Words no longer mattered; his soul was reaching heavenward. He lost awareness of everything around him, so vast was his desire to move the heart of God on behalf of his people. He was unaware that the men, women, and children around him had joined him in lifting their voices in a chorus of prayer.

The bomber grabbed his ears in agony and wailed, "Enough!"

Daniel's body dripped with sweat, so great was his exertion. But he remained resolved. He would keep praying until he could pray no more. The floor beneath him began to rumble and shake. His prayers became more urgent, words tumbling from his lips. When the bomber screamed, a booming explosion of hot air enveloped Daniel. He was engulfed with a strong sense of déjà vu. Just like the explosion that killed his squad, he found himself disoriented. He sat up, tiny bits of debris floating in the air around him. He turned to his church family.

Dumbfounded, Daniel realized every person standing against the wall was still there, alive and breathing. Shrapnel, pieces of glass, nails, and metal were lodged in the wall, clearly outlining the shapes of everyone who had stood against it. But no one's flesh had been pierced. No one was injured. It was as if something or someone had stood in front of them, blocking the bomb's destructive force. And yet, nothing remained of the bomber, his body torn apart by the explosion.

"It's a miracle," the people around him cried. "We've been saved."

He tried to stand, but his legs wouldn't obey. His father rushed to help him.

"My precious son, your faith, your prayers called the mighty power of heaven down. God protected us."

"Yes, but how, Father? I'm not sure I understand what just happened."

"We have just witnessed the miraculous, Daniel. You must mark this day and never forget God's provision for His people. Never underestimate the power of faith and prayer."

"Yes, Father," he promised. "I will remember."

After the authorities arrived and took everyone's statements, Daniel took his parents back home and then made his way to his own. He climbed the stairs, bypassed his apartment, and instead headed straight for the roof. He was exhausted. He had spent countless hours in church praying, but never with the intensity he had experienced this morning. Reviewing the events of the morning again in his mind, he felt an unexplainable fragility in his spirit. What kind of agony leads a man to seek out so much destruction? His heart was heavy because he knew that the bomber could have made another choice. The man didn't have to let his grief overwhelm him, filling him with anger and bitterness. He didn't have to strike out at others to assuage his aching soul. He didn't have to choose death; he could have chosen life.

Gingerly, Daniel touched the tingling skin behind his ear. He must have sustained a minor burn in the blast. How was it possible that they had all remained unscathed? He knew God was all-powerful, but he had never witnessed the magnitude of His authority before. His soul cried out in praise. He had never felt such an unquenchable thirst for communion with God as he did now at this moment.

"I'm sorry, I didn't know anyone was up here!"

He didn't recognize the man. He must be a new tenant in the building.

"No problem, this roof is big enough for both of us. I haven't seen you before. Just move in?"

"My name is Ira. What about you?"

The stranger's white teeth flashed in a big grin against his dark brown face.

"I'm Daniel Sharon."

"Hey, man, I don't mean to pry, but you look pretty upset just now," the stranger returned.

"Yeah, it's a long story."

"I've always been a sucker for a good story. And I've got nothing but time."

"I'm not sure I even know where to begin."

"At the beginning?" he encouraged.

"Okay, it's pretty fantastic, so hang with me till the end."

"Sure."

"At church this morning with my family, a man burst through the door with a bomb strapped to his chest."

"Seriously? What happened?"

"He demanded that everyone stand in a circle facing the walls. I've never been so scared. But I wasn't afraid for myself. My time with the IDF pretty much conditioned me. It was my family. I didn't want them to die."

"What did you do?"

"I prayed."

"You prayed? You're kidding me?"

"Not in the least. I can't really explain it, but I had a strong feeling in my gut that I needed to lie down on the floor and pray. I didn't even know what words to pray. I just focused on God and the faces of my family. I started to shake and sweat, my arms were aching, and my head was pounding, but I kept praying. The bomber didn't like it. He shouted for me to stop. But I didn't."

"Well, what happened?"

"The ground started to shake, he screamed, and then the explosion. It was so strange. I've been in an RPG explosion before, and this was nothing like this. It was just a whoosh of hot air. And to beat it all, nobody was hurt. Only the bomber, he didn't survive the blast."

"Sounds like you were protected somehow."

"My father said it was a miracle."

Ira whistled in amazement. "Well, I guess it was a miracle for sure. You said you felt it in your gut, didn't you? I always follow mine; it hasn't failed me yet."

"Yeah, but it still doesn't make any sense. I believe in God's power and in His ability to perform miracles. But this? How did the explosion miss all of us? Not a scratch on one person. It was like someone stood in front of us and absorbed the blast."

"Well, it must have been your guardian angel. In this case, lots of angels. They must have deflected the debris from the bomb blast. The angels shielded all of you from harm."

Daniel studied the man. There was something about him that made Daniel trust his explanations with no question.

"God sent His angels to you today to perform a miracle."

When the man shed his human form, transforming into a glowing warrior, Daniel wasn't even fazed.

"You have a gift, Daniel. Age or circumstance makes no difference to God. He will use whomever He chooses when He chooses. He chose you today. And I believe He has chosen you for what is to come."

"What do you mean?"

"You'll know soon enough."

From the shadowed recesses of the arena, Keket watched the demon horde settle into their seats around the battle floor. Icy blue eyes flamed, casting the space in an eerie spectral glow. Flawless faces and forms disguised their disfigured souls. Once they had been beautiful angels who served the mighty Elohim. But they had wanted more.

When Lucifer acted in rebellion against the Creator, others followed suit. Defeated and cast down to earth, the fallen angels became Scáths. They were driven by a singular purpose, the destruction of Elohim's creation. She shared their deadly goal. Under the command of Cain, her master, the Scáths had been waging war for thousands of years. They had experienced great success and were gaining ground in the fight, and yet Cain had grown impatient and dissatisfied with his army of demons.

So, he decided to forge a new evil, stronger, smarter, and infinitely more wicked than a Scáth. From each generation of Sorcha, her master had stolen a particular female member to enact his abominable plan. Taking each one and making her his own, he had created a superior army of assassins.

Keket had been the first. Born from the unholy union of a Sorcha and a Scáth, she was a Mescáth. Embodying both good and that which would destroy life, she was a fascinating and lethal combination of extremes within one being. The darkness and power within her were magnified because of the light that also dwelt within her. She was no lowly Scáth. She was perfection itself.

Now, legions of Scáths had arrived from all over the world to bear witness to the prowess of their commander's most prized creation—her.

Keket had no peer, and tonight she would prove it. All would behold her sheer brilliance and total domination. Her victory would secure her position as chief warrior in Cain's demon army.

Chapter 20

Lucas was thrilled. Tonight, after weeks of waiting, training would finally begin. Even though he had worked with Nolan for several years, there was still much for him to learn about wielding the power of the light. Nolan had asked him to bring the others to the church, where their guardians would be waiting. His guardian had always been so secretive about the Dìonadain sanctuary. He had often wondered what it looked like, and in just a few minutes, he would see it for himself. When the church bells rang four times, marking the hour, he pushed the heavy oak door open. He went inside, followed by Zoe, Beni, and Rafe.

The interior of the old stone church was cool, in stark contrast to the warm and humid summer afternoon. The comforting scent of candles hung in the air, helping to mask the mustiness of the aged sanctuary. The last rays of the setting sun shone through the stained-glass windows, casting prisms of color on the stone floor. Ornately carved oak pews, aged and worn, flanked the center aisle.

"This church is beautiful," Zoe whispered.

"It reminds me of my church back home," Beni added.

"I think it's downright creepy," Rafe whispered. "It looks like a church in one of those horror movies about vampires and witches."

He had to agree with Rafe. But he also knew things were not always what they seemed to be, especially if the Dìonadain were involved. At the altar at the end of the aisle, the warrior, Ira, was waiting with an unfamiliar young man.

"Meet Daniel Sharon. He has traveled a great distance to join us," Ira announced.

Daniel bowed in greeting. "I am thankful to join you in service to God, my brothers and sister."

He embraced Daniel. "Same here, Daniel. This is Zoe, Beni, and Rafe.

Never one to be shy, Zoe blurted out, "How old are you, Daniel?"

"I just had a birthday. I'm twenty-one."

"That makes you the oldest so far," Zoe commented. "You're not from around here, are you? I can tell by your accent."

"Zoe, the man doesn't need the third degree," he warned.

"Lucas, I'm just trying to get to know him. You don't mind, do you, Daniel?"

"Not at all, Zoe. My home is in Israel, Tel Aviv, actually. At least it was until about thirty-six hours ago," he offered kindly.

"Israel, very cool," Rafe interjected. "What did you do there?"

"I served for the last four years in the Israel Defense Forces. I just got back from my last tour when Ira found me and brought me here."

"Wow, a soldier," Beni mused, pumping his fists in the air. "Will you teach me how to fight?"

"Me too!" Zoe added excitedly. "I bet you're great at hand-to-hand combat. What else can you show us?"

While Daniel was busy answering Beni and Zoe's questions, Rafe moved closer to him and whispered under his breath, "Did you see his arm?" Rafe asked.

"Yeah, so?"

"Well, he's not gonna be any good in a fight if he can't use his hand," Rafe declared. "What do you think happened?"

"It's not our business, man. If Daniel wants us to know, he will tell us."

"Well, I think it is our business. We're supposed to trust this guy and fight with him against some tough opponents. We need to know if he can handle what's up ahead," Rafe retorted. "Identify our weak spots and compensate for them. We don't want to be blindsided."

He wasn't sure why Rafe was being a jerk, but something about Daniel had obviously gotten under his friend's skin.

"If you want to know, you are welcome to ask," Daniel said softly, his gaze fixed on Rafe.

He cringed. Daniel must have heard their entire exchange.

Not one to back down, Rafe asked sharply, "What happened to your hand? Can you even use it?"

Seemingly unruffled by Rafe's questions and obvious rudeness, Daniel simply offered, "I got too close to an IED. I was lucky; my unit was not," he continued, flexing his fingers, "and yes, I can use my hand."

"Sorry, man, I crossed a line. Didn't mean to push so hard," Rafe apologized, appropriately reading the looks the others were sending his way.

"Are you finished with this useless banter?" Ira asked sharply.

"Ira is correct. We have significant matters at hand and do not have the luxury of wasting time," Nolan chastised, making his way down the aisle.

He hadn't noticed Nolan's arrival. Hearing Nolan's voice quieted any further discussion from the group.

"Tonight, we begin your training, Sorcha. Beyond this door is the greatest challenge you have yet faced. Follow me," Nolan ordered.

At the plain wooden door behind the large pipe organ, Nolan paused. He wasn't surprised when Nolan extended his hand in a slight movement toward the iron lock, and it clicked open. He had seen his guardian do the same and more. Down the circular staircase hewn into the rock, Nolan led them underground through a series of torch-lit tunnels. The ancient passages appeared to have always existed as if the granite simply happened to form itself into a well-constructed path. Despite the depth that they traveled, the air remained soft and clean.

With every step Lucas took, his senses were heightened. He knew there must be a great many Dìonadain in the great hall below. He could hear the swoosh of their wings and feel the energy that radiated from their bodies as he got closer to them. Due to their silence, he figured his friends must be feeling like they had entered another world entirely, so unusual were their surroundings. Nolan paused at a large natural archway in the rock and faced them.

"Beyond this gate lies the Hall of the Sorcha. Only those chosen by God may enter this chamber. Within, you will learn how to wield your gift of light."

When they stepped through the archway, a bright light shining from the silver orb suspended from the stone ceiling illuminated the chamber. Gargantuan stone columns covered in ancient script lined the circular space. Between each column stood a life-size marble statue. At the foot of each statue was a seat carved into its base. He felt the significance of the moment.

"The chiseled likenesses you see before you are the first Sorcha, your ancestors," Nolan spoke reverently and continued to walk slowly around the space, pausing at each statue. "Here is the Perceiver, who can see both worlds, discerning the natural and supernatural."

He looked into the eyes of the first Perceiver. He marveled, thinking that he had also been gifted with this great power. Who was he to have been blessed with this incredible gift?

"Communicating and understanding languages, no matter their origin, just as you can do Beni, is the gift of the Speaker," Nolan continued. "The ability to heal all living things from physical, emotional, or psychological sickness and injury is the gift of the Healer, your gift, my dear Zoe. The Believer's unshakeable faith connects the twelve and moves the heart of God. Daniel bears this gift. And you, Rafe, just as the Knower who stands before you, can harness the illuminating power of knowledge, using it to solve the unsolvable. And the Crafter, who can fashion any substance into a weapon used to fight evil."

"My father was the Crafter. I remember watching him create a shield out of ice and snow. I didn't understand then the great gift that he wielded," he mused.

"I wish I could have seen him do those things as you did," Zoe whispered to him.

"What about the others, Nolan?" he asked.

"Strength beyond measure is the gift of the mighty Warrior. The Wielder can accomplish the fantastic, even the miraculous, in the name of God to alter the course of nature. The interpretation of visions and prophetic dreams is the gift of the Dreamer."

"Like mom," Zoe whispered.

"The Psalter has an extraordinary gift of music with a voice that can instill fear in the enemy and hope when all is thought to be lost. The one who wrestles with evil spirits and demons banishing them from those they control is the Exiler. And finally, the Leader of the twelve. A strategic mind and courageous spirit for battle are this Sorcha's gifts from God."

"Now, take your seats, Sorcha," Nolan commanded. "To unite your gifts and defeat the prince of darkness, you must understand the history of your quest and meet the man who started it all. His name was Simon."

Lucas shivered as a swirling mist filled the room. Within the thick vapor, a small cluster of rough-hewn buildings surrounded by a wooden fort atop a grassy moor took shape. A steady rain was falling from the darkening sky. A man was standing at the door of one of the ancient dwellings.

Standing in the small village he called home, Simon looked across the windswept moor. It was late, and all was quiet. His clan slept peacefully, unaware of the supernatural struggle going on around them. Because he was the leader of his people, their welfare was his own. He had led them here across the ocean to a place where they could begin anew. Marriages, births, and deaths—the cycle of life—were all shared here on the tor.

Closing the door of his dwelling place, Simon sat heavily in his chair. There was still much to do, much to record, and he felt as if his time was running out. He had been plagued of late with an increasing sense of dread. People in the neighboring villages were acting strangely toward his clan, whispering among themselves about witchcraft and sorcery. When his clan had first arrived on the island in the north, the people had welcomed them, eager to hear the Word of God. But their attitudes had shifted dramatically of late.

Simon believed evil had taken root in the hearts and minds of many in the nearby villages. Those who committed their lives to God were no longer safe. Even though he and his people were protected within their fortified encampment, he still couldn't shake the feeling that they were being watched. Simon knew the task he had been charged with long ago must be completed if the future of the Sorcha were to be secured. Before Jesus had come into his life, Simon had been a warrior, a zealot, a man who fought for the freedom of his people and their cause. He was no stranger to battle. He knew this was the very reason he had been given this task.

He ran a weathered hand through his thick dark beard speckled with grey. He had not eaten much over the last few weeks, and the effects of his sparse diet had only accentuated his hooked nose and angular jawline. He looked at the bowl of soup and hunk of brown bread Marhe had prepared for him hours ago. He smiled wistfully. His wife worried about him but would never speak it aloud. It was just her way.

Seated again at the rough-hewn table, he picked up his quill and wrote on the parchment scroll before him. His brothers had all been charged with specific tasks; he was to record and protect this sacred testament. Once the book was finished and Lucifer discovered its existence, he knew the dark angel would stop at nothing to destroy the scroll and the powerful words contained within it. The book would usher in the destruction of evil itself. So far, he had lived undetected, but he knew that Lucifer's demons would find him soon. Maybe they already had.

He labored on; the light from the oil lamp burning brightly in the night. Just before dawn, he put down his quill and rolled up the scroll, binding it with a thin strip of leather. Exhaling deeply, he said, "It is finished, Father."

A hard rap at the door startled him. He crossed the dirt floor quickly and opened it to find his most trusted companions, his beloved sons.

"Amhlaid? Alphaeus?"

Simon recognized the urgency in the young men's expressions. Amhlaid, the eldest, was a younger version of himself, dark, strapping, and passionate about justice. And Alphaeus favored his sweet mother, slight with reddish-blond hair and pragmatic to a fault.

"Come in, my sons; I must show you something."

"There is no time, Father. We must go!" Amhlaid declared, sweeping past his father.

"He's right," Alphaeus continued, shutting the door behind him. "They are out for blood this time."

"We have been watching the people in the village," Amhlaid recounted. "Someone has stirred their hatred against us. They are screaming sorcery and death."

Bowing his head, Simon said gravely. "My sons, I will not leave my people."

"Please," Alphaeus begged earnestly. "You and Mother must come with us."

"You know as well as I do, Father, our defenses will never hold against the mob marching upon us now," Amhlaid stated.

Simon moved to the table. He untied the binding and unrolled the scroll. The pages glowed warmly in the lamplight.

The danger was forgotten for a moment; Amhlaid gasped. "You have finished it."

Simon pulled one of the pages from the rest and then bound the scroll again. He tied the single page he had removed with a worn piece of leather and offered it to Amhlaid.

"You must keep this safe, no matter the cost, even if it means your own life," Simon said with conviction. "It is the key to understanding what I have written. The twelve will find you when it is time."

Amhlaid took the scroll without question and tucked it under his cloak.

"Alphaeus, guard your brother's back. You two must get to safety."

"Please reconsider, Father," Alphaeus insisted. "And what about Mother?"

"We must travel different paths," he said. "Remember all I have taught you. Yes?"

"Yes, Father," his sons declared.

"Your mother and I love you both." He kissed the forehead of each son in blessing. "Go now, quickly, my dearest boys."

He watched his sons until they disappeared into the thick dawn mist. Simon had prepared them as best he could for what was surely to come. He knew the key to the book would be safer parted from the whole. He sat before the dying embers of the fire and waited.

"And so, it begins," he whispered.

When the mob came, their bloodlust was palpable. They dragged him from his home and forced him to watch as they cruelly slaughtered his whole village—every man, woman, and child. His people's screams rent the air, their blood soaking the ground. They saved Marhe for last. His eyes never left hers, willing her to be brave. He cried out in anguish when they slit her throat. Then, a sudden blow to his head turned his world black.

When he came to, his hands were bound, his nose broken, and his body felt heavy with pain. He only had the use of one eye, the other swollen shut. The metal taste of blood in his mouth made him queasy. He surveyed the dark, crude space he was in. It was small and dank. A light rain fell through the hole above him. The patch of sky his one good eye could see was grey and ominous. He shifted his body, and the rope cinched about his waist and connected to something above the hole grew tighter. He could hear people above arguing and shouting.

He bowed his head, asking God for strength and Christ for courage and resolve. He knew his time had come. He grieved the loss of his people—his wife—but he knew he would be with them soon. His mission on earth was complete. The scroll was written, and its true message would remain a secret. His sons had the key, and he was confident in their ability to keep it secure. The path was now paved for the Sorcha to awaken and discover their power to destroy the darkness. He knew this, so his heart was at peace. He could face the terrible death he knew would be his with hope for the future.

The ground where he was kneeling trembled, and a winged man appeared in the corner of the small space. He knew he would come. It was his Dìonadain guardian, Cain. His protector had exchanged his once beautiful golden wings for leather-like appendages and eyes that burned with a cold blue flame. He hadn't been surprised by his guardian's betrayal. When Cain had disappeared from his side days ago, he had feared the worst. And his fears had not been unfounded. Cain had chosen to abandon the light and align himself with Lucifer, the prince of darkness.

When Cain moved closer to him, he wasn't at all surprised to see the scroll clutched in his betrayer's hand. He had planned for this actuality when he had removed the page that was the key to unlocking the mes-

sage in his book. The contents of Simon's book would remain shrouded in mystery, kept safe by his sons until the appointed time. Cain was blissfully unaware that the scroll in his possession was incomplete. The fallen angel had underestimated the strategic guile of the Sorcha.

"Come to gloat?" Simon taunted, a renewed sense of purpose welling up in his soul.

As Cain approached him, a triumphant smile spread slowly across the fallen angel's face, "You are going to die, Simon. And I, well, I will live on. Know that the work you and your brothers of light began will be for naught. The darkness will not suffer the light."

"Woe to you and all your wicked kind," Simon roared. "When the morning dawns, you will be destroyed."

Cain disappeared as quickly as he had come, his odious laugh echoing in Simon's ears. Someone above yanked on the rope and pulled him roughly from the hole. He landed in the mud, surrounded by a mob of feral faces, all singularly focused on his doom.

When the image of Simon faded, and the room returned to its normal state, Lucas was burning with a hundred questions. But before he could ask, Nolan spoke.

"Simon was a very brave man. He knew the extraordinary knowledge contained within his book would defeat the march of darkness across the earth. That's why he protected it by separating the key to understanding the language the book was written in from the scroll itself. The immeasurable power within Simon's book cannot be understood without that key."

"Where is the key now?" Lucas asked.

"Only when the twelve unite will you have the ability to discover the answers you seek, Lucas."

"What about Simon?" Rafe nudged. "You can't leave us hanging, Nolan."

"I will share the rest of Simon's story another time," Nolan answered.

"But how will we find the others?" Zoe asked.

"The task of locating the others rests with the Dìonadain. You must focus now on mastering your gifts. Learning to use the power of the light within you is all that matters now."

"Cain was there the day my father died. I'll never forget his face," Lucas said bitterly.

"Cain was tempted by greed and the promise of great power from Lucifer. He betrayed Simon for his own selfish gain."

"Does Cain know about the key?" Beni asked.

"When he studied the scroll, he soon realized a part of it had been removed. He knows he can't decipher Simon's book without the missing page. And he has no idea where the key might be. He has tried for centuries to find it."

"That's why he hunts the Sorcha, right?" Rafe asked. "If he destroys us before we can unite, the key is lost forever."

Nolan nodded, "Yes."

"Nolan, once we are all together, do you believe we can find the key? Can we really stop the darkness?"

"Darkness can't withstand the light," Daniel said reverently.

"Yes, Daniel, even the smallest fraction of light illuminates the darkest of nights. You must all believe this. Now, enough talk; let us train!" Nolan ordered.

Vowing to avenge his father, Lucas followed the others into the training room, intent on doing all he could to prepare himself for the fight ahead.

"Silence!" Cain boomed from the dais. "Let the champion come forth! Rao!"

Opposite Keket's position, Rao, the most fearsome warrior in the Scáth army, appeared. The demons roared their approval for their champion. He stopped in the center of the floor and bowed low in deference to Cain. She knew her opponent's face, underneath his silver shroud, was taut and smooth as marble. His iridescent green tattoos writhed like serpents across his mighty body. She wasn't afraid; instead, she felt a rush of adrenaline like none before.

"Who challenges the champion?"

Leaving the shadows, she exploded with a crack of lightning into the center of the arena. Her supple body encased in black leather was humming with electricity. She wanted it all, and tonight she would get it.

"I, Keket, descendant of shadow and light, challenge!"

There were no cheers for her. It didn't matter. By the time she finished with her opponent, they would be chanting her name!

In deference to her master, she bowed and then faced Rao. Confident that he would make the same mistake so many other creatures did, her full red lips curved into a seductive smile. He would underestimate her deadly skill because of her great beauty. When the warrior's eyes widened in appreciation, Keket knew she had won already. Breathing deeply, Keket prepared to strike.

When the gong sounded, she catapulted and landed behind the Scáth. He turned in surprise.

Flaming darts shot from her hands, striking him squarely in the chest. Rao maintained his stance without so much as a wobble. She noted that she would have to increase the power of her darts if she wanted to knock him down the next time. Rao extended his wings and began to spin like a wild tornado. She was enveloped in a maelstrom of dark shadows. Blinded, she focused her other senses. She heard the darts hissing through the darkness and dodged them with a complex series of acrobatics.

"Is that the best you have, Scáth?" she taunted, jumping from the vortex.

When she pummeled him with a deluge of flaming darts,

Rao stumbled.

Quickly the warrior shot up from the arena floor and swooped down on her again. Picking her up, he tossed her to the far side of the arena. The Scáths' chant amplified. Choking on a mouthful of sand, she repositioned herself, and at a dead run, she crossed the floor, pummeling Rao with her sizzling darts. The force of her attack knocked him back forcefully into the dirt. She approached him slowly.

"Is that the best you have, Mescáth?" Rao bellowed.

He clapped his hands together, sending a surge toward her. The potency of his flames suspended her in midair, contorting her body. She struggled to break Rao's powerful embrace. When she heard the taunts and laughter from the crowd, something in her snapped. She had wanted to give the demons a show, to draw out her defeat of the Scáth. She had longed to savor the thrill of it all.

But no one was going to laugh at her. Her eyes burned intensely, and then she went limp.

Roaring in triumph, Rao released his stranglehold, and she fell unceremoniously into the dirt. He saluted his fellow Scáth around the arena, acknowledging their chants of victory. When the Scáth warrior knelt before Cain, the crowd hushed.

"Scáth scum!" Keket shouted.

Rao jerked around but not in time. Violet flames shot from Keket's eyes like a blowtorch. The horde gasped. No Scáth had ever achieved the destructive finality of a violet flame. Nothing could withstand the intensity of that kind of assault. Rao fell, writhing in agony. The silver shroud melted, exposing his face to Keket's blaze. She advanced, continuing to release her violet darts, coming now from both her hands and eyes. Her opponent was helpless, outdone. The once great warrior folded his wings and sunk lifelessly to the ground.

Her opponent obliterated; she stepped over Rao's charred form and proudly approached her master. She climbed the steps to the dais and knelt before him. Cain embraced her.

"My wicked daughter, so beautiful, cunning, and brutal. Today, you have earned your greatest desire," Cain whispered, then turned to the crowd. "Behold, your new captain, Keket, the Mescáth!"

The roar that filled the arena was music to her ears. She had done it!

The day of the Mescáth had dawned. Her destiny lay before her. She would usher in the final destruction of the Sorcha. Her bloodlust would never be satiated; she would not rest until the Sorcha were destroyed for good. After all, she was her father's daughter.

Chapter 21

When her alarm went off a few hours later, she moaned. It was Sunday, and the last place she wanted to be was in church. Mia insisted they all go to church as a family. Ugh! She resented being told what she should or should not think or do. She was eighteen, for crying out loud. It was her life—she could decide for herself. Her phone buzzed with a text message. It was Jude.

"Going to church?"

"Unfortunately," she texted.

"I'll save you a seat."

The smiley face emoji that ended his message made the morning a little less dreadful. Jude had quickly become her best friend. On a whim, she texted him an invitation.

A few weeks ago, Lucas had come home raving about rafting on the Ocoee River. Since that day, Zoe hadn't stopped begging Mia to take her on a rafting adventure. Zoe was tenacious, and Mia soon gave in. Today, the whole family was going to the river for rafting and a cookout after church. This was to be their first family outing since moving to Cleveland. Her mother was a homebody and didn't like to venture out much. But the new job and Aunt Audrey's contagious high spirits must have loosened her up a little. Lily was beyond excited; she wanted her best friend to be with her. If Jude was there, not only would it be more fun, but it would also save her from having to interact with her mother and Lucas so much.

"Going rafting after church. Wanna join?"

"Yes!"

"Bring a change of clothes, then."

"Will do."

After showering, she checked the time on her phone. It was already 9:30 a.m. She pulled up her unruly hair, brushed her teeth, and applied some lip gloss. At her closet, she took out a blue sundress and sandals. After slipping them on, she ran down the stairs.

"I was about to come get you," Lucas said, holding the front door open. "Mom won't like it if we are late."

She ignored her brother and got into the back seat of the car. Zoe was sitting up front, smiling as usual, "Aren't you excited? Our first Sunday in our new church!"

"Yeah, can't wait," she answered sarcastically.

"Oh, don't be so moody," Zoe admonished, lightly touching her sister's forehead with one finger, "Your face gets all crinkly right here when you do, and you're gonna regret that one day."

"Stop it, okay," Lily laughed.

Reaching their destination, Lily was the last one out of the car. She wanted to delay the agony of congregational hymns, prayer, and the pastor's message for as long as possible. When she spied the coffee shop across the street, she knew she could add a few more minutes to her delay.

"Aren't you coming?" Zoe asked.

"In a minute. I need some coffee first. I slept terribly last night."

"I'll come with you," Zoe offered.

"No need; I promise I'll meet you inside."

When Zoe looked unsure, she pushed, "If I don't get some caffeine, I'll just sleep through the sermon. Go on. Jude is saving me a seat."

"Fifteen minutes, and you better be in the pew beside me," Zoe warned and ran up the front steps of the church.

"Seriously, Lily, it's just one hour out of your day," Lucas said, slamming the car door to get her attention. "You know you just might learn something! Besides, it's important to Mom. And you know it was to Dad, too."

Lily swore under her breath, watching her brother's back as he walked away from her. She was here, wasn't she? She was going to church. She crossed the street and went into a little coffee shop. After placing her order for a latte, she noticed Aiden Talbot at a small table in the corner. He was gorgeous in his linen suit and tie. Her heart skipped a beat. He was with a stunning dark-haired young woman. Lucas had told her that Aiden was dating a Barbie look-alike. So, who was this girl? And why did it matter so much to her anyway?

She felt her face flush when Aiden caught her staring at him. A slow smile spread across his gorgeous face.

He waved and called out, "Mornin', Lily."

She waved back, too embarrassed to even open her mouth. She made a beeline for the door and crossed the street to the church.

"Ugh, I forgot my coffee," she said under her breath.

Entering the packed sanctuary, she looked for Jude. He was sitting beside Lucas on a pew with the rest of her family toward the back. The congregation was already standing and singing a hymn when she slid into the space at the end of the row beside Jude.

"Thanks for saving me a seat," she whispered.

Jude smiled. "A few minutes more and Lucas..."

"Would have chased you down and drug you into church!" Lucas finished, leaning across Jude to give her his best glare.

In return, she flashed her best smile and said sweetly, "I made it, didn't I? Just like I said I would."

After the third hymn ended, the pastor motioned for everyone to be seated. Reverend Gregory Bennett had stopped by Audrey's house the day after the Quinns had arrived to welcome them to Cleveland. Then, Audrey had invited the pastor and his wife, Margaret, to join them for dinner one night last week.

"Good morning, everyone. Before I share the message, I want to take a few minutes to recognize a very special family," the pastor announced. "Mr. Talbot, would you and your precious children join me on the stage?"

"You've got to be kidding me?" Lily muttered, her leg beginning its usual bob up and down.

"What's wrong?" Jude asked, placing his hand on her knee to steady it.

"Nothing, just ready to go rafting, that's all," she answered quickly.

When she recognized the young woman from the coffee shop following Aiden and his father up to the stage, she cringed. How stupid was she? Of course, she must be his sister.

Why hadn't she seen the resemblance before? Stylishly dressed and coiffed, the Talbots carried themselves like a royal family. The trio joined the pastor on the platform.

"The Talbots have been members of our congregation here at St. John's for many years," the pastor stated. "And today, I want to publicly thank Flynn for his extraordinary contribution to this church and its ministry. He has humbly offered to donate a piece of land right here in the heart of downtown, as well as the funds needed for construction, to develop a state-of-the-art recreational center for our young people. Their generous gift will allow us to serve families in our community in more diverse and effective ways."

The congregation stood, joining the pastor in a burst of applause to show their gratitude for the gift so freely given by the Talbots.

"Thank you, Pastor Bennett," Flynn Talbot said graciously. "My children and I have been blessed beyond measure and are so thankful to be able to give back to our church family. I am proud to be part of this congregation and thankful my children have grown in their faith in this church. I believe one of the greatest gifts God has given to us is family. So, I hope this wonderful new space will provide you and your families with many opportunities to laugh and play together."

Once again, the congregation offered their thanks by applauding. After the Talbots returned to their seats, Pastor Bennett delivered the message. Lily tried her best to pay attention to the sermon but found herself instead thinking about Aiden Talbot. She was startled back into the present when Jude nudged her shoulder.

"Earth to Lily," he said softly.

She grinned and sat up straighter, hoping her mom hadn't noticed her lack of attention. When the pastor concluded his message, he asked everyone to stand for prayer. Before the final amen, Lily was out the door, pulling Jude along with her. They made their way over to a large oak tree in the churchyard.

"What's your hurry?" he asked.

"I need some fresh air."

Her pulse quickened ever so slightly when she noticed Aiden approaching them. She tried her best to appear nonchalant, but who was she kidding?

"Hey, Lily," Aiden drawled. "I didn't know your family attended St. John."

"Hi, yeah, it's actually our first Sunday," she managed, her voice sounding a bit higher pitched than usual to her ears.

"It's a great church. I've been going here my whole life. The Bennetts are good people. They really helped my sister and me after my mom passed."

"Oh, Aiden, I'm so sorry. I didn't realize."

"It was a long time ago. I was three years old," Aiden responded. Then he turned to Jude and extended his hand."Hey, man, I've seen you around, but I don't think we've been formally introduced."

Her friend shook Aiden's hand but remained silent. Lily understood Jude's response. Aiden Talbot was a bit intimidating, to say the least.

"Um, this is my friend, Jude Butler," she interjected.

An uncomfortable silence followed. She couldn't think of anything else to say. She avoided looking at Aiden because she was so nervous. She was thankful when Jude spoke up.

"What your dad is doing for the community is cool. It means a lot."

"I think so too. The rec center will give a lot of kids in this town somewhere to go to have fun and to stay out of trouble. My dad didn't have the easiest childhood. So, he cares about giving kids opportunities he didn't get growing up. I respect him for that."

"He's lucky to have you for a son," she said softly.

She had spoken from her heart. Unfortunately, she didn't mean to say it out loud. So stupid! But when she met his eyes, she realized that Aiden had been surprised by her comment. He was the one blushing now! He turned when his sister called out to him.

"Well, gotta go. Great to meet you, Jude. And Lily, I'll see you soon."

It wasn't a question but a statement. Lily wasn't sure what to think about that. She watched him walk away, totally caught in the moment.

"You like him," Jude stated slowly.

"Am I that obvious?"

"Yep, but he probably didn't notice," Jude laughed.

"Oh, stop it!" she pushed on him playfully. "He doesn't notice me at all, I'm sure of it."

"Keep telling yourself that if it makes you feel better."

"Let's change the subject; are you ready to go rafting?"

"Absolutely. Just let me grab my things, and I'll meet you at your car."

As she hurried to the car, she checked herself. She felt like she had boarded a fast-moving train and wasn't entirely sure she wanted to get off. She was reading into things; she was sure of it. Aiden Talbot was just being nice. But the way he had just looked at her did make her wonder. Either way, she was most definitely in a world of trouble!

On the way to the river, she and Jude rode with Lucas and Zoe, while Mia and Audrey followed close behind. Lily had heard all about the Class 3 and 4 rapids from Jude. In 1996, the Ocoee served as the whitewater venue for the Summer Olympics. The challenging five-mile rollercoaster ride was not for the faint of heart. It was a mecca for first-time rafters and kayakers, as well as those who were more experienced, affectionately known as river rats.

Arriving at the rafting center, Lily was the first one out of the car. The two-story log cabin that served as the rafting office was already crowded with groups checking in, all anxious to brave the Ocoee rapids. Lily and the others gathered around one of the picnic tables scattered around the property.

"Now, everyone, please be careful. Rafting can be dangerous," Mia urged.

"Relax, Mom, I got it all under control," Lucas grinned. "Jude and I will take care of the girls."

"Love you, Mom," Lily hugged Mia unexpectedly. She could tell her mother was surprised by her unsolicited show of affection. Mia kissed her cheek before Lily stepped away.

"Be fearless," Audrey called cheerily, earning a frown from her overprotective sister. "We'll have dinner ready when you get back." Then she turned to her sister, "Mia, let them have their fun. They aren't kids anymore."

"I know. It's just nerve-wracking to think of them out there on those crazy rapids."

"I guess you've forgotten the parasailing fiasco when we were their age?"

"Enough said," Mia agreed with a smirk.

"Details, please," Lily urged.

"Not on your life," Mia laughed. "Now go..."

"Okay, okay, I'm going," Lily laughed and followed her siblings and Jude.

When the foursome walked into the rafting office to check in, Lily was surprised to see Aiden at the front desk. He was with a group of people who were obviously his friends.

"Aiden, I didn't know y'all were rafting today," Lucas commented excitedly.

"Last minute decision! You all should join us. It would be a blast to go down together," Aiden answered.

"Yeah, sounds great; let's do it," Lucas agreed.

"Introductions, please?" Zoe asked, nudging her brother's shoulder.

"Oh yeah, sorry," Lucas said sheepishly. "You know Aiden already. And this is Rachel, Jenna, Marshall, Gray, and Daryl. Y'all meet my sisters, Zoe and Lily, and her friend Jude."

Lily didn't miss the look of displeasure that crossed the face of the pretty blonde named Rachel. She guessed the girl, who must be Aiden's girlfriend that Lucas had told her about, wasn't happy to have their company on the trip downriver. Surely now, after meeting Rachel and seeing just how much she didn't compare to the girlfriend, Lily would be able to keep things in perspective about the lack of any future relationship with Aiden.

After getting their paddles, helmets, and lifejackets, Lily and the others walked outside to await their guide.

"Y'all ain't lived till you've ridden the Ocoee," Daryl hooted good-naturedly.

"Yeah," Marshall agreed, using his paddle to joust with Lucas. "I came close to meetin' my Maker the first time I braved these rapids."

"How comforting," Jude whispered to Lily.

She giggled and was just about to say something back to Jude when Aiden moved close and spoke directly to her.

"You're gonna love it, Lily. It's a real adrenaline rush—nothing like it in the world, and I've been to a lot of places."

"Not sure I'm a fan of adrenaline rushes," she offered with a slight smile.

"Don't worry. It's just like riding a rollercoaster."

"Aw, Aiden, you're not exactly being truthful with our sweet Lily," Rachel said, with a sweetness that didn't ring true for Lily. "The Ocoee should always be taken seriously. Accidents can happen; in fact, people have been hurt badly; in fact, the rapids have knocked them out of their boat into the rocks."

"Some have even died," Gray added innocently.

"Cut it out, you two," Aiden warned.

Lily swallowed hard, refusing to let the girl's words unnerve her. She challenged quietly, "Well, if you're that scared about the trip, Rachel, I'm sure everyone will understand if you decide to stay here."

When everyone laughed, Lily knew she had just made an enemy for life.

"Well, my goodness, aren't you quick?" Rachel returned sarcastically.

"So, who's ready to brave the rapids?" a dark-haired river guide interrupted.

Even though the guide stood only about five feet three, it was obvious to Lily, by her demeanor, that she was very much in charge.

"All right, let's get to it, then! I'm Ali, and I'll be taking you down the river."

After, Ali reviewed safety procedures and gave everyone a quick lesson in paddling, the group grabbed their gear and boarded the bus for the short drive up Highway 64 to load-in. Lily wasn't sure if she was more nervous about navigating the rapids or the chance that she might end up sitting next to Aiden Talbot for the hour-long trip.

When the bus parked in the lot next to the load-in point, Lily and the others donned their life jackets and helmets, picked up their paddles, and lined up outside the bus.

The noise was crazy. Guides were yelling instructions, rafters were laughing and shouting, and the water was roaring. When it was their turn, Ali directed them to their positions around the raft. Daryl and Lucas took the back with Ali. Zoe, Rachel, Gray, Marshall, and Jude were in the middle. And as luck would have it, Lily was in the front with Aiden. They picked up the raft and carried it to the edge of the swift river.

Taking their positions in the raft, they pushed off into the foaming water. There was no turning back now. Aiden must have noticed her nervousness because he shouted with a smile, "No worries, Lily. I've got ya."

Before Lily could respond, Ali yelled, "Here we go!"

The raft hit the ledge of the first rapid and jumped into the air, splashing back down hard into the water. Lily laughed. This was fun, after all!

Ali yelled, "Paddle!"

The raft was sucked into the rapid by the hydraulics created by the water hitting the riverbed rocks. Successfully navigating the first rapid, everyone cheered. When Lily looked at Aiden, he flashed a wide grin and winked.

"Don't get too confident—it was only the first one," Ali teased.

"Hold on, Lily," Jude urged from behind her. "Hook your feet under the seat in front of you."

Lily did as Jude suggested and prepared for the next rapid.

"See that big rock up ahead?" Ali shouted. "It's called Table Saw, and he's tricky. We need to paddle hard. Right after Table Saw, there's Double Suck, and he's a real beast. If we get trapped, it will be very hard to get out."

"Bring it on!" Daryl and Marshall stood, raising their paddles in the air.

The boat jerked hard in response to the guys' shenanigans. "Sit down, hot shots," Ali commanded.

"We'll be fine, Lily, I promise," Aiden encouraged.

"We won't be if your friends don't stop rocking the boat," Jude countered from behind. He reached up and squeezed her shoulder. "I got you, Lily."

"Would you both stop treating me like I'm helpless?" Lily retorted. "I got this."

Ahead, Lily could see the next rapid. It was a big one. She adjusted her feet and position, readying herself.

"Here they come. Now, paddle!" Ali shouted.

When the raft dove over the first ledge, the sound of the huge rapid roared in Lily's ears. She dug her paddle into the water and focused on listening to Ali's commands. She screamed when the raft spun and hit Teeter Totter broadside. The force of the impact against the monstrous rock flipped the front end of the raft into the air. She lost her paddle and toppled into the swirling whirlpool.

Chapter 22

Lily fought to get her head above the churning water. When she broke the surface, she gasped for air but instead got a mouthful of river. The force of the rapid sucked her back into the powerful vortex. Spinning head over heels, it was impossible to get her bearings. She knew she was in trouble. She fought against the current but with no success. Panic set in. For a moment, her head broke the surface again. The quick puff of air she managed to gulp wasn't enough to fill her lungs. She saw the raft in front of her, but the water pulled her down once again.

Her body, battered against the rocks that lay beneath the surface, screamed in pain. Her foot was caught in a small crevice between two rocks. She fought but couldn't free herself. Her chest ached from the pressure. She knew she was going to die. Desperate to breathe, unable to hold her breath any longer, she would open her mouth, and the cold water would rush in, filling her lungs. She was suddenly filled with an overwhelming sense of regret. She would never see her family again. She would never be able to tell her mother how much she loved her or tell Lucas how sorry she was for being so terrible to him. And

Zoe? She would never see her little sister grow up. In that moment, her disbelief, her anger, and her pride all melted away. She wondered if this was how her father had felt before he died.

She closed her eyes and prayed, "Please, God, if you're real, if you really do care, please save me; give me another chance!"

When she opened her eyes, she was startled by a warm light glowing faintly in the distance. This was it. She must be dying already. She remembered hearing stories about going into the light when a person died. She squinted as the light drew closer. The light took shape. It was a man surrounded by an aura of sparkling light. His giant wings waved in the water, propelling him toward her. She knew she must be dead now because what she was seeing couldn't be real.

The figure swimming toward her looked like the angels she remembered her mother telling her about at bedtime. Only, he was larger and more breathtaking. As soon as the rainbow of light around the man touched her, she felt calm. She no longer fought to breathe. It was as if she needed no air. She felt the man dislodge her foot.

When he lifted his head, she received the biggest shock of her life. Time stood still. The beautiful, powerful man whose body pulsed with warm golden light was her best friend. Her rescuer was Jude. Her best friend wrapped his arms around her and swam swiftly away from the rocks and churning water. She closed her eyes, giving in to the great peace that flooded her.

A sharp slap on her back brought her back to reality. She gulped precious air into her lungs. When hands lifted her to a sitting position, she began to cough and sputter.

"Lily? Lily? Are you okay?"

She looked at Jude, who knelt beside her on the bank of the river. He was soaked to the skin, hair plastered to his head, and his glasses were askew. He was just as he always was. But how? She reached out her hand to his face and whispered, "It was you?"

He nodded solemnly. He covered her hand with his and stared fiercely into her eyes. Before she could demand an explanation from him, the rest of the group pulled up in the raft.

"There she is!" Aiden shouted.

Aiden and Lucas jumped out of the raft and raced toward it.

"Lily! Are you okay?" Lucas exclaimed, dropping to his knees. Her brother ran his hands swiftly over her legs and arms and winked at her. "Nothing broken?"

"I'm good," she answered.

When he hugged her, Lucas whispered in her ear, "I thought I had lost you." Then he announced loudly, "She's okay. Thank God for Jude! Crazy guy dove in after you, Lily, before we could stop him."

"I'm just lucky I got to her in time," Jude offered shyly.

"Yeah, real lucky," Aiden agreed. "Stand back; we need to get Lily back to the rafting center."

Aiden bent and lifted Lily easily into his arms. "Let's get you somewhere where you'll be safe."

Aiden carried her to the raft. Ali had the first aid kit ready, and Zoe helped her quickly wrap her bruised and swollen ankle. Jude loped awkwardly back to the raft. Lucas sat behind her, so she leaned back against him.

"You seriously had us all worried, Lily," Marshall said. "I wasn't serious about the whole "meeting your Maker" thing!"

Lily smiled tremulously. “I was worried for me too.”

“I’m just glad you are all right,” Marshall returned kindly.

“Yes, we all are,” Rachel agreed lightly.

“Don’t ever do that again, okay?” Zoe declared. “You scared me to death.”

“I’m okay, Zoe, really. Just a little banged up,” she assured her little sister.

Ali steered the boat along the bank of the river, guiding them to a place where they could disembark. A couple of park rangers were already there waiting to take them all back to the river center in their jeeps.

Once there, Aiden and Lucas helped her from the vehicle. Then Aiden lifted her again and carried her to a chair near the picnic tables where everyone gathered around. Mia ran over to her daughter and enveloped her in a fierce hug.

“Ali called us to let us know what had happened. Are you sure you’re okay, honey?”

“Fine, Mom, I promise. Just super tired and sore all over. I don’t think I’ll be going rafting again anytime soon.”

“You got that right, honey—not for a good long while. Do we need to head back and get you to bed, or do you want to eat? I bet you feel awful.”

“That’s an understatement,” she returned ruefully. “If it’s okay with you, I would like to stay here for a while.”

“All right, if you’re sure,” Mia responded. “I’ll get the burgers going.”

Audrey brought Lily a steaming cup of hot chocolate, “Drink this, Lily. You’re shivering.”

She took a sip of the dark liquid, thankful for its heat. “Where’s Jude?” Lily asked, anxiously searching for the group.

"Right here," Jude spoke up from behind her. He pushed his glasses up on his face and frowned. He looked like he would rather be anywhere but where he was at that moment.

"Man, I still don't understand how you did it. That rapid was wicked," Gray mused.

"Yeah, you are either the craziest or bravest guy out here," Marshall pondered.

"Really brave," Rachel agreed sweetly. "Lily is lucky to have such an amazing guy looking out for her."

"Yeah, he's a real hero," Aiden said without much feeling.

"Jude, what you did took real guts. Thank you for saving, my sister," Lucas said sincerely.

"Well, as much as I would love to hang out and hear more, we better be going," Rachel announced.

"Don't rush off! We have enough food for everyone," Mia invited.

"Thanks, Mrs. Quinn, but we're supposed to be at a party," Rachel answered.

Marshall and Gray followed Rachel to the car.

"Coming, Aiden?" Rachel prodded insistently.

"Go ahead. I think I'll take Mrs. Quinn up on her offer. Lucas will give me a ride home later, yeah?"

"Sure, no problem. Come on; you can help me get the grill going."

When Aiden turned his back and followed Lucas to the grill, Lily watched Rachel's face change. For a split second, her beautiful countenance twisted. Obviously, she didn't like what was happening. But just as quickly as it had appeared, it was gone, replaced by a chilly smile.

"All right, then. Y'all enjoy."

Rachel turned on her heel and stalked up the slight hill to Marshall's jeep. When Aiden's friends drove away, Lily exhaled a breath she hadn't known she was holding. She settled back in her camp chair and closed her eyes. She was a bundle of nerves and emotions. She replayed the events of the day repeatedly in her mind. She couldn't believe it, but the truth was right there in front of her. Whatever or whoever Jude was, he was not what she had thought him to be. So many questions and so few answers didn't help her pounding head.

"Here you go, Lily. I made your hamburger just the way you like it, extra ketchup and pickles," Zoe served a plate to her sister.

"Thanks, Zoe."

Zoe leaned down and gave her a peck on the cheek. "Don't you ever scare me like that again, got it?"

"Don't worry; I'm done with water sports for a while."

"Hey, Zoe, your burger is ready," Lucas shouted.

"You better be," Zoe returned before walking away.

"Mind if I sit with you, Lily?" Aiden asked quietly.

She nodded her pounding head. She was too overwrought to be nervous around him.

"What a day, huh? I bet you feel terrible?"

She laughed. "Ha, like I've been through the heavy-duty cycle on my mom's washing machine."

"No doubt. You were very lucky."

"I know I was," she said. "I'm just glad Jude was there."

"We all are, Lily," Lucas said, joining them. "No more rafting for you, at least until next week, brother's orders."

"Not a chance! I've had my fill of the river," Lily smiled.

They ate their burgers and talked about anything and everything.

When Lucas walked back toward the grill, Aiden mused, "You've got something special." "What do you mean?"

"Your family is very close. Don't ever take them for granted, Lily. My family doesn't get to spend much time together. My dad is always traveling. Lysha goes with him most of the time. I didn't realize how much I miss my family until now."

She was surprised at Aiden's transparency. Without thinking, she took his hand in hers. She felt an immediate connection, a hum of electricity crackling just below the surface. He didn't move but kept her hand enveloped in his for a moment.

When he finally let go, he didn't look at her but whispered, "Thank you."

They sat in companionable silence, both lost in their thoughts. Lily stared into the night sky with a hint of a smile on her face.

"What are you smiling at?" he asked.

"Hmmm, the stars. It's so clear tonight; you can see millions of them."

"Yeah, they're really beautiful."

"They remind me of my dad. When I was little, he would take Lucas and me out onto the roof of our house. We would spread out a blanket and lay side by side, looking up at the stars."

"You miss him."

"More than I can even say. But especially on starry nights like this one. But it's on nights like this that I feel close to my dad again."

"Then I wish many more starry nights for you, Lily."

Lily turned toward Aiden. He was looking at her with genuine care. She realized she liked that look very much.

"Aiden, lend a hand?" Lucas shouted. "Come on, man. I need some help over here."

Aiden smiled and asked, "Talk again? Soon?"

"Yes," she whispered, returning his smile.

After Aiden walked away, Jude joined her at the fire.

"How are you feeling, Lily?"

"No secrets, Jude. I must know what really happened in the water," she said urgently. "Who are you?"

"Promise me you'll listen?"

"Yes, I promise."

"I've known you all your life, Lily. The moment you came into the world, I have been watching over you, protecting you."

"Like a guardian angel? You're saying you aren't human?"

"Yes, and yes. Most people have no idea we exist. We live outside your awareness. But can show ourselves in human form if needed."

"And how did Lucas know about you?"

"Your brother has a special gift, one that I will let him share with you when he wants. Let's just say Lucas can see what others cannot."

Lily shook her head, trying to organize the riotous thoughts jumbled in her head. Her whole world had changed in an instant. And that should have made her nervous; instead, she just felt excitement and a little awe.

"My very own angel," she mused. "You know what's crazy? I believe you. So, many things are starting to make sense to me now. But why are you pretending to be a regular guy when clearly you aren't?"

"We thought it best I take human form for a time. I needed to gain your trust so that I could help you come to terms with the truth you have been avoiding."

"We?"

"The elders of my order. The Dìonadain Council directs my movements, as well as those of the rest of my brothers. We often take human form, but we are careful not to draw undue attention to ourselves in the forms we choose. Even though we walk and live among you, most people never notice us. We look like everyone else, act like everyone else; we blend in. I must admit I have enjoyed experiencing the world from a more human perspective, especially eating the food."

She bowed her head, her eyes welling with tears. "You saved my life today. Why didn't you save my father?"

"I'm your guardian, Lily, not your father's. What happened to Eli was out of my control."

"Where was his guardian? If the Dìonadain are so strong and mighty, why didn't they save my father?"

"That question is not mine to answer. God's plan is beyond our comprehension, but I can tell you this—there are no mistakes."

Lily laid her head on Jude's shoulder and gazed up at the stars.

"Lucas was telling the truth, wasn't he?"

"Yes," Jude answered quietly, "he was."

Chapter 23

Lily woke up slowly. A steady rain drummed on the roof. Shivering, she burrowed deeper under her blanket. She winced when a sharp pain shot down her leg. Memories of yesterday came flooding back. She pushed herself up to sit and leaned back against her pillow. She had only one thought: Jude. As if on cue, he walked into her room carrying a lunch tray. He put the tray on her bedside table and sat on the edge of her bed.

"Your mom asked me to bring this up and check on you," he said gently.

"I hurt all over."

"You got knocked around pretty good yesterday. It could have been a whole lot worse."

"If you hadn't been there," Lily mused.

"But I was," Jude assured. "And I always will be."

A range of emotions played across Jude's face. She knew him well enough, at least in his human form, to know that he was wrestling with something. She knew he had decided when he took his glasses off and stuffed them in his pants pocket.

"I want to take you somewhere."

"Of course," Lily answered without hesitation. "Where?"

"You'll understand when we get there. Get dressed. I'll be waiting outside."

Lily pulled on her clothes quickly and made her way to the backyard. The rain had tapered off to a light mist.

"Trust me, Lily," he whispered cryptically as he took on his full glowing Dìonadain form.

She gasped at his transformation. Under the raging waters of the Ocoee, he had amazed her, but it had all happened so quickly that she had not had the chance to study him. His towering form was intimidating in its perfection. His wavy hair framed his flawless countenance. He wore his great strength and beauty like a mantle. His incredible wings, large and shimmering, were folded behind his back. Lily thought him the fairest of all creatures.

Before she could think about the mystery of his words, he spread his wings and hugged her closely. They rose in the air hovering about six feet off the ground.

"So much for my fear of heights!" she exclaimed, grabbing him tightly around the neck. "You won't let me fall, will you?"

Jude smiled. "You aren't going to fall, Lily. You're going to fly."

And then they were. Lily should have been frightened out of her wits, but she wasn't. She was amazed at her profound sense of calm. She was enjoying the freedom and rush of it all. Flying high above the clouds, she reached out to touch their whispery softness. Too soon, Jude set her gently on the ground.

"That was fantastic," Lily laughed, stepping out of the shelter of his wings.

Her heart stopped. Her eyes took in what her mind struggled to admit. She was standing in the exact spot where she had seen her father for the very last time. The clearing.

"Why did you bring me here?" she asked uneasily.

"Trust me," Jude urged.

Her guardian waved his hand; the green grass and warm summer sun were replaced by a winter snow and frigid air. The clearing looked just the same as it had all those years ago.

"Take me back home now!"

"I can't do that, Lily."

"Please, Jude, I'm begging you to take me away from this awful place."

"Lily," Jude soothed, folding her into his embrace, "You need to remember, Lily, all of it; it's time."

"I can't," she sobbed into his chest. "It hurts too much."

"You need to be free from the past." He gently stroked her hair and whispered, "Trust me."

She knew in her heart that her guardian was right. For too long, she had been carrying the burden of what had happened in the clearing. She had willed a part of herself to die that day. And she had been living from one day to the next with no real joy or peace since.

Taking a deep breath, Lily pushed away from Jude and warned, "You won't leave my side?"

"Never," Jude vowed.

Leaving the shelter of his arms, she went to a gnarled stump and sat. She allowed her mind to drift back to that day.

"It was early. My dad loved to take long walks, especially in the snow. That morning, he asked Lucas and me to go with him. We were having so much fun. It was snowing. We raced to this very spot. We made snow angels. Mine was so much better than Lucas'," she smiled, remembering.

"Go on," Jude encouraged.

"I remember my stomach growling because I was so hungry. Daddy must have felt the same because he wanted to head back to the house for breakfast. We started walking back, but Lucas didn't move. Daddy called to Lucas, but he..." She grabbed Jude's hand and pleaded, "I can't do this, please."

"You must, Lily. I know this is difficult; I can feel your fear and your pain. But you must remember."

She inhaled deeply, finding strength in the cold air, and pressed on into her memories.

"Lucas didn't move. He was so still like he was frozen. Daddy shouted at him, but Luc just stood there, right there."

She pointed to the exact spot, remembering the glazed look of terror in her brother's eyes. Jude knelt beside her in the snow and put his hand over hers.

"I tried to push him, pull him. Daddy did too, but we couldn't make him move. I was so scared. I knew something was wrong. But then," she paused.

She stood abruptly and turned slowly in a circle, peering at the dark trees surrounding the clearing. Memories she had kept locked up deep in her mind flooded her.

"What is it, Lily? What did you see?"

"They were all around us, so very beautiful. I knew my father didn't like them because he pushed me behind him. One of them threatened us, and it made my father very angry. I remember his eyes, so blue. When he hit my daddy, I realized

I had been wrong. These people weren't beautiful at all. They were ugly!"

Hot tears slid unchecked down her cheeks. She felt the terror and powerlessness of that day all over again. It was all coming back to her now, so clear and unquestionably true, unbelievable, yes, but true.

"A woman dressed in black attacked, and my father fought back. That's when I grabbed Luc's hand. But it was so cold.

I didn't know if I was dreaming or if what I was seeing was real."

"It was all real, Lily," Jude said. "You can see that now, can't you?"

She nodded and continued recounting her memories, "I had never seen my father like he was at that moment. My father used the snow to make a weapon. And then the golden man came from the sky. He glowed as you do. He said something to my father. And then he disappeared."

"What happened next, Lily? It's important that you remember what happened next."

"Daddy's eyes were sad when he smiled at me. He must have known what was going to happen next. When he shouted at us to run, I couldn't leave him. All I could think of was getting to him. But these horrible black beasts jumped on him. I could see him struggling. I had to help him. But Lucas—he ran away. He left us. I must have blacked out after that because I don't remember anything else."

She dropped onto her knees in the snow. Rocking back and forth, gut-wrenching woeful sobs racked her body. Jude came to her and held her until she was spent.

"I couldn't save him," she hiccupped. "And when Luc left—he didn't even look back." Lily pushed back out of his embrace. "Where were you, Jude? I was completely alone."

"But you weren't, Lily. Let me show you. You need to see what you could not before."

He placed his warm hands on either side of her face. Her vision blurred and then revealed the events she had just recounted in real time. But this time, she saw things differently. Encircling the clearing behind the beautiful ones were rows of golden soldiers with shields and swords. They stood quietly, ignoring the taunts the beautiful ones flung at them. When the glowing man appeared next to Eli, the golden warriors snapped to attention.

She gasped. The man from the sky was Nolan Gable. He spoke to Eli and then left him in a flash.

"How could they just stand there and watch my father die? They did nothing! Why didn't they fight?"

"We grieved when Eli fell. But it was his time, Lily, his destiny."

"I don't understand."

"Do you wonder what Nolan said to your father before he died?" Jude asked.

"Yes, of course."

"Nolan brought your father a message from God."

"A message? What did Nolan tell him?"

"That Lucas would carry on what he was not able to complete."

"So, my dad knew before he died that Lucas was part of the next generation of the Sorcha?"

"He did. He sacrificed himself so that Lucas and your family would be safe. God never allows suffering without a purpose, Lily."

"I can't pretend that I understand all of this, but I want to. I want to know more about God and the light that Lucas talks about. For too long, I denied the truth of all that happened here. I won't do that any longer," she pledged. "I owe my mother and Lucas a big apology. I've been incredibly awful to them."

Jude picked her up and held her close in his warm glowing embrace. The winter scene disappeared. Lily felt the summer sun on her face. She gazed at her protector, feeling an unexpected lightness in her soul and mind. The past no longer had any power over her; it couldn't harm her. She was free. She couldn't wait to get back home and share everything with her family. She couldn't go back to the years she had lost with them, but she could start today, making sure she didn't miss another moment of the love and happiness that her family offered her. She loved them more than she had realized.

"Lily, I know being here again, reliving that day, broke your heart all over again. I'm truly sorry that I caused you such great pain."

"It's a lot to process, but there's no need to apologize," she admonished with a bright smile.

"Let's get you home," Jude encouraged.

When they arrived back at Centenary, Jude quickly took his human form again.

"Can we take the long way? I just want to be outside for a while."

"Of course," Jude responded.

Hand in hand, they slowly made their way through the rose garden, by the dancing fountain, and across the quad. The trees were awash with the golden and red colors of fall.

"You know why I'm not sad?" Lily asked abruptly.

"Tell me."

"God had a plan for me. Knowing that there is so much going on around us that I can't see or even understand, I know that He has been watching over my family and me the entire time. My mom always told me that our circumstances don't mean we can't choose to be joyful. I never believed her until now. When you realize that even the bad stuff is working for your good, it's a lot easier to have faith even when it hurts."

When they reached Audrey's house, Lily announced, "It's game night tonight, and I promised Zoe I would help her bake cookies. Talk later?"

Jude nodded.

She moved toward the house, but then Jude pulled her back.

"Wait, Lily; I need to say something."

"Okay, what is it?"

"I need you to know that I'll always be here for you. Don't ever doubt it."

"I won't, I promise," she smiled softly and then climbed the steps to the front door. Before going in, she announced, "Jude Butler, I'm so grateful we have each other because I'm sure I wouldn't be able to handle any of this without you!"

Chapter 24

Lucas was still floating on air. Lily believed him! Yesterday, his sister had asked for a family meeting. After her tumble in the river and the realization that her best friend had provided her with a supernatural rescue, Lily had finally accepted the truth. She shared in detail with all of them exactly what had happened after her fall from the boat and then her visit back to the clearing. After many tears and apologies, the Quinn family had stayed up most of the night talking, laughing, and remembering. As a result, he had slept through his alarm this morning.

Lucas hurried down the aisle of the old church. Grimacing, he checked the time on his watch and picked up his pace. He burst through the doors and hurried down the aisle of the old church. He was very late. Bad move! It was a training day, and Nolan was a stickler for punctuality.

Before coming to Cleveland, training sessions with Nolan had been conducted secretly in whatever city the Quinns were living in at the time. Over the last seven years, Lucas had matured in his gift. He could now experience, process, and understand any number of sensory messages without becoming overwhelmed by the power of them all. Nolan had taught him so much. Even still, he doubted sometimes if he was worthy of the light within him. Buried in his thoughts, he ran right into the back of a rather large and imposing Dìonadain guarding the entrance to the Hall.

"Careful, young man," the sentry warned. "Mind your path."

"Right, excuse me," he answered respectfully.

He didn't think he would ever get used to the sight of the Dìonadain in all their splendor. Walking around the warrior, Lucas crossed the hall quickly and entered the training chamber. It was a large three-story room with solid rock walls. Opening off the main circular space were smaller rooms hewn into the stone. Everyone else was already there. A curt nod from Nolan was all Lucas needed to understand that this best be the last time he came late to a training session.

"Bout time, man," Rafe muttered under his breath. "Nolan's been scowling for ten minutes."

"Just catchin' up on my beauty sleep," Lucas quipped.

"And that's why I was on time; I'm already beautiful," Rafe bantered back.

"Enough! We begin the next phase of your training today, the Light Trials. Lucas has already successfully completed his series of trials. It is your turn now," Nolan said. "Please enter a chamber and join your guardian."

"Here goes nothing." Rafe grinned. "Wish me luck."

"You got this," Lucas encouraged. "No pain, no gain!"

"That's what I'm afraid of," Rafe replied before entering the first chamber.

Lucas was thankful he had already mastered this stage of training. The Light Trials were incredibly demanding. Each one of his friends would be required to use their gifts while remaining keenly focused, having relentless control over mind and body, all while experiencing significant levels of pain and fear. Lucas knew this challenge would be greater than any of those his friends had experienced before. They would need to be brave, committed to action, and persevering to the end—that was the true test.

Taking a seat beside Nolan outside the training chambers, Lucas said, "I'm sorry for being late."

"You are forgiven. Just don't make it a habit."

"Lily believes me now. That's why I was late. We stayed up all night just processing everything."

"Yes, I thought as much." Nolan smiled.

Turning his attention back to the training chambers, he asked, "We can see and hear them, right, but they can't do the same?"

"Correct. Each Dìonadain warrior has created a barrier to seal off the chamber from any distracting stimuli. Invisible and very powerful. Rafe will be first. Watch closely."

Lucas focused on Rafe. He was seated at a small desk in the chamber with Yona next to him.

"On the desk in front of you is a cryptogram," Yona explained.

"A mind puzzle; yeah, I've solved hundreds of these. An unreadable block of text that can't be understood without the use of a substitution cipher or key. Figure out the cipher. Solve the puzzle. Piece of cake!"

"Focus the light within, Rafe," Yona replied. "You may begin."

Rafe manipulated the cryptogram. Within moments, Lucas could see that Rafe was shivering. The temperature in the chamber must have dropped dramatically. His friend's shivers soon developed into the shakes. But Rafe pressed on.

"I have two letters. Working on the third," Rafe chattered.

"As it is written in the book of Proverbs, 'By wisdom, the light laid the earth's foundations; by understanding, He set the heavens in place; by His knowledge, the depths were divided.' You can do this," Yona encouraged.

"I have the third and fourth letters in the sequence."

Rafe had stopped shivering and was soon wiping away perspiration from his face. The temperature in the room was rising. Lucas noticed that the metal table Rafe was working on was glowing hot with heat.

"I have the fifth letter."

"Keep going," Yona urged.

"My hands are burning!" Rafe shouted in agony. "I can't do this."

"Solve the puzzle," Yona commanded. "Press through the pain!"

Lucas was now genuinely concerned for his friend. The burns must be excruciating. He cringed when Rafe howled, jerking away from the table. That's when he saw them. Hundreds of bugs creeping across the puzzle, the table, and the chamber's walls. They were everywhere. Vile creatures with black horns crawled up Rafe's arms and legs, across his face, and into his clothes. Rafe growled in disgust, wincing when the creatures' dagger-sharp stingers pierced his skin. Still, he didn't give up. Lucas was impressed with his friend's persistence. No way Rafe was not feeling everything Lucas was seeing.

"Finished!" Rafe screamed.

The bugs disappeared instantly. The room was just as it had been before the trial began. No cold, no fire, and no bugs.

"Well done, warrior," Yona said, folding Rafe into the comfort of his wings. "Today, you gained much in strength and focus. I am proud of you."

"Next time, I'm wearing gloves and bringing a blow torch," Rafe responded ruefully.

"And now, Beni will be tested," Nolan said.

Lucas turned his attention to the second chamber. He was glad Beni wasn't aware of what had just happened to Rafe, or he might have run. Instead, Beni sat quietly on the floor in the center of the chamber. Asher stood directly behind him.

"The key to wielding your gift, Beni, is complete focus," Asher instructed. "God has given you the ability to speak in known and unknown languages, as well as the ability to interpret what is being said. Trust your gift and interpret the written words you see before you."

Lights danced around the chamber, forming words and phrases that floated in the air. All were unfamiliar to Lucas. But not for Beni. It wasn't long before his friend was translating the different languages aloud, detailing the specific dialect. Lucas could hear confidence in Beni's voice growing with each interpretation: Hebrew, Gaelic, Russian, Ancient Egyptian, Latin, and many Lucas had never heard of.

"Excellent, Beni—remain focused," Asher instructed.

Then, a voice rang out in the chamber. An unknown tongue that Beni translated immediately. More voices sounded, speaking different languages simultaneously; some were loud and sharp, while others were soft as a whisper. Lucas could distinguish at least ten different languages being spoken at once, and Beni was translating them all. Beni was doing it!

Then, there was silence. When the next language echoed within the chamber, Lucas felt Beni's profound anguish and fear because the sound of it, the high-pitched screeching, caused all the warmth to drain from Lucas's body. He had heard this cursed demonic language before. Beni collapsed, curling into a fetal position. Clearly, the sound and whatever the words meant were paralyzing Beni.

Asher knelt beside Beni and urged, "The spoken Word of God is like a powerful sword in your mouth—use it!"

Beni rolled onto his back and shouted, "His light is within me. I am not afraid!"

Suddenly, the chamber went silent. Then, Asher began to sing. The angel's voice rolled like the waves of the ocean—rhythmic and peaceful. Pure and divine, it was the most beautiful melody Lucas had ever heard. Beni stood, tears of joy streaming down his face.

"I have never heard anything more wonderful in my whole life," Beni whispered in awe.

"The language of the Dìonadain is unknown to man. Soon, you will be strong enough to understand my song and speak my language, wielding its comfort and power."

"But what of the cursed one?"

"The Scáths tongue is so cold and painful it fills the soul with fear. We do not speak it, for it brings destruction. But you, Beni, focused the light within, banishing the fear from your soul. You leashed the tongue's darkness."

"I want to try again," Beni asked.

Asher smiled. "I appreciate your enthusiasm, but let's review all that you have learned first."

Now that Beni had completed his trial, Lucas knew Zoe would be next. Rafe and Beni had both been faced with extraordinary and sometimes painful obstacles. He had to admit he was afraid for her. Zoe, of course, was totally oblivious to the potential challenges of her session. Lucas was thankful the soft-spoken, gentle Tov would be Zoe's guide during her trial.

The first thing Lucas noticed about Zoe's chamber was its transformation into an outdoor scene alive with activity. A bright sun was suspended in the clear blue sky. Birds chirped in the lush shade trees. Bees buzzed, flitting from flower to flower in the colorful garden. Zoe looked happy and content; her bare feet sunk into a carpet of green grass.

"This is amazing, Tov. I could live here forever," she said.

Tov passed his hand over the flowers surrounding Zoe.

Lucas watched as each one withered.

"Can you make this rose bloom again, Zoe?"

His sister studied the flower intently. As she touched each petal with the tips of her fingers, the bloom became a vibrant pink once more.

"Well done, Zoe. Now let's try something else," Tov encouraged. "Remember to focus."

A bird flew from its perch in a tree and across his sister's line of sight. Lucas grinned; besides Jack, birds were Zoe's favorite animals. When Tov picked up a rock and threw it at the bird, it was knocked to the ground. Lucas knew Zoe would waste no time helping the bird. She picked up the bird and placed her hand on its broken wing. Again, almost immediately, the wing was mended. Zoe giggled with pride and tossed the bird into the air. A loud hiss drew his sister's attention quickly.

Lucas tensed up when he saw Tov struggling on the other side of the chamber with two Scáths. How did they get inside? He quickly realized the demons were not real because his senses had not responded to danger. But he knew there was no way that Zoe would know that. His sister screamed when the demons shot their fiery darts at Tov. Beni must have heard Zoe's scream because he burst through the door of his chamber into hers. Before he could reach Zoe, one of the Scáths released a wicked blue dart piercing Beni's heart. Beni grabbed his chest, stumbled, and slid down to the grass. Even from a distance, Lucas could see that Beni labored to breathe. Obviously in shock, Zoe was frozen to the spot. Her friend had collapsed, and her guardian was still being pummeled by Scáths.

"Help me, Zoe," Beni groaned.

Zoe ran to him, knelt, and placed her hand on Beni's heart. Her head shot up when she heard a hiss. The Scáths had beaten Tov, his body pierced by dozens of deadly darts. They were coming for Zoe now.

"Please, help me," she called out to Tov. "He's dying."

"You can do this, Zoe," Tov managed. "Use your light."

Lucas started to pray. Zoe must overcome her fear. When she spoke, her voice soft but steely, he realized she was digging deep for the courage to do what she needed to do. Turning away from the approaching enemy, she placed her hands on Beni's chest once again.

"God, give me strength. Use me to make him whole."

Lucas knew his sister had successfully completed her trial when the Scáths disappeared from the room. Beni sat up; his injury was gone. She had done it! Lucas was so proud. Zoe must have been reeling from what had just happened to her, but she had gained undeniable strength and confidence today. They all had. Except for Daniel. The chamber he had entered earlier remained shrouded in darkness.

"What about Daniel?" Lucas asked. "When will his trial begin?"

"Look for yourself." Nolan waved his hand and illuminated Daniel's chamber.

Lucas gasped. Daniel was kneeling on the stone floor. His body was soaked with perspiration. Blood dripped freely from his nose. His arms were painfully extended, bound on either side by thick iron chains. The effort it must have taken Daniel to lift his shackled arms into a posture of prayer was almost inconceivable to Lucas. His friend's tortured muscles appeared to be strained to the point of ripping in two. Daniel's eyes were tightly shut, and his mouth moved wordlessly. He was praying despite the punishing amount of exertion it must require. When Ira moved his hand over his charge's bent form, the chains broke. Daniel slid to the floor, completely spent.

"The Believer is willing to go where others will not," Nolan said quietly.

"Incredible," Lucas whispered.

Chapter 25

When Lily discovered the quaint café that served afternoon tea and scones, she knew she had found her special place. The cute blue and white striped awning, small tables, and chairs lining the sidewalk were just waiting for someone to sit down and lose themselves in their favorite book. And she loved to read. Next to running, reading was a favorite pastime. Getting lost in a book allowed her to relax; unfettered by the stresses of her life, she could just be in another world.

Today, she was reading *Pride and Prejudice* for what must have been the twentieth time. She knew Mr. Darcy didn't exist in the real world, but it was still nice to imagine what life might be like if he did. She was a closet romantic, to be sure. Lucas would have teased her mercilessly if he ever found out. Lost in her book, she didn't notice the black sports car that was pulling up in front of the café.

"Hey, Lily!"

Startled, she looked up and came face-to-face with the last person she had expected to see.

"Aiden, what are you doing here?"

Even though he was dressed casually in shorts and a gray T-shirt, Aiden still looked like he had just stepped off a page of a magazine. Suddenly, she wished she had taken more time on her appearance. Her ponytail, athletic shorts, T-shirt, and flip-flops were hardly a match for his stylish look.

"Get a hold of yourself, Lily," she said to herself. "Stop worrying about impressing him."

Aiden took his black sunglasses off and smiled. "I actually came to see you. I went by your house, and your mom told me you might be here."

When she didn't reply, he jammed his hands in his pockets and rocked back on his heels. If Lily didn't know better, she would have thought he was nervous.

"Uh, okay," she finally responded. "Do you want some tea?"

"Nah, I'm good, thanks."

"Well...what did you want to see me about?'

"I wanted to ask if you would come for a drive with me?" Aiden asked. "I'd like to show you something."

"A drive?" she asked awkwardly.

She was flabbergasted by his invitation. Her leg began to bob up and down under the table. She placed her hand on her stomach to calm the butterflies dancing inside. Why did this guy always have this effect on her?

"Yeah, I promise we won't be gone long," Aiden implored.

He looked so earnest and sweet that she couldn't think of a reason to say no. Besides, her curiosity was piqued.

"Okay, I'll go with you. Let me text my mom."

She sent Mia a message to let her know she was going for a drive with Aiden. She knew her mom and aunt would be full of questions when she got home.

"Your chariot awaits." Aiden gestured to his car.

His boyish smile made her weak in the knees. She settled in the buttery leather seat. Aiden shut her door, walked around to the driver's side, and joined her in the car.

"I hope you know what you're doing, Lily Quinn," she said to herself. "You're definitely playing with fire."

Pulling away from the curb, she fought the urge to ask Aiden to stop the car. She wasn't a spontaneous person, so this outing was very much out of her comfort zone. On the other hand, Aiden was devastatingly handsome and smart, and the bonus, he seemed to truly want to get to know her better. Quickly weighing the pros and cons, Lily decided to relax and enjoy the adventure, trying to focus on anything else but the butterflies in her stomach that were ever present when Aiden was nearby. They talked and laughed. Lily was surprised by how comfortable she felt. Until Aiden slowed the car and stopped in front of an old, three-story building that looked as if it had been abandoned decades ago. Mass of bricks and broken windows. Graffiti decorated its exterior and large metal doors. It was striking, haunting, empty, and rich, all at the same time.

"We're here."

"Where is here, exactly?"

"The old textile mill, it was a beautiful building back in the day. It's just a bunch of bricks and broken windows, now."

"A relic of the past. Very cool. Thank you for showing it to me."

"Sure, but that's not why I brought you here. Not exactly. It's around the back of the mill."

"What is?"

"You'll see. Patience is a virtue, you know."

"That's what my mother keeps telling me, but it hasn't really stuck."

"Come on," he encouraged. "It's not too far."

Aiden exited the car and came around to open her door. Exiting the car, she was greeted by a warm breeze and the sweet scent of honeysuckle. They traversed some uneven ground before turning a corner. The sight that met her eyes was truly lovely. The summer sun was beginning to set, and its red-gold and purple hues streaked the sky, reflecting off the water in the small pond behind the mill. An abandoned railway car sat in the middle of a beautiful field of summer wildflowers. Lights hung from the ceiling and along the open doorframe.

"This is amazing, Aiden.

"I was hoping you would like it."

Catching the uncertainty in his eyes, she replied, "It's perfect. How did you find it?"

"I've been coming here since I was a kid. It's private property, but I've got connections with the owner."

"Let me guess...your dad?"

"Yes, ma'am, guilty as charged."

Turning in a circle and surveying the incredible view, she continued lightheartedly, "I bet this has been a slam dunk with all the girls you've brought here."

"I've never brought anyone else here...only you."

She turned her head to look at him. He was just studying her intently. She had no quick comeback to the revelation that she was the only girl he had ever shown this place to. The silence hanging in the air did nothing for her already heightened nerves. So, she did the only thing she could; she changed the subject.

"Can I get inside that rail car?"

"Of course."

She walked past him and climbed the five metal steps that led up to the rusty railcar. She wasn't prepared for what she saw.

"Your favorite things all in one place," Aiden announced from behind her. "The outdoors, the stars in just a few minutes, I hope, and of course, what would a picnic be without tacos!"

She couldn't help but giggle. "Who told you I love tacos?"

"Well, I may have asked your little sister. And you know how Zoe likes to talk." He smiled.

As afternoon faded into night, they laughed and talked while they ate their simple dinner. Their conversation was much more than words. It had an energy that she was unfamiliar with, like a ripple in a pond that becomes a fast-flowing river. The string lights were glowing softly overhead in the rail car. Still, they talked—about anything, everything, and nothing at all. It was so easy—like they had known one another forever. Before tonight, she had thought Aiden was so very different from her, but she was realizing they had more in common than she knew—likes, dislikes, goals, and dreams. When they spoke of the parents they had both lost, she discovered in Aiden a sensitive heart and compassionate spirit. He continued to surprise her.

"Thank you for a lovely picnic, Aiden. You really know how to impress a girl."

"You're the only girl I care about impressing, Lily."

She couldn't help but blush. Maybe she had been wrong. Maybe there were men like Mr. Darcy in this world after all.

Aiden reached into the basket. His fingers shook slightly as he gave her a single white lily. She looked up into the eyes of the young man who had no idea that he had just turned her whole world upside down. Gone was the perfection and nonchalance of his practiced expression. Gone was the mask he wore everywhere he went, the one he believed protected his heart. In its place was the earnest and unguarded face of a young man who yearned to be loved.

She touched the cool softness of the white bloom. “It’s beautiful, Aiden. I don’t know what to say. No one has ever given me flowers.”

“Well, I guess I will have to make sure you get them often, then.”

She wasn’t sure how to respond. She felt very overwhelmed suddenly. Her silence didn’t seem to bother Aiden, and he went on.

“Remember the first day we met? I’ll never be able to forget it. It’s like the whole world came alive. Everything was brighter, warmer, better. Every time I see you, it’s like that for me. Since I met you, I’ve been trying to figure out how to make you notice me.”

“Aiden, I don’t know what to say...”

“You don’t have to say anything. I’m not sure I can even explain it, but when I’m with you, I feel a hundred things at once. I’m different, you know. I feel like I could do anything, be anything. I know this is happening fast, Lily, but I want you to know what I’m feeling.”

“Feelings don’t come easily for me, Aiden. I’ve tried for a very long time never to let my emotions get the best of me. Relationships are difficult, and they hurt.”

She stood and walked a few steps away from him. She looked up at the stars twinkling brightly in the sky.

"I've tried to ignore you, to avoid you even, and standing here right now with you, I'm not so sure I want to do that anymore. But I need time."

Aiden moved to stand beside her. He put his hands in his pockets and rocked back on his heels. He said softly, "Take all the time you need, Lily. I'm not going anywhere."

They both stood silently, just looking at the stars. Lily was a riot of emotion and thought. Strange—she wasn't scared—she was hopeful. Moments ticked away before Aiden took her hand in his. She turned toward him. He was gazing at her so intently as if he needed to find an answer in her eyes.

"The gala is a few days away. Maybe we can talk again?" he whispered, lifting her hand to his lips for the barest whisper of a kiss, "Give me a chance, Lily; I promise I won't disappoint you,"

With his pledge, she knew she was lost. He must have known it, too, because a heart-stopping smile broke across the hard planes of his face.

"Let's get you home. If I keep you out any longer, your mom will send a search party." He winked, picking up the blanket and packing up everything in the basket. "Besides, the gala is just a few days away."

She shook her head, a little disconcerted by his quick change of mood. One thing was certain—Aiden Talbot was full of surprises, and time with him would never be boring!

Chapter 26

Catching his reflection in the mirror, Lucas had to admit he looked pretty good. Tonight was the gala at the museum center. It would be his first fancy party, black tie and all, and he was ready to start the evening. Waiting at the bottom of the stairs, he checked his watch. He hated to be late, but apparently, the women in his life didn't share his feelings. Impatiently, he studied the mask Audrey had given him to wear. Simple in design, the black leather half-mask was accented with silver piping. His aunt had purchased it in Venice, Italy, on one of her summer trips abroad. He bet the ones his mother and sisters would wear were even more intricately designed.

"You look so handsome," Audrey said from behind.

Lucas turned with a grin. "A real heartbreaker, huh?"

His aunt wore a simple yet classic black gown. She was wearing pearls—her favorite—on her neck, on her fingers, and in her ears. Her silver mask was also decorated with tiny seed pearls. As always, his aunt was lovely in every way.

"Come over here, Romeo, and let me straighten your tie."

"They are going to make us late, Aunt Audrey," he said with frustration. "And..."

"You like to be early," she teased, dusting off the lapels of his jacket. "I know. But I hear being fashionably on time is all the rage right now!"

Zoe whistled as she came down the stairs. "You clean up real nice, bro. James Bond ain't got nothin' on you."

His little sister wasn't so little anymore. Her emerald-green party dress, heels, and colorful mask made her look much older than he liked. He felt his protective instincts kick in and gave his sister his best smile.

"Wow, Zoe, you look so pretty, so grown up."

"Thank you, Lucas," Zoe smiled shyly.

"You both know this is a big night for your mom," Audrey said. "Mia is a ball of nerves. I'm worried because she hasn't eaten all day."

"Mom never eats when she's anxious," Zoe commented.

"Don't worry, Aunt Audrey; Mom will be fine. I'll make sure she eats something," Lucas promised. "Mr. Talbot is sending a car for us, and it will be here any moment. I wish they would come on."

He opened the front door and walked out onto the porch. The sweet scent of honeysuckle hung heavy in the night air. Even though he was excited about the party, he was tired. The responsibility for all that lay ahead weighed heavily on him. He and the others had been training hard this past week, so he hoped the gala would be a great diversion. A little light-hearted fun would give them all the energy they needed to jump back into training tomorrow with a renewed focus. Even though they were leaving the protection of the Centenary grounds, Lucas knew Nolan and the Dìonadain would be close tonight. He was confident they would be safe. When a sleek black limousine stopped in front of the house and the car horn sounded, he grinned with anticipation.

"Thank you, Mr. Talbot. The Quinns will be riding in style tonight."

Lucas considered his mom's association with Talbot Industries and the great man himself to be a real opportunity. Even though he had been spending all his time either training or with Aiden in the last few weeks, he hadn't had the opportunity to interact much with Mr. Talbot. He hoped he would have a chance to talk with him at the party. He could learn so much from a man like him.

"Mom, Lily, come on, the car is here!"

"We're right here, Lucas," Lily answered lightly, joining him on the porch. "You don't have to shout."

His sister was a vision in midnight blue. Her shimmering organza dress with its scooped neckline, cinched waist, and flowing skirt complemented her figure and coloring perfectly. Her thick blonde hair hung in waves around her shoulders. Her gold mask was in place, but he immediately recognized the faint glimmer of insecurity in her eyes. Lily needed approval but would never ask for it. He knew she didn't see what everyone else readily saw. She was beautiful. He wished she thought so too.

"So, what do you think?" she asked nonchalantly.

"Stunning," he said with meaning.

"Really?" she asked softly.

"Really," he returned.

Flashing a brilliant smile, she warned, "Wait till you see Mom."

Lucas turned back toward the wide front door and watched as Mia descended the staircase in her strapless crimson brocade floor-length gown. The sequined crimson mask she wore accented her elaborate updo. His mother was beaming.

"You look amazing, Mom, and tonight is your night," Lucas offered her his arm. "Shall we?"

Lucas helped the beautiful women of his family into the limo. It was a short drive to the museum.

"When I left earlier this afternoon, everything was set and just as it should be," Mia mused. "I pray it all goes off without a hitch."

"No worries, Mom, your event is going to be just perfect!" Zoe declared.

"Zoe's right," Lucas agreed. "It will be a smash!"

"You've put your whole self into making sure this evening is a success, Mom. Now it's time to enjoy it all. We are so proud of you," Lily said.

"Ditto," Audrey offered with a laugh.

"My beautiful, encouraging family. I don't know what I would do without you," Mia said. "How much I love you all."

When the limo stopped in front of the museum, Lucas reached for the car door. His mother grabbed his hand and gave it a little squeeze as he exited the vehicle.

"You good?" he asked, extending his hand and helping her from the back seat.

Mia squared her shoulders and nodded her head confidently before she sailed by him in a crush of brocade and satin.

He turned to his aunt and sisters, "Ladies, let's get this party started."

The entrance to the museum was ablaze with thousands of sparkling lights. The lobby was alive with costumed street performers and acrobats reminiscent of the formal Venetian masquerades.

Once inside, Audrey said, "You guys have fun. I'll be around if you need me. I promised I would help your mom make sure everything is lined up for the silent auction later."

The Quinn siblings, Lucas in the middle, with a sister on each arm, entered the ballroom. It was spectacular. Voluminous cream-colored silk covered the walls while tall silver candelabras held shimmering candles. Large, intricately carved ice sculptures adorned the tables of food and drink. An orchestra played while the masked attendees circled the space serving scrumptious cold and hot finger foods. Couples swirled around the room in a dance in a kaleidoscope of colors. It was quite the show!

"Wow, Mom really did it, didn't she?" Lily said with wonder.

"She sure did," Lucas agreed.

He had about lost hope that his sister would ever say nice things about their mother again, much less feel them. Ever since her accident at the river, she had been a different person. And he was grateful.

"Here comes Beni," Zoe announced, waving at her friend as he crossed the ballroom floor.

"Is there anything about those two that I should know about?"

"Shh, Luc, they're just good friends." Lily winked.

"Your mom really knows how to throw a party," Beni remarked when he joined them.

"Lily, tell Beni he looks handsome?" Zoe asked. "He won't believe me."

"Stop it, Zoe," Beni said sheepishly, his cheeks flushed with discomfort.

"She's right, you know. You do look very dapper in your navy suit," Lily complimented warmly.

"Thank you," Beni answered. "I've never worn anything so grand before."

"Ooh, look, it's a chocolate fountain," Zoe interrupted.

Beni's eyes widened. "A chocolate fountain? Seriously?"

"Absolutely, let's go," Zoe urged, tugging on his arm.

"I love America," Beni said with conviction, following Zoe to the dessert table.

"Those two are funny," Lily remarked.

"Yeah, for sure," he laughed. "I still think something might be going on between them. Did you see them look at each other with those puppy eyes?" Lucas offered.

"Seriously, Luc, not everything is something," Lily admonished. "They're just friends."

"Until they aren't," he joked back. "Do you want some punch or something?"

"Truth? I do, but—don't laugh—I'm afraid I'll spill it all over me," she whispered.

"Come on, Lily. I would never laugh at you," he teased. "Okay, maybe I would."

"Oof, here comes Aiden," she said quickly. "Act like I just said something funny!"

"You like him, don't you?" Lucas mused, recognition dawning. "I'm not so sure I'm okay with that."

"Shh, save it for later," she urged quickly, then turned to greet Aiden brightly. "Hi, Aiden!"

"Wow, Lily, you look beautiful," Aiden replied with appreciation. "And Quinn, you don't look half bad, brother," he drawled.

Lucas noted his sister's blush at Aiden's compliment. He was torn—frustrated because he wasn't comfortable with the idea of Aiden and his sister together, but he was also happy. He wanted Lily to feel pretty and knew that a few words from Aiden had done just that. Maybe his sister dating his best friend wasn't the worst idea after all.

"Watch yourself, Talbot," he warned good-naturedly before walking away.

He made a beeline to one of the long buffet tables. He grabbed some punch and sipped while he scanned the crowd. All of the Sorcha were in attendance tonight. Rafe was across the room in conversation with the eldest Talbot sibling, Kayanga. Funny, he had never seen Kay look that relaxed, but with Rafe, he seemed at ease. His friend had a way of making everyone feel comfortable. Daniel, as expected, was standing solemnly against the wall, looking as if he would rather be anywhere but here. It was no surprise to him—in the week he had come to know Daniel, it wasn't hard to miss that the guy wasn't exactly the party type. Beni and Zoe were at a table, enjoying their spoils from the chocolate bar.

He finished his punch, determined to find a certain young woman. He had promised himself that he wouldn't leave tonight's gala without asking Lysha to dance. He had rehearsed it all in his head. But when he found her in the crowd, he frowned. Rafe had beaten him to the punch. His friend, no longer talking with Kay, was instead in a corner chatting up the woman of his dreams. Drop-dead gorgeous in a skin-tight red dress, Lysha was stunning. So much for practicing his opening line in the bathroom mirror! Time for Plan B, he thought.

Lucas looked down at his empty glass and knew exactly what he was going to do. After visiting the punch bowl again, he made his way across the room and headed right toward Rafe's back. When he got close enough, he turned his head ever so slightly and proceeded to bump into his friend. Red punch ran down Rafe's shoulder, soaking his grey suit jacket. Just as Lucas had hoped, Rafe was startled. His friend spun around immediately, with a few chosen words hanging in the air.

Lucas was only too happy to smirk and say, "Oh man, I'm so sorry. I bet if you get some soda water on that jacket right away, it won't stain."

The realization that he had been beaten at his own game slowly dawned in Rafe's eyes.

"Don't worry, I'll entertain Lysha while you're gone," Lucas called out as Rafe stomped away.

"Impressive. For a college boy." Lysha smiled.

"Impressive enough to convince you to dance with me?"

She smiled flirtatiously, "You just don't give up, do you?"

"Not easily, no. Just one dance?"

"It will have to wait, handsome," Lysha said easily. "My dance card is already full."

And with that, she simply walked away. Lucas was dumbfounded. He wasn't used to making a total crash and burn! But he wasn't going to be deterred that easily. He squared his shoulders and decided he needed to develop a new strategy if he was going to have a chance with Lysha. But his planning would have to wait. He had promised Mia that he would help her with the fireworks show that was scheduled to take place later in the evening. He circled the ballroom, weaving through the crowd, but his mother was nowhere to be found. He decided to check the outdoor patio and the property beyond where the fireworks were set up. Maybe she was already there waiting for him. He opened the French doors and was surprised to see his mother and Flynn Talbot embracing on the moonlit patio. Something twisted deep in his gut. He moved into the shadow of a yew arbor next to the door and tried to make out their hushed conversation.

"I'll take you anywhere you want to go," Mr. Talbot insisted. "Come away with me, Mia."

"I can't, Flynn, at least not right now. The children are just settling in, and my new job..."

"After the success of this event, your boss will be happy to give you a few days off."

Lucas was relieved when Mia pushed lightly on Talbot's chest to put some distance between them.

"I love being with you; I do. I didn't think I would ever feel this way again. But I think maybe things are moving a little too fast."

Lucas was shocked and angry. How could she have feelings for another man?

"I understand. I really do. I loved my wife very much, just like you loved your Eli. I had resigned myself to being alone because I didn't truly believe I could ever feel passionate about another woman. But then I met you."

Flynn closed the distance and took Mia in his arms again. Lucas drew in a quick breath. He didn't want to see what he was seeing, but he couldn't tear his eyes away from his mother and Talbot.

"Our paths were meant to collide, Mia," Flynn declared, placing one of Mia's hands against his heart. "I feel alive again. And I know you feel it as well."

"I do have feelings for you, Flynn; I just need some time to sort it all out."

"Take all the time you need. I'm not going anywhere."

When Talbot bent his head toward Mia and she leaned into his kiss, Lucas couldn't remain silent any longer.

"Take your hands off my mother," he shouted explosively, leaving the shadow of the yew arbor.

Startled, Mia broke away from Talbot's embrace. Her embarrassment at being caught by her son was etched plainly on her face.

"Lucas, let me explain," she pleaded. "And please lower your voice."

"No explanation needed! I can see—clearly!"

"Lucas Elijah Quinn, you will not speak to me in that tone."

"Your mother is right, Lucas. Calm down, and let's have a civil conversation," Flynn urged quietly.

Lucas didn't spare Flynn a look. His hero worship of Flynn Talbot had died a quick death. He only had eyes for his mother.

"How could you? You don't even know him."

"It's not for you to say what I should or should not do, young man. You know nothing about my relationship with Mr. Talbot."

"So now it's a relationship?"

Mia looked at Flynn and then back to Lucas. "I was going to tell you; I was just waiting for the right time."

"When? After you spent a weekend away with a man? I don't even know you anymore, Mom."

"Lucas, please, it's not what you think."

"I'm just glad Lily and Zoe weren't here to see."

"Look, we can talk about this when we get back home, after the gala. All of us, I want to explain everything."

Nonplussed, Lucas shook his head. "Why? I mean, how could you just forget about Dad? Please, help me understand."

"I could never forget your father, Lucas. But I can't stop living my life just because he is gone," Mia declared. "My choices are my own to make, Son. I would think I have earned your trust and respect by now."

"Yeah, obviously, we have different ideas about trust and respect," he offered sarcastically. "Can't you see? You're just an easy mark, Mom. You don't know about him. You're just one more woman in a long line of women that he has taken advantage of."

His face stung from her slap. Mia looked at her hand and then at her son's face.

She reached for him. "Luc, I'm so sorry."

He turned on his heel and walked away, leaving Mia alone with the man that was no longer a hero in his mind. Flynn Talbot was a user and a heartbreaker. He was an adversary now, and Lucas vowed to do everything in his power to stop the man from destroying his mother's heart.

Chapter 27

"Thinking about me?" Aiden whispered in her ear.

Lily blushed. It had been two days since their picnic at the mill, and all she had been able to do since was think about him. Was this really happening to her? On the arm of the most gorgeous guy in the room, she felt like the heroine in her very own fairytale. Aiden Talbot was becoming rather important to her. The walls around her heart showed a few cracks now that he was in her life. She wasn't sure where it would all lead, but she wanted to find out.

She answered with a newfound sense of confidence, "Maybe."

Aiden responded with a woeful grin and stabbed the left side of his chest as if he had a dagger in his hand.

"You're killing me, sweetness, but I promised I would be patient, and so I shall."

Lily smiled brightly. "I've never been to a party this grand. It's magical."

"It certainly is," he stated, gazing intently at her.

She felt herself blushing again. She couldn't deny that she was falling fast for Aiden, and she wasn't sure she wanted to slow things down any longer.

"I bet you've been to many parties like this."

"Yeah, quite a few, but this one is the best we've ever had. Your mom knows what she's doing when it comes to parties."

"She has been so nervous; she's never planned an event before. But I think she's a natural. I'm proud of her."

"You should be. And now, I think it's time for a dance," he announced, taking her hand in his.

"Yes, please."

"I have to warn you, I'm not very good," she responded, walking with him to the dance floor. "My aunt gave Luc and me a few lessons this past week but—"

"No buts. I bet you are better than you think. Besides, you're in luck with me for a partner. My dad insisted I learn early, so I've been dancing for years now."

When the music swelled, Aiden took her in his arms, guiding her expertly around the floor. She realized immediately that Aiden had been right about her luck with a partner; he was a fine dancer. Wanting to soak up every detail of the evening, especially the time she spent with Aiden, she forced herself to relax. Once she did, she enjoyed herself.

"You're smiling," he said. "I'd like to think it's because of me."

"Truth?"

"Always."

"It is you. And it's tonight, this place, my dress, and dancing." She laughed. "It's just all magical. And you were right earlier, you know; I have been thinking about you."

He flashed a brilliant smile. "Then we're even because I haven't been able to stop thinking about you."

Lily surprised herself with the transparency of her next words.

"I am falling for you, Aiden Talbot. And that should scare me to death, but it doesn't. Instead, it makes me feel happy and hopeful. I told you at the mill that I needed time, but I'm not so sure I do anymore."

"Well then," he said gently.

Whirling around, she caught sight of her brother.

"There's Lucas." She nodded toward the end of the ballroom. "And he's headed straight for your sister with a very determined look on his face. What's he up to?"

"Flirting, I bet." He grinned.

"No way your sister would give him a second glance. He's so much younger than her."

"Hmm, you might be surprised. Age is just a number. Besides, Luc has some serious skills when it comes to charming women."

"You're as bad as he is." She giggled.

When she and Aiden circled back around the room again, Aiden asked, "So, how's he doing?"

"Well, your sister just walked away from him, and he's just standing there with his mouth hanging open. Epic fail."

Aiden laughed. "You two have that whole brother-sister love/hate thing going on, don't you?"

"We sure do, and we're very good at it. But seriously, I don't know what I would do without him."

"Your secret is safe with me. Lysha and I have our moments too. Half the time, she can't decide if she wants to be my mother or my big sister. But I wouldn't trade her for the world."

When the dance concluded, Aiden asked, "Hungry?"

"I'm dying to try the chocolate fountain."

He laughed. "Let's start with dessert, then. I'll be right back."

Watching Aiden circle the table, filling a plate with all sorts of sweets dipped in chocolate, she thought about how much her life had changed since coming to Cleveland. She had found a place that felt like home, her relationship with her family was better than ever, she had discovered her best friend was also her guardian angel, and now, maybe, just maybe, she had met a guy she could see a future with. She couldn't remember the last time she had so much to smile about.

"I wouldn't look so smug if I were you. It's not as if you really mean anything to him."

Lily turned and met the furious eyes of Rachel Pooley. She was dazzling in a gold-sequined strapless dress that hugged her every curve. Lily frowned. She had never thought kindly of catty girls, and Rachel was the queen of them all. This girl was quickly becoming a thorn in Lily's flesh. She decided she needed to show her she wasn't an easy mark.

"I'm not really clear on your meaning. Care to explain?"

"Don't play the dumb blonde. Everyone knows you've been after Aiden since the day you first laid eyes on him. But your pathetic little plan isn't going to work. He's mine."

"If that were true, he wouldn't be talking to me, would he?" Lily asked directly.

"That's where you're wrong!" Rachel's shrill voice was garnering people's attention. "You're just a plaything—not even a pretty one at that! Your new girl scent will wear off soon enough."

Lily had had enough. Lowering her voice, she said, "That's enough. You are making a scene. Stop it!"

When she tried to walk away, Rachel grabbed her arm, twisted hard, and wouldn't let go. Lily stumbled back, ripping the hem of her gown in the process. When Rachel let go suddenly, Lily fell to the floor. Humiliated, she pushed herself up and stared back into her attacker's vindictive face. Rachel's minions stood behind her.

She couldn't decide which was worse—Grayson and Marshall's snide laughter or the look of pity from both Jenna and Daryl. Her magical evening had quickly become a nightmare. She fought hard to keep her tears at bay and attempted awkwardly to get up without tearing her dress again.

"Easy now, I've got you," Aiden said softly.

With a gentle touch, as if she were something precious to him, Aiden helped her stand.

"Are you hurt?"

"Nothing but my pride," she managed ruefully. "It stings a little."

"Not for long," he promised.

Aiden's warm expression disappeared and was quickly replaced by one of cold fury.

"Enough, Rachel! All of you, back off."

"Aiden, honey, don't be so serious. It was just an accident. Poor Lily just tripped over herself," Rachel drawled, feigning an air of innocence.

"That's not the way I saw it," he returned.

Rachel moved closer to Aiden, "It was just a bit of fun. Besides, I know you're paying her attention because you want to make me jealous. Well, mission accomplished."

When Rachel leaned in to kiss Aiden, he stepped back abruptly.

"Wrong. I couldn't care less about what you think, Rachel. And to be clear, whatever you think is between us, it doesn't exist for me."

The color drained from Rachel's face at Aiden's words. Lily instinctively scooted closer to Aiden. Rachel was angry, very angry.

When she turned her murderous glare to Lily, Aiden warned, "Don't even think about it."

"We aren't over, not by a long shot," she declared before leaving the room in an incensed whirl.

"You didn't have to be so ugly to her, Aiden," Jenna complained. "She loves you."

Lily didn't think it was possible, but the look Aiden gave Jenna was so icy she shivered.

"That's not love. Rachel is malicious and controlling. She can't love anyone but herself. And the rest of you? You're supposed to be my friends, have my back, I thought you would have been above something like this!"

"As Rachel said, we were only having a little fun. Like we all used to do before she came." Marshall nodded at Lily.

"No harm, no foul, dude! She's just a girl," Gray quipped.

At that remark, Aiden lunged at Gray. His momentum was halted when Lucas grabbed him from behind.

"Shake it off, man," Lucas urged. "They aren't worth it."

Aiden nodded. "You're right. I couldn't see it before, but they were never my friends in the first place."

"Exactly," Lucas replied.

Aiden straightened his jacket, and in a clear cold voice, emphasizing every word, he commanded, "Get out of here, or I'll have you thrown out!"

As if on cue, the intimidating form of Aiden's older brother appeared behind Aiden and Lucas.

"No need," Marshall said deliberately.

"Yeah, this party has become tedious," Gray responded stiffly, never taking his eyes from Aiden's. "Another time, friend."

After his so-called friends left the room, Aiden turned back to Lily. "I am so sorry, Lily. Please forgive me."

"Forgive you? Are you kidding? You saved me," she said. "If you hadn't come back when you did, I'm pretty sure Rachel would have had another go at me."

"She's right; you did. I owe you, man," Lucas said. Then he grabbed her shoulders and squeezed. "And if Rachel Pooley ever comes near you again..."

"Don't worry, big brother. I'll be ready for her next time," Lily responded with a grin.

"Are you sure you're okay, Lily?" Aiden asked again earnestly.

"Promise. Now, how 'bout my two favorite men take me to get some punch?"

"I think I'm partied out. Time for me to head home," Lucas said quickly.

Lily noted her brother's deflated look. Maybe Lysha's rejection earlier had thrown him for a loop. She gave her invitation one more try. She didn't think Lucas should be alone right now.

"It's still early, brother, and there are lots of pretty girls that would love to dance with you."

"Next time, maybe. Enjoy the night, Lily," Lucas said and gave her forehead a quick kiss. "Take care of her, Aiden."

"He's okay. Give him some space," Aiden urged. "I'm sure it's nothing."

"I don't know. Something is bugging him, though. Lucas has never been very good at hiding his feelings," Lily agreed. "I just worry about him, you know."

"He's lucky to have you," Aiden returned. "We can go after him if you want."

"No, I'm sure you're right. He just needs a little space. If he wants to talk about it, he'll tell me when he's ready."

"Okay, want to try the chocolate fountain one more time?"

"Hmm, I think I'd rather have you spin me around the dance floor again."

"Happy to oblige, ma'am," Aiden drawled before twirling onto the dance floor.

Chapter 28

Sitting on the couch in an oversized sweatshirt and leggings, Lily was grateful for some time alone. Everyone was busy doing something else tonight, so she had the house to herself. So many wonderful things had happened in the last several weeks, and although she appreciated every single one, she was looking forward to some time to decompress from the whirlwind that was her life right now. She needed to turn her brain off for a while. Some hot buttered popcorn and one of her favorite movies were just what she needed for self-care. She had just started the movie when the doorbell rang. Lily wanted to pretend no one was home. But at the second ring, she begrudgingly gave in, pausing the movie and leaving the comfort of the couch to see who was at the front door.

"Aiden!"

"How's my favorite girl?" Aiden grinned.

"I'm good, but what are you doing here? I thought you had an event with your family."

"Dad let me off the hook. So, here I am. Do you have plans tonight?"

"Just watching a movie. Everyone else is out doing things."

"Want some company?"

"Sure, come on in."

She waved him into the den and then joined him on the couch. Sitting close to him, she felt the familiar hum of electricity she experienced whenever she was close to him. She didn't think she would ever get used to it. And maybe she didn't want to. It had been two weeks since the masquerade, and she had seen Aiden almost every day. Romantic dinners, a concert, a carnival, waterskiing at the lake, and hiking. He had even joined her family for their Friday game nights. She was crazy about him, and she was sure he felt the same because he never let a day pass without expressing his care for her somehow.

Text messages, flowers, handwritten notes, and conversations about real things that mattered; in all their time together, Aiden had never failed to be intentional toward her. He didn't just shower her with pretty words and compliments. He showed her in everything little thing he did that he respected her and wanted to know her. In a very short time, Aiden Talbot had become very important to Lily. He was the kind of young man she had wished for and the type of man her mom had told her that one day she would find.

"*Star Wars*? It's on my top ten list," Aiden said. "I didn't take you for a sci-fi fan."

"You don't know everything about me yet! When Lucas and I were little, we pretended we were Luke Skywalker and Princess Leia. I loved it as much as he did."

"Same! Lightsaber fights with my brother and sister were epic," he explained, grabbing a handful of popcorn from the bowl. "And since we're talking about favorites—this right here is the snack of champions! There's never a good time not to eat popcorn."

"Same!" She laughed. "I can't watch a movie without it."

"I'll make sure to put that fun fact on my list."

"You're making a list? Of my favorites?"

"Absolutely. Impressing you has become my favorite past-time."

Playfully, she pushed his arm. He caught her hand, intertwining his fingers with hers.

"Happy?" he asked.

"You know I am." She giggled.

"Good, then I'm doing my job."

He winked and then focused his attention on the TV screen. Lily laid her head on his shoulder and relaxed against him. Much too soon, the movie was over. Time always flew by must too quickly when she was with Aiden. She wasn't ready for the night to end yet.

"Want to watch another one?" she asked. "I can make us some more popcorn."

"I want to, but I've got to get home and pack. Dad decided he wanted to start our family vacation early. We were supposed to leave next week. He left today with Lysha and Kay. I'm headed out tomorrow to meet them."

"Why didn't you just go with them?"

"I wanted to have the chance to see you again and say goodbye."

Lily blushed and quickly changed the subject. "This is your trip out west, right? To Montana? I bet you're excited."

"I do love it there. Somehow, the world is just bigger in Montana. Undisturbed land as far as the eye can see and the mountains...words can't do them justice. The ranch is home to me. I've thought seriously about living out there full-time once I graduate."

"I understand. I felt the same way about Colorado. We lived there when I was a little girl. I miss the mountains and the snow. And you must be looking forward to being with your family."

"We're all so busy now; our trips to the ranch have been the only quality time we've had with no distractions in the last two years. My dad told me he has something special planned for me this time."

"That's great. How long will you be gone?"

"Probably three weeks. I won't be back until right before the semester starts."

"Wow, that's a long time. What will you do while you're there?"

"What cowboys do." He grinned. "I gotta admit I've missed it."

Lily laughed. "A cowboy?

"Yes, ma'am," he drawled. "Riding, roping, and branding cattle in my boots and Wranglers with my hat pulled down low."

"Now that's a picture I'd like to see!"

"Our place is in the middle of nowhere, so I don't always have good cell service. I've never minded it before, at least until now..."

"Don't worry. Lucas won't do anything remarkable while you're gone," she teased. "You won't miss a thing."

"It's not Lucas I'm worried about. It's you, Lily. You need to know that I have feelings for you. And that I've never felt this way about anyone before. I want to show you Montana someday, Lily; I want to look at stars in the Montana night sky with you."

"I would like that very much," she said wistfully.

"I was hoping you would say that."

Aiden reached for a strand of her hair and gently twirled it around his finger before letting it fall back into place. She caught her breath. Lily's wish had finally come true. Time had slowed and came to a full stop. She couldn't tear her eyes away from his. She knew she had just jumped into the deep end of the pool. She wasn't falling in love with Aiden; she realized at that moment, she was in love with Aiden.

How had that happened so fast? It didn't matter, fast or slow; there was no denying her feelings for him. When he leaned in, she met him halfway. It was their first kiss, tender and sweet. It was a promise. When he leaned back, all she could do was stare at him. He must have been pleased by her stunned expression because a heart-stopping smile broke across the strong planes of his face.

"I'm gonna miss you, Lily Quinn."

And with that, he stood up, placed a small blue box and a card on the table in front of her, and walked out her door. Staring at the box, Lily touched her lips and replayed their kiss again in her mind. Scared but excited nonetheless, she decided to open the card first. It was a handwritten note from Aiden.

Lily,

Remember the night at the river? You told me the stars reminded you of your father. And when you looked at them, you felt closer to him. Well, I want you to have stars with you always. And know there won't be a day while I am gone that I don't think about you.

Aiden

She opened the blue box and gasped. Inside, a pair of diamond earrings shaped as stars sparkled. Aiden Talbot was full of surprises.

Chapter 29

Aiden had only been gone for two weeks, but it seemed like a month. Lily burrowed deep under her quilt. She prayed the stillness of the house would somehow flood into her being, bringing peace. Last night, she had experienced a vivid and frightening dream. After waking up in a cold sweat, she called out to Jude. Instantly, he was at her side. His presence had helped to quiet her spirit, but she couldn't entirely shake the fear that was still clutching her heart. Jude had urged her to tell her brother. So, she went to Lucas' room to wake him.

After sharing all the details of her dream with her brother, Lucas told her something that had shocked her to the very core of her being. Only after Lucas had shown her the star-shaped sign on the skin behind her ear and his as well did she reluctantly accept the truth of who she was.

Her father had known too. Jude purposefully kept that knowledge from her when he told her about the message Nolan gave her father before he died. It's why Jude had been her protector from the start. She was the Dreamer, the Sorcha gifted with the power to interpret prophetic dreams and visions.

All day she had struggled to wrap her mind around the reality of what she now faced. Jude had told her that her dreams would only grow stronger and come more often. If that was true, she wasn't looking forward to the future. Last night every ounce of energy was drained from her. It was as if her dream was a thousand pounds of chain wrapped around her body, heavy, cold, and unforgiving. Until she solved the mystery, the hidden secrets of the dream, the meaning of the images running rampant through her mind, she knew she would continue to feel the heaviness of the burden.

Tomorrow, she was set to begin her training, joining the other Sorcha in their preparation for the war that was ahead. A war she had no idea about just twenty-four hours ago. Everything was happening so fast, and there was so much for her to learn. But Jude would be with her, and he had vowed to help her grow in her gift.

Longing for a dreamless sleep but knowing that it would not be so, she closed her eyes. A few hours later, she woke screaming and shivering despite the warmth of her bed. The dream was different this time, and she needed to tell Lucas. She fought for control as she walked unsteadily to her brother's room. He was sleeping on his stomach and snoring as usual.

"Luc, wake up!"

"Lily? What is it?" He rolled over on his back, groggy, and rubbed his eyes.

"I had the dream again."

Lucas was immediately alert. He sat up and asked, "The same one?"

"Yes, but it was different this time. It was stronger, more powerful."

"Lily, you're shivering." Lucas pulled his blanket around her shoulders. "Better?"

She nodded.

"Tell me."

She took a deep breath, and then the words just spilled out.

"I was running down a long hallway. But it wasn't dark this time. I could see things that had been hidden before. There was a metal door. I went through it and ended up in a huge room. I think I was in an art gallery because paintings were hanging on the walls. And I wasn't alone. There were people, strangers, but their backs were turned, so I couldn't see their faces. They were standing silently, looking at the art. I felt so afraid; I felt lost. When I asked for help, the strangers just ignored me."

"That's super weird. Go on."

"Well, that's when I saw him."

"Who? Who did you see?"

"A little boy. He was so cute. He was standing across the room. He called out to me. He knew my name. He motioned for me to come to him, so I did. The closer I got to him, the colder I felt. It was like I was frozen from the inside out."

When she paused, Lucas put his arm around her and gathered her close.

"Go on," he said and encouraged softly.

"I reached out my hand to him. When he took it in his, my hand started to burn. He wouldn't let go. I begged him, but he wouldn't let go," she whispered. "And then his face contorted, and his eyes flamed hot blue. It was...grotesque. That's the only word I can think of that even comes close to describing his face."

"That sounds awful, Lily. I'm sorry."

"I screamed and struggled, and then suddenly, he let go. I ran across the room, trying to get back to that hallway. But he chased me. You know, I think he meant to do it. He wanted me to run. The more I ran, the further off the hallway was. It was like I was on a treadmill going nowhere fast. Then I heard this hideous roar; I thought my ears would explode with the sound. It stopped me in my tracks. I turned around and...and..."

"What, Lily? Tell me."

"The little boy, he changed suddenly; he morphed into this enormous green dragon, a very angry dragon."

"You're kidding, right?"

"I wish. And it was so real, Luc. It was like I was truly there. When the dragon opened its mouth, I could see the fire inside, but the flames were blue. I ran to the opposite side of the room, hoping I would find a way out. But then I stumbled and fell. The floor underneath me was shaking with every step the dragon took. I could feel his hot breath on my neck. I managed to get back up, and I turned to face him. Then a girl, out of nowhere, shoved me out of the way when the dragon roared and spat flames at me."

"The same girl from the dream last night?"

"Yeah, but I still have no idea who she was. I think she might have been Asian. I don't know. But she gave me a small red bag and pointed me down another passage. This time you were there, Lucas, waiting on me with the others. You took my hand, and that's when we heard the woman's voice moaning. It was dreadful; she sounded like she was in so much pain. We all followed her voice. The passage twisted and turned. It must have been going deeper underground because the air was getting colder with every step. We rounded a corner, and it was a dead end. But..."

"But?"

"A large painting was leaning against the wall. There were thick black swirls of paint crawling all over the canvas. I touched one of the swirls, and it exploded with blood. More and more blood kept pouring out, filling the space. And then blood swallowed us, and everything went dark."

"That's a horrible dream, Sis. Do you have any idea what it means?"

"No, not really. I wish I could make sense of it. All I do know for sure is that something bad is going to happen, and it's going to happen soon."

Lucas squeezed her hand in support. "You will figure it out; I know you will."

"And that's what I'm most afraid of, Luc, I think someone is going to die. Someone I love."

"Lily, we can't be sure what your dream means yet."

"But you can't be sure I'm not right, either. I keep thinking about what Jude told me before I came to you. He said my vision is waiting for its appointed time. He said it hastens to the end, and it will not lie. He told me not to chase the meaning but to wait for it to be revealed."

"Then we'll wait," Lucas said confidently. "You will figure it out. I believe in you, Lily."

"Thank you, Luc," she whispered and hugged him tightly.

"Hey, as long as we are both awake, we might as well ask Nolan and Jude to start your training. It's almost dawn anyway."

"Sounds good. I'll get dressed and tell Mom. I'll meet you downstairs in ten."

She went back to her room and dressed in jeans and a T-shirt. She pulled her unruly hair back in a ponytail and looked at her reflection in the mirror. The diamonds in her ears sparkled against the paleness of her skin. If only her dad were here. He would tell her to pull herself together and have some confidence in herself. She sighed, "I'm trying, Daddy. I'd appreciate a little help, though."

"You ready?" Lucas asked, leaning against her door.

"Yeah, but I still need to tell Mom."

"We can both go."

The twins made their way to their mother's bedroom. Lily knocked faintly on Mia's door. No answer.

"That's weird; Mom's a light sleeper," Lucas said. "She hears everything."

Lily opened the door and slipped inside her mother's room. Mia's bed hadn't been slept in.

"Mom never gets up this early," Lucas commented. "Hey, what's wrong?"

She stood speechless at the foot of her mother's bed. She felt like she was going to vomit. When she swayed abruptly, Lucas steadied her.

"Whoa, Lily, what is it?"

"It's the painting in my dream. The black swirls. The canvas. It's the color of blood."

"Aunt Scarlet painted that picture?"

"Yeah, I think she did. And you know what happened to her?"

"Let's not go there, at least not yet; I'm gonna wake Aunt Audrey," he said and left the room.

Lily fought the waves of nausea rising from the pit of her stomach; the mystery of her dream unraveled before her eyes. Mia wasn't in her bed because Mia was gone. Something had happened to her, something awful and terrifying. Every fiber of Lily's being knew that her mother had been taken sometime last night. And if her dream was true, Mia didn't have much time. She was going to die if they didn't find her quickly. The clock was ticking.

She pointed to the picture and cried, "Oh no, Luc, I think Cain has Mom!"

Unobserved, hidden in the dark recesses of the room, she relished the opportunity to study the woman that had so enthralled her master. A familiar pang of delight coursed through her as she watched the woman's confusion slowly turn into panic as she surveyed the windowless green silk-covered walls, the magnificent crystal chandelier hanging from the high ceiling, and the dark wood four-poster bed. All were foreign to this wretched woman but familiar to her. This was the room her master kept for his special captives. She had visited it many times over the years to prepare the chosen for all that was to come.

When the woman went to the thick mahogany door and turned the knob, Keket's pouty lips curved into a devilish grin. Humans were so predictable. Soon, the woman would discover that escape was futile. But, instead of fleeing the room and giving her a good chase, the woman stood at the door, seemingly transfixed by the faint voices on the other side. It was her father and mother. Keket's languid move from the shadows went undetected.

"Lower your voice, little dove—you will wake our guest," her father commanded.

"Why is she here?" her mother asked in frustration.

"You know why."

After a period of silence, her mother said softly, "All the years I gave up for you. All the horrible things I did for you. They meant nothing to you. You never loved me, did you?"

"No. You served a purpose. You gave me a perfect child, one born of light and shadow."

"And for that, I will never forgive myself. You have fashioned her into something I barely recognize. There is no kindness in her, no goodness. You have ruined her."

"Ruined? I have exalted her. Keket is powerful, cunning, loyal, and oh-so-deadly. And very soon, all my children, the Mescáths, will take this world for me. And Keket will lead them."

"It's too much, Cain. I won't do it. Not anymore."

Keket wasn't surprised by the uncompromising sound of her father's blow and the pitiful cry that escaped her mother's mouth as a result.

"You will do this and anything else I ask of you, my little dove, because you have no choice. You belong to me for all eternity," he said coldly. "Now, get out of my sight!"

When the Quinn woman sank to the floor in tears, Keket felt nothing. Her mother had been right about one thing. She was incapable of compassion or empathy. Her father had beaten that out of her long ago. When the woman looked up and realized she wasn't alone, her eyes grew wide and fearful.

Keket laughed wickedly. She was going to enjoy this!

Chapter 30

Everyone gathered at Audrey's house, anxious for news about Mia. Beni and Zoe were conversing in hushed whispers on the couch, with Jack settled between them. Rafe kept vigil by the front door, hoping Mia would return at any moment. Daniel stood by the window, praying quietly. Audrey was making phone calls to anyone who might have seen Mia before she disappeared.

Lucas paced the den floor; it had been less than an hour since he and Lily had discovered their mother was gone, and they were no closer to figuring out what had happened to her. There was no doubt in anyone's mind that Cain was responsible, but how did he manage to get through the supernatural boundary that surrounded them? It made no sense. Passing by Lily, he noticed his sister's leg in its familiar shaking movement. She was more agitated than he had ever seen her. He knelt crouched down by her chair and placed his hand lightly on her knee.

"I need my big brother now to tell me everything is going to be all right," Lily begged.

"We will find her," he promised. "Together, we will figure this whole thing out. I just wish I hadn't been such a jerk at the gala. If anything has happened to her, I'll never forgive myself."

"You can't think like that, Lucas, but if I'm honest, all the times I treated Mom badly are running across my brain right now too. And then I can't stop visualizing all the awful things that could be happening to her."

He didn't want to think about it either. Cain was evil personified. That day in the clearing, he had proved that. He had already lost one parent to the demon commander; he was not going to lose another. He had to stay calm and be a leader if he was going to keep his promise.

"I know, but we have to try. I need you to keep a cool head so you can figure out what else your dream might be showing us. Okay?"

"Okay."

He left Lily and joined Audrey at her desk. She had been calling everyone trying to get a lead on Mia's whereabouts.

"Any news?" he asked.

Audrey frowned. "I talked to Mrs. Bradley at the historical society—no Mia. I contacted Della's, the park, and even the library on campus, and no one has seen her. Her car is still in the garage. I even took a long shot and called Flynn Talbot."

"Did he have any idea where she was?" Lucas asked.

Audrey shook her head. "No. He said he hadn't seen her since the gala. He was very concerned, though, and wanted us to let him know the moment she turned up. He offered his help with the authorities, but I told him we had already called the Sheriff's Office and filed a missing person report."

"Did you talk to Mom last night?" Lucas asked.

"Yes, around 8 p.m. She seemed fine," Audrey answered. "I was tired, though, and I turned in early. The last time I saw her, she was on the couch there, reading."

"Nolan is here," Rafe announced.

When Nolan walked into the room, Lucas blurted out the one question that had been burning in his mind for the last hour.

"How did Cain break the supernatural boundary around the house?"

"He didn't," Nolan answered gravely. "Mia left the house late last night and went beyond the boundary; Cain must have taken her then."

"Must have taken her? Don't you know?" Lily asked sharply.

"Mia is not my assignment, Lily. But you can be assured that her guardian is with her wherever she is. She is not alone," Nolan assured.

"But why didn't her guardian stop Cain? Why didn't he send some kind of distress signal?" Zoe cried.

"It doesn't work that way, Zoe," Nolan said. "Only God knows the details of Mia's situation right now. But I am confident that all will be revealed as He wills it."

"But why?" Lucas demanded. "If he's after this generation of the Sorcha, why would Cain take Mom?"

"Cain's purpose is not yet clear," Nolan said. "But if he can succeed in filling your hearts and minds with fear, he knows you will lose your focus. The Dìonadain are combing the globe looking for any clue to Mia's whereabouts, but her location remains a mystery."

"If the Dìonadain can't find her, how will we ever be able to?" Zoe said miserably, leaning her head on Beni's shoulder.

"Wait a minute!" Lucas exclaimed. "Look, God gave us our gifts for a reason. We can do things that others cannot. Together, we can find my mom. I'm sure of it," Lucas declared. "Lily's dream has already told us the "who." Maybe the "where" is in the dream too."

"Luc, I've gone over the dream again and again. Even though it was more vivid last night than ever before, I still don't understand it. I even wrote it all down. Here, look."

She picked up a piece of paper and showed everyone what she had drawn. The page was covered in curious symbols, words, and pictures.

"Let me try?" Rafe asked.

Lily gave him the paper, and he studied it intently. Lucas felt the first inkling of hope that they would find Mia in time. No one was better at puzzles and mysteries than Rafe. But his optimism was quickly dashed.

"I'm sorry. I can't even make sense out of any of it," Rafe said.

"The clues in Lily's dream are not for you to interpret, Rafe. They are Lily's alone," Nolan offered.

"Okay, spit it out then. Tell us everything, Lily, the whole dream, start to finish," Rafe suggested.

"That's a great idea," Audrey agreed. "Maybe talking it through will help."

"Go on, Lily, you can do this," Zoe urged.

"You can find her, Lily; you've just got to believe that you can," Daniel offered. "Open your heart to God's guidance."

Lucas took Lily's hand in his. "You've got this."

Zoe took Lily's other hand. "You do."

Lily inhaled deeply and began. "There was a long hall and a metal door. Behind the door is a room with paintings hung all over the walls. I'm sure it was an art gallery."

"You think Mia is in an art museum?" Beni asked.

"No, I'm sure she isn't; the art gallery represents something else; I just can't see it."

"It's okay, Lily, go on," Lucas urged.

"The gallery is full of people, strangers. I want to leave, but I can't find a way out. When I asked for help, the people just ignored me. I believe this part of my dream means that Mom is hidden in a public place, and nobody notices the evil right there in front of them."

"That makes sense," Rafe interjected. "But it doesn't narrow down the location for us."

"Then there's a cute little boy—I know he was a demon, I'm sure of it because when I got close to him, his hollow eyes flamed blue, so I ran. He chased after me. And I felt his breath hot on my back."

"That's horrible," Zoe whispered.

"And frightening," Audrey added.

"When I turned around, the little boy shape-shifted into a monstrous green dragon. It roared and spat violet flames at me, but out of nowhere, this girl appeared and pushed me into another passage."

Lily paused.

Lucas asked, "What is it?"

"It's so weird. She gave me a red purse. She told me I was going to need it. Then she pointed to another passage that I hadn't seen before. I ran and turned a corner. Lucas, Daniel, and Rafe. That's when I heard the woman moaning. I knew we needed to find her, but then the paintings exploded with blood, and everything went dark."

"The woman is Mom, isn't it?" Lucas asked.

"I don't know why I didn't catch it before, but it's her voice I heard; I'm sure of it."

"That's good, right? She's moaning, so she's still alive," Zoe offered.

"We need to go now. She doesn't have much time," Lily said.

"But where exactly?"

"Chinatown, New York City," Lily said confidently.

Lucas stared at his sister in disbelief. "You're sure?"

She smiled brightly. "The girl that rescued me from the dragon was wearing a New York Yankees baseball cap. And the paintings that exploded with blood were covered in Chinese script. Isn't it obvious?"

His sister's confidence was contagious.

"I knew you could do it," he whispered, then turned to the others. "We know where to go, so let's go!"

"Look, man, I know you want to rescue your mom, but we aren't ready to fight Cain. We can't fully control our gifts yet," Rafe said.

"I agree with Rafe," Daniel said. "The Dìonadain can rescue Mia now that we know where she is," Rafe insisted.

"No, they can't," Lily declared. "The Dìonadain were not in my dream. We were. It must be me, Lucas, Rafe, and Daniel who go. I'm sure of it."

"But what about Beni and me?" Zoe asked.

"Neither of you were in Lily's dream, Zoe. Her vision is prophetic, so we must honor it if we are going to find Mom," Lucas said.

"Please," Zoe stood up with her fists clenched by her sides. "You may need me. If Mom is hurt, I'm the only one that can help her."

Lucas tipped his sister's angry, tear-stained face up to his. "We'll bring her home, Zoe. I promise."

"All right then," she said bravely. "I'll trust you. But don't take too long."

"Let's go outside," Nolan encouraged.

Lucas and the others followed Nolan out of the house to the backyard. He knew they were headed into the fight of their lives—untried and largely unprepared—but he also knew the power of God's light would lead them. It was a time for courage, perseverance, and, most of all, trust.

When Nolan spoke, he echoed Lucas' thoughts.

"Each one of you must have faith. Trust in your gifts and in each other. And remember, you must only speak our names if you need our help."

Anxious to get going, Lucas asked, "So, how are we gonna get to New York City?"

"I know," Daniel answered, lifting his face to the sky. "Almighty God, make a way."

The ground trembled, and five very familiar winged warriors radiant with the power landed in the yard. One was a big surprise to the rest. Clearly, one of the guardians took everyone by surprise when everyone besides Lily and he said in unison, "Jude?"

Rafe recovered quickly, "No offense, man, but all this time, I just thought you were Lily's nerdy tagalong."

"None taken," Jude replied with a grin.

"That's gonna take some time getting used to," Rafe murmured to Lucas. "Of course, you knew. You could probably feel it."

"Yeah, the day I met him. Lily didn't know until the day at the river."

"Well, a lot of things are making sense now," Rafe returned and then continued seriously, "Luc, we are gonna bring your mom home."

"I know," he said, digging deep to find the strength and confidence he knew he would face what was surely ahead of them.

"It is time," Nolan declared. "As your Dìonadain guard, we will transport you to the city and be with you every step of the way. Lucas, trust your senses. Be mindful of the signs in your dream, Lily. Stay focused and sharp, Rafe. Keep your mind clear. And Daniel, keep them balanced. They will need your powerful faith."

Lucas and Lily hugged Zoe and Audrey, saying their goodbyes. When he met his little sister's gaze, he whispered, "I will keep my promise."

"I know you will. Just get everyone back in one piece."

"Lucas," Nolan called, unfurling his mighty wings.

Joining the others who were already enveloped within their guardian's wings, Lucas stepped into Nolan's embrace.

"We will be moving very fast through space and time. Keep your eyes open; it will help with the queasiness," Nolan advised.

"Got it," Lucas said.

"Hold on, this will be the ride of your life," Nolan smiled.

Chapter 31

"Wicked ride!" Lucas shouted.

The Dìonadain had flown them within moments from Audrey's backyard onto a subway train barreling through a dark underground tunnel. Lucas looked around at the others, who were all trying to get their bearings while fighting to remain balanced and upright on the fast-moving train. The car they were in was empty except for the four of them, their guardians no longer visible.

"I feel like I'm going to puke," Lily moaned.

"Breathe, Lily. It will pass in a moment," Daniel assured.

"My face is numb," Rafe said to no one in particular.

The train slowed to a stop, and the doors slid open. Canal Street was emblazoned on the brick wall opposite them. People filed out of the other subway cars onto the platform.

"This is it," Lily announced.

"Okay, let's go," Lucas said.

Lucas exited the train and found the stairs to take them up to street level. Leaving the crowded subway station, Lucas was immediately assaulted by the sights and smells of Chinatown. Located in the lower portion of the island of Manhattan, Chinatown was home to one of the densest populations of Chinese immigrants in the Western Hemisphere. Canal Street was bustling with activity. Street vendors and food trucks lined the busy streets selling everything from hotdogs to ancient Chinese herbs.

"Umm, I'd know that scent anywhere. Shawarma!" Rafe remarked.

"No distractions, man," Daniel said pointedly.

"I'm not distracted," Rafe returned. "I'm just hungry. Everything happened so fast this morning; I forgot to eat breakfast."

"We don't have time for this, Rafe," Lucas admonished. "Okay, Sis, where to?"

Lily was quietly studying everything around her. He figured she was revisiting her dream, looking for clues as to where they should go.

"We need to go shopping," she said abruptly.

"Shopping?" Lucas questioned. "Are you sure?"

"Very. We need to buy a purse."

"A red purse, I bet," Rafe offered.

"Exactly," Lily answered. "We need to find a store that sells handbags."

"There's one," Lucas pointed. "Across the street."

Just then, a young woman walked up to Lily and asked softly, "Hey, lady, you want Gucci or Prada?"

Lucas was astounded. Could it be? He looked at Lily and knew instantly from her huge smile this was the girl from her dream. She was petite with long dark hair, and she was wearing a New York Yankees baseball cap.

The girl cut her eyes toward him and asked, "I take you to secret place, no cops. Follow me?"

Lucas responded immediately, his heart racing, "Yes!"

"This is it," Lily said with wonder. "My dream was real."

"I never doubted you. Let's go get Mom," he said.

Weaving in and out of the crowded streets, Lucas and the others soon left the hustle and bustle of Canal Street behind. He had no idea where this girl was leading them, but he was ready to get there.

"How much farther?" he asked.

"Almost there," she answered. "Hurry now."

"Are you sure this is a good idea, Lucas?" Rafe questioned from the back of their little group. "I grew up in the city. A quiet neighborhood is trouble."

"I don't sense any danger," he replied. "But stay alert."

At the corner of Crosby and Howard Streets, a kid who couldn't be more than eight years old, wearing an "I Love New York" T-shirt, was waiting for them.

"He will take you to the pretty purses," the girl said before hurrying back the way they had come.

"I think we just got passed off," Rafe remarked.

"Is this kid the little boy from your dream?" Daniel asked softly.

"No, he isn't. I think we're off script now," Lily replied.

"You come, quick," the kid urged.

"You heard the little guy," Lucas declared. "We don't have another choice."

They walked a short block and followed the kid into a small storefront. When Lucas stepped inside, the fragrant scent of jasmine filled his nostrils. Multicolored Chinese umbrellas hung from the ceiling. Little Buddha statues, tea sets, and colorful embroidered clothes were displayed around the room. On the shelf covering the back wall, dozens of pairs of shoes were stacked. Behind the counter, an old woman was smoking a pipe. She looked like she was a hundred years old, with wispy white hair and deep grooves lining her leathered face. She just stared at him.

"This way, to the back," the kid said, pulling on Lucas' arm.

Reaching the shelves, the kid let go of Lucas' arm. When the kid stuck his hand in a shoe on the end of the fourth shelf, Lucas was unnerved. There must have been some type of concealed button in the shoe because a panel in the wall to the right slid open.

"You go in," the kid pointed.

"This just keeps getting weirder," Rafe whistled.

Stepping through the opening, Lucas and the others found themselves in a room the size of a very small closet. When the panel in the wall behind them slid shut, another door opposite opened. A small woman with eyes that disappeared in her chubby face motioned them forward into the dark space. A single light bulb hanging from the ceiling provided the only light. She led them down a long metal staircase to a steel door. The woman rapped on the door three times. Immediately, the door cracked open, and a man with an ugly scar running down his cheek peered out. The man and woman exchanged a few words in Chinese. Then the man invited them into a brightly lit windowless room. It was stacked from floor to ceiling with hundreds of counterfeit designer purses, wallets, bags, and belts. Three other shoppers already in the room had already selected their purchases from the impressive array of Coach, Gucci, Louis Vuitton, and Prada in every color and size.

"Jackpot," Luke announced. "And Mom's close. I can sense it."

"But where?" Lily asked, looking around the small space impatiently. "We came in the only door."

"You buy? You stay. If not, you leave," the man with the scar demanded.

"Stall him," Lucas whispered.

Daniel pointed to the Louis Vuitton duffle bags and backpacks on the far wall and asked, "How much for this one?"

"We need to be quick. Look for another door," Lucas urged.

Pretending to look at the bags and purses, Lucas, Rafe, and Lily searched the entire space with no luck.

Lily whispered dejectedly, "I know the clues in my dream led us here. I don't understand."

"I'm sorry, Lily," Lucas answered. "But we can't give up."

"There!" Rafe interrupted, pointing to a row of handbags stacked on the floor against the far wall. "It's a red purse, the only one in the whole room, from what I can see. Is it the same as your dream?"

"Yes!" she responded, giving Rafe a quick hug.

"Time, you go. Must make room for others," the scarred man ordered.

"If we leave now, we'll never get back in," Rafe said.

"We have no choice. We'll just have to figure out how to get back in later," Lucas said.

He was frustrated. Worse than that, he was bordering on giving in to the feelings of hopelessness that he had fought to keep at bay all day. He was sure his mom was close by. But they had to leave the room. If they didn't, the scarred man might make trouble, and that would bring them too much attention; maybe worse, it might alert Cain to their presence.

The group made their way back upstairs to the store and headed for the door.

"You find what you were looking for, pretty boy?" the old woman at the counter rasped.

Turning back, he answered, "No, ma'am, not yet."

"You wait; it will come," she promised.

He wished he could believe the strange old woman. Outside the store, he saw the others had crossed over to the opposite side of the street. They were standing in front of a five-story red-brick and limestone structure.

"Lucas!" Lily motioned excitedly.

He jogged across the street and joined them.

Peering through the large windows, Lucas could see marble statues, Oriental vases, and antique oil paintings; all looked very old and expensive.

"Look up there," Lily pointed impatiently.

Following his sister's gaze, he drew in a shaky breath. Above the front door, painted in gold letters, was the name of the building: Dragoni Ltd., Antiquities and Fine Art. Above the letters, there was an emblazoned image of a green dragon.

"It's the dragon from my dream," she said.

"She must be in this building, somewhere," he said. "That's why I could feel her presence."

"Do you still? Feel her close?"

"It's faint, but I'm positive that's where she is being held."

"Hey, kids, you need to move along," a burly police officer announced from behind them.

"What's the trouble, officer? We were just window shopping," Daniel explained innocently.

"No trouble, just police business. I need you to clear on outta here," he finished. "Capisce?"

"Sure thing," Daniel answered pleasantly. "Anyone up for some coffee? We passed a place a couple of blocks back."

"I'd love some coffee," Lucas returned, leading the group away from the cop. "We need to plan our next move anyway."

Reaching the coffee shop, they positioned themselves at an empty table by the front window. After ordering some coffee for everyone, Lucas asked, "Lily, think hard. Are there any other clues from your dream that could help us?"

"Nothing that makes sense right now."

"Well, let's review the events of the day thus far. Mia was taken. Lily had a dream. Our guardians took us on a vomit-inducing thrill ride to New York City. We followed a girl who probably speaks three words of English into a sketchy store in what might as well be another country. We entered a hidden room to buy a counterfeit purse. Illegal, by the way. And then we leave without a purse or your mom," Rafe said dryly.

"That about sums it up, yeah," Lucas responded.

"As hard as it is, we need to be patient and wait. Our path will be revealed to us a step at a time," Daniel said.

"Easy for you to say, man. It's not your mom being held and possibly tortured by demons at this very moment," Rafe responded hotly.

"Arguing isn't going to help us find Mia any quicker," Daniel said pointedly.

Rafe shook his head. "I can't believe I'm gonna say this, but you're right. Arguing leads nowhere."

"Apology accepted, my friend," Daniel said seriously.

"So, why don't we put our heads together and figure out the best way to get into the Dragoni building?" Lucas suggested.

"I think we may need some help right about now," Rafe offered.

As if on cue, Yona entered the coffee shop.

"Brilliant!" Rafe exclaimed. "You never cease to amaze me, man."

Yona offered a quick smile and said, "Ask, and you shall receive. How can I help?"

"We're pretty sure our mother is being held somewhere in the Dragoni building down the street," Lucas explained.

Yona nodded. "I believe you are correct. There is an unusual concentration of Scáth activity in this area. They are everywhere. You will need to find a way to enter the building undetected."

"Most of these older buildings should have their floor plans on file," Rafe mused, pulling his laptop from his backpack. "I'm on it. Stay tuned."

While Rafe's fingers moved deftly across the keyboard, Lucas noticed the same young woman they had met on the street with another group of people outside the coffee shop. She happened to look, and he caught her eye through the window. She appeared to be anxious. The glance lasted no more than a second before the girl and her group of potential bag buyers disappeared.

"I got it," Rafe announced. "The Dragoni building is built on top of some underground tunnels that were never fully developed by the city transit system. If we can get into one of those tunnels, then we can get to Mia."

"Rafe, memorize those plans, every nook and cranny," Lucas said.

"Done," Rafe said, staring at his computer screen.

"Hey, look out the window. Isn't that the girl from before?" Daniel asked.

The girl with the Yankees cap ran past the window. Lucas wasn't surprised to see the burly police officer chasing after her.

"Lucas, why are you smiling?" Lily asked.

"I think I know how we can get in," he laughed.

Lucas was out the door in a flash. He could barely see the girl up ahead, which meant she was fast. But, despite his size, the burly cop was close behind—too close. Lucas knew he had to get to the girl before the cop caught up to her. She was their ticket into the Dragoni building. He felt a rush of energy flow through his body, and he stumbled. His senses had been triggered and were humming at a very high frequency, the Dìonadain kind.

Three Dìonadain warriors, disguised as NYPD cops, joined the chase. One yelled at the burly cop and pointed him down a side street. The burly cop didn't hesitate; he shifted direction and sprinted away from the main street. Two of the warriors followed him while the third stopped Lucas.

"Down the alley," he said. "Quickly."

Lucas edged quietly into the alley between two apartment buildings and paused by a fire escape ladder. From behind a battered green dumpster, she lunged. Knocking him to the ground, she hopped up, ready to run. But he was too quick. He grabbed her ankle and pulled her back down. Rolling on top of her, he pinned her to the concrete.

"Get off of me," she spat defiantly.

"Stop struggling! I'm here to help."

Her movements stilled, but her expression told him she would bolt if he let off the pressure. "The cop chasing you will be here any moment. I'm the best shot you've got," he said fiercely.

For a split second, he thought the girl wasn't going to comply. But a slight nod of her head was all the agreement he needed. He helped her up and took her hand.

"Come on," he shouted.

He led her to the end of the alley, where a taxi was waiting.

"Get in," Nolan ordered.

They jumped in the backseat. The taxi tires squealed as Nolan left the alley at breakneck speed.

"I owe you, whoever you are," she said.

Her broken English had been replaced by a perfectly American accent.

"I'm Lucas Quinn," Lucas replied. "And you are?"

"Wei Sung," she said. "Why did you help me?"

"Because I need your help with something."

"Such as?"

"I want you to get my friends and me back into the room with the purses below the shop. Tonight."

"Why? If it's a purse you need, I can get that for you tomorrow morning."

"It's not a purse. I need a way into the Dragoni building, and I think the small door in the purse room might get me there. Will you help me?"

Wei slumped back against the seat. Lucas held his breath. This girl was his only shot at getting into that building and to his mother. And time was not on his side. He met Nolan's gaze in the rearview mirror. His guardian's concerned expression matched his own.

"Please, God, let her say yes," he prayed silently.

When Wei did answer, Lucas didn't think he had ever heard three better words.

"I'll do it."

Chapter 32

Nolan stopped the cab in front of a five-story walkup in the heart of Chinatown. The others had already arrived, apparently having no trouble finding the address he had texted them. When he and Wei got out of the car, Nolan pulled away from the curb, merged into the street traffic, and disappeared. Immediately, Lucas felt his guardian's invisible presence beside him. With Wei's help and the protection of the Dìonadain, his confidence in his rescue plan had increased tenfold. Tonight, he vowed his mother would be home with her family.

After introductions were exchanged, Wei said bluntly, "You're all crazy to try to get into that building. Evil surrounds that place, but I always repay my debts. We need to talk to my grandmother first."

Lucas and the others followed Wei up to the fifth floor. When they reached their destination, Lucas' eyes started to burn.

"Sorry about the incense," Wei offered. "My grandmother loves the stuff."

Before Wei could insert her key into the lock, the door was flung open by the little boy from the shop.

He cocked an eyebrow and asked, "Who are they?"

"Just some friends. This is my little brother, Junjie," she introduced. "Come on in."

"Hello again, pretty boy."

Somehow, Lucas wasn't surprised to see the old woman from the store sitting in a recliner in the living room. Of course, they were all related and running the counterfeit purse scam together.

"Nainai, this is Lucas Quinn. He helped me get out of some trouble today. And this is his family."

"Trouble? Was it that cop who was in the shop yesterday? The one with muscles on his muscles?" she asked.

"Yes, Nainai. I'll be more careful, I promise.

The old lady waved her hand nonchalantly, "No mind. Thank you, Lucas Quinn, for your help. And please call me Nainai."

"I'm pretty sure she would have done just fine on her own, Nainai," he returned.

"My girl, she's very smart, here and in here," Nainai explained, pointing to her head and then her heart. "Been working the streets since she was Junjie's age. Now, she's in charge of our little business." Then, she turned to her granddaughter and asked, "How will you repay the young man for his service to you?"

"He wants me to help him get into the Dragoni building."

"No! I will not allow it," Nainai said forcefully. "Remember the promise."

Lucas interjected, "Nainai, let me explain. Our mother is being held captive somewhere in the building by a very evil man capable of terrible things. My friends and I must rescue her before it's too late. I'm afraid if we don't get to her soon, she might die. That's why I asked Wei to help me."

Lucas watched as a myriad of emotions played across Nainai's wrinkled face.

"I owe him, Nainai," Wei said. "I would be sitting in a jail cell right now if it wasn't for Lucas."

"Yes, that is true," she answered quietly. "Come close, my children. You must all hear my words and heed their warning."

Everyone did as she asked, finding a place on the floor at her feet.

"The path you seek lies behind a small door in the room in the basement where we keep the purses. Wei knows it," Nainai explained. "No one in my family has ever opened the door. You see, long ago, my grandfather vowed to never go beyond the barrier. Breaking his promise would mean the death of my entire family. The door has remained locked ever since, each generation remaining loyal to my grandfather's vow. My grandfather was sure that a great evil dwelt beyond that door. He never spoke the name of the man who had demanded his vow, but I know he was very afraid of him."

"Believe me, I wouldn't ask if there were any other way," Lucas said.

She nodded. "When you walked into our store today, I knew the time had come for my grandfather's vow to be broken."

She removed a long golden chain from around her neck. Dangling from it was a key. She clasped it around her granddaughter's neck.

"Take this," she said to Wei. "Be watchful, little one. Evil lurks in dark places."

"Yes, Nainai. I promise."

Wei hugged her grandmother tightly.

"What you all are about to do will put you in great danger," Nainai said. "Don't hesitate, be quick and sure. Mistakes will get you killed. Now go, all of you, before I change my mind!"

"Thank you, Mrs. Sung," Lucas said before following the others out the door.

Back outside, Rafe was the first one to speak, "Well, that's it then. This is really going down."

There was no mistaking the apprehension in his friend's expression, but Lucas knew Rafe was as resolved as he was to rescue Mia no matter the danger.

"It won't be if we don't get a move on," Wei urged impatiently. "Come on."

The blazing summer sun had disappeared, replaced by a humid darkness. With Wei in the lead, they moved quickly through the maze of now empty streets back to her family's store.

"I thought this was the city that never sleeps," Rafe mused.

Wei whipped her head around, putting a finger to her lips—the unmistakable sign for "shut up."

"Sorry," Rafe whispered. "My bad."

When they arrived at the store, Wei asked quietly, "Are you sure you want to do this?"

"We have no other choice," Lucas answered. "We're all committed, right?"

Lily, Rafe, and Daniel nodded in agreement.

"Okay, here goes nothing," Wei said and entered the store.

Lucas' senses were triggered the moment he walked into the store. As the group made their way down to the basement to the room of purses, the sensations grew stronger. As he entered the purse room, his heart began racing.

Wei went straight to the door. She pushed the purses stacked against it to the side. She reached for the golden chain and held up the small key.

"After I unlock this door, you're on your own, okay?"

"I understand. Consider your debt paid in full. Thank you for bringing us this far."

When Wei slipped the key into the lock and turned it, the door popped open, releasing a cold blast of air. Lucas inhaled a foul and familiar scent from the darkened crawlspace. There was no turning back now.

"Can I come too?" a small voice sounded, surprising them all.

Whirling around, Wei snapped, "Junjie, what are you doing here?"

"Be still!" Lucas whispered fiercely.

Wei and Junjie froze, responding to Lucas' direct command.

"What is it?" Daniel demanded.

Lucas's whole body tensed. His senses fired on red alert. It was just like the day his father had been murdered. Overwhelming, but this time, he knew how to control his gift. He had mastered his physical response, so he no longer experienced muscle paralysis or loss of speech when his senses were triggered like this. Speaking to no one in particular, he announced, "Upstairs. I can smell them."

"Who?"' Wei demanded.

"Death."

"What are you talking about?" Wei demanded.

As soon as the words came out of Lucas' mouth, he regretted his bluntness. There wasn't time for explanations. They needed to get out of the purse room immediately.

"Everyone in the crawlspace, now!"

Rafe dove through the door immediately, followed by Lily and Daniel. Wei and Junjie went the opposite way and hugged the far wall. Lucas could see both were panic-stricken. He extended his hand.

"Wei, you have to trust me," Lucas said firmly.

"No! Whoever is up there is after you, not me and Junjie."

"It won't matter. They will kill you and your brother," Lucas declared. "Please."

Still, she remained flattened against the wall holding Junjie's hand. Her indecision was written plainly in the furrows of her brow.

"We should go with him," Junjie said softly.

Obviously surprised at his urging, Wei looked down at her brother. When she returned her gaze to Lucas, he extended his hand again, mouthing the words, "Trust me."

Wei nodded her head. Her indecision was replaced by determination.

"Let's go, little brother!"

Wei led Junjie to the door and pushed him through. Before diving into the passage after her brother, she turned back to Lucas.

"You better not let me down," she warned.

Lucas followed her in and slammed the door behind him. He had crawled about twenty paces through the narrow tunnel when it dipped sharply. He slid a short distance and was dumped unceremoniously into a larger chamber. He stood and dug in his pocket for his cell. When he clicked it on, the faint light from the screen barely illuminated the chamber. But it was enough for him to see that everyone had made it through in one piece.

"We need more light down here," Lucas suggested, turning on his cell's flashlight.

Everyone except Junjie pulled out a phone and followed suit.

"What now?" Lily asked.

"We keep moving," he said. "Rafe, you got this?"

"Relax, man." Rafe pointed to his head. "It's all right here."

Rafe took the passageway to his left at a dead run. He never paused, anticipating every zig and zag of the path. Lucas knew his friend's gift of knowledge would guide him in expertly navigating the underground maze. When his razor-sharp sense of smell was triggered, Lucas knew the demons were gaining ground. Suddenly a bitter blast of air rushed through the passage. Lucas grimaced. The stink was overwhelming. Lucas' lungs burned, and running became increasingly difficult. His ears rang painfully with the Scáths awful shrieks.

When Junjie stumbled, Daniel reached for him and hoisted the little boy on his back.

Junjie whimpered, "I want to go home."

"Hang on, little man," Daniel urged.

"I promise I'll get you home, Junjie," Lucas assured before continuing down the passage.

When it snaked to the right, Lucas halted abruptly. It was a large room with thick concrete walls and overhead fluorescent lights that colored the space a sickly green.

"Why are we stopping?" Lily asked.

"Dead end, man," Rafe said, shaking his head.

"We have to go back, find another way," Wei pushed.

Lucas put Junjie down, and the little boy ran to his sister.

"We can't," Lucas said. "The only way out of this is forward."

"I thought you knew where you were going." Lucas admonished.

"This wall wasn't in the schematics," Rafe explained, tapping the concrete. "It must have been put up after they were drawn."

"We just need to find a way to get through that wall," Lucas declared.

"Last time I checked, people couldn't walk through concrete walls," Rafe retorted.

"I'm not giving up, and I won't let you either!"

"Lucas is right," Daniel pressed. "We can do this. We just need to work together."

"Everyone take a part of the wall; maybe there is a trip lever or hidden door or something," Lucas said, running his hands over the wall.

Each one took a part of the wall. After a thorough and frantic search, no escape had been discovered.

"It's no use," Rafe said. "We have to think of something else."

Peering into the passage behind him, Lucas recognized familiar silver lights twisting and writhing at great speed. They were out of time. He looked over at Wei, who was crying now. He had broken his promise. Wei and Junjie wouldn't be going back home. Worse, he had failed his mother, his sister, and his friends. He was startled by his dark thoughts when Wei slammed both of her hands against the concrete wall.

"Please, God," she cried. "Don't let us die. Give us a miracle!"

Lucas was dumbfounded when the concrete wall began to shimmer and move. He watched as Wei's hands passed through the wall as if it was liquid. Wei didn't even notice. Her head was bowed, and her lips were moving furiously in Chinese.

"Whoa!" Rafe exclaimed.

"Wei!" Lucas shouted. "Look at your hands."

Wei opened her eyes and inhaled sharply. She pulled her hands out of the shimmering wall and then pushed them back in again.

"Whatever you're doing, keep doing it," Lucas urged.

Wei's furrowed brow returned as she concentrated on the wall. The shimmer in the wall continued to grow until there was an opening large enough for them to pass through.

"That's freakin' amazing," Rafe whispered in awe.

"Go," Lucas shouted.

Daniel grabbed Junjie and passed through the wall to the other side. Rafe and Lily followed. The shimmering opening started to shrink.

"Go," Wei pleaded. "I don't know how much longer I can hold this open."

"I'm not leaving you," he answered. "We go through together."

Blinding silver lights exploded in the room. Lucas turned back toward the passage. Two beautiful, silver masked Scàths were gliding toward him. Lucas grabbed Wei and threw them both through the opening. It immediately closed behind them. It didn't stop the demons; they passed through the concrete wall easily.

"Oh no, you don't!" Wei shouted, rising to her knees.

She clapped her hands. A pulsing barrier of shimmering golden light appeared between them and the demons. The Scáths hissed in anger. No matter how hard they tried, the demons couldn't breach the barrier. Screaming, they turned and disappeared back through the concrete wall.

"They're going for reinforcement! We gotta move, Rafe," Lucas commanded.

He reached for Wei and helped her to stand. She wavered and lost her balance. Lucas caught her and hugged her closely.

"What you just did is the most amazing thing I have ever seen. And I will explain everything, I promise, but we can't stay here."

Wei tensed and pushed away from Lucas. "I feel like I just got a swift kick in the gut. My whole body is buzzing with electricity, and I have no idea what just happened to me. I'm not going any further until somebody talks."

"You have a gift, Wei, a very powerful one. God has given you the ability to do the miraculous, the impossible," Lily explained gently.

"Yeah, like that beautiful hole you made in that wall," Rafe smiled.

"I am freaking out right now!" Wei exclaimed.

"I know you're scared, Wei, but Lucas is right; if the Scáths catch up to us, they will kill us," Daniel added.

"Wei," Lucas urged. "I need to find my mom, please,"

"Okay, but once we're out of here, you all have a lot of explaining to do," she said.

"Thank you," he offered. Turning to Rafe, he asked, "Where to?"

"If my calculations are correct, and they usually are, we are now in one of the sub-basements of the Dragoni building," Rafe boasted.

"There's the hallway in my dream," Lily pointed.

Just as she had described, the hallway was white, and a metal door stood at the far end. Lucas had no doubt that the path ahead would lead to Mia. He led them to the door. Along the way, the bright fluorescent lights flickered. It was so quiet. He paused at the door and reached for the knob.

"Whatever might be behind this door, no matter what happens, we stay together, okay?"

"We're right behind you, boss," Rafe assured.

Lucas opened the door, and the Sorcha entered the unknown.

Chapter 33

"Aunt Scarlett?"

Lucas struggled to believe the truth in front of him. She was a carbon copy of his mother, and yet it wasn't her. Same face and body, but instead of Mia's pale blonde hair, this woman had fiery auburn hair. Her long black dress accentuated the paleness of her face and willowy frame. Purple bruises mottled her lower jaw, and dark shadows smudged her stormy blue eyes.

"But you're supposed to be dead," Lily mused, moving close to Lucas.

"I'm afraid I am very much alive." The woman smiled faintly. "And I would recognize you two anywhere; you're the images of your parents."

"Where is my mother?" Lucas asked. "Is she alive?"

"For now, but she's in trouble, and so am I," she answered. "I managed to escape the room where I've been held captive and made it down here. Wherever here is! I was going to go get help. And here you are."

"How long have you been here?" Lily asked, studying her aunt closely.

"Too long," Scarlett frowned. "It doesn't matter anymore. All that matters is that we need to get Mia out before the worst happens."

"What do you mean? The worst?" Lucas questioned abruptly.

Scarlet looked directly at him and said, "He wants your mother to bear him a child."

"That's just crazy!" Lucas announced in disbelief.

"Cain is a demon. Is that even possible?" Lily asked.

"Very much so. I know because that's what he did to me. You see, the union of a Scáth and a Sorcha produces a child of great power and strength. And when that child becomes an adult, well, let's just say he or she is invincible. They are known as Mescáths—both darkness and light."

"He's creating an army," Lucas said.

"Yes, it's been his plan all along."

Lucas swore. "I'm not gonna let that happen. He's not laying a hand on her."

"Can you take us to her, Aunt Scarlett?" Lily asked.

"Yes, but you don't understand; we can't beat him. Cain is too powerful. And he was surely alerted to your presence the moment you entered his domain. His Scáths are everywhere."

"Yeah, we've met a few already."

"So much for a surprise rescue, huh?" Rafe smirked.

"I'm glad he knows," Lucas said. "We don't fear him."

"Maybe you should," Scarlett admonished.

"You don't have to come with us," Lucas returned. "Just point us in the right direction."

"No, I'm not leaving my sister behind," she announced. "It's time for me to get back into the fight."

"Stay sharp," he warned. "Scáths are crawling all over this place."

Scarlett led them from the room through a series of short hallways to an elevator.

"This will take us deep underground. That's where we'll find Mia," she suggested. "I suggest you hold on; this thing moves fast."

Scarlett wasn't kidding, Lucas thought. The elevator plummeted to its destination. When the doors slid open to reveal a long torchlit tunnel, he said, "Stick close. We don't get separated. Daniel?"

"I've got him," Daniel answered, holding Junjie's hand. "I'll keep him safe."

Leaving the elevator, they followed Scarlett deeper into the tunnel.

"Anyone else think it's weird that we haven't run into a single demon since we left the room upstairs?" Rafe asked.

"Well, I, for one, am happy about that!" Wei returned.

"They're here, even if we can't see them," Daniel said. "Just watching us, waiting."

"Be quiet," Lily shushed. "Do you hear that?"

There was a faint sound of moaning echoing off the rock. Lucas couldn't quite make it out, but with each step, the sound grew stronger.

"Yeah, it sounds like someone is in great pain," Lucas answered grimly.

"It's Mom. I know it, Luc," Lily whispered frantically. "We have to find her."

"It's coming from that direction," Daniel pointed to another tunnel that branched off from the one they were in. At the entrance to the tunnel, carved into the rock, were two intricately detailed serpents, intertwined, fangs exposed, that formed an archway.

"We can't go that way!" Scarlett declared, moving to stand in front of the group, her arms spread wide. "They will catch us for sure!"

"We have no choice," Lucas answered.

"You don't understand," Scarlett pleaded. "That path will lead you straight to Cain."

"We do understand, Aunt Scarlett. We all knew this rescue was going to be dangerous. But we're committed. We aren't gonna turn back, no matter what you say," Lucas declared.

Lily added, "Look, you got us here, so you don't have to go any farther if you don't want to. You've done enough."

Scarlett began to weep, but she dropped her arms and moved aside.

"Lily and I will take the lead. Rafe, you bring up the rear," he directed, then glanced at Lily. "Let's go get Mom."

He took his sister's hand, and together they entered the tunnel. They left Scarlett behind and moved into the passage. Lucas frowned. There was still no sign of any Scáths, even though the air reeked with their stench. There was no doubt that the woman moaning was Mia; her voice was unmistakable now that they were drawing closer. Reaching the end of the tunnel, they found a massive gate fashioned from black iron. When Mia's moan turned became a scream, Lucas and Lily ran through the gate into a large circular arena.

It resembled a coliseum from ancient times where spectators would come to view the bloody fights of seasoned gladiators. There was no visible ceiling, only obsidian blackness above. When a single light shone from above and bore down on a spot in the center of the arena, Lucas saw his mother. On her knees in the dirt, Mia's scream was once again a painful moan. Her outstretched arms, riddled with angry welts and purple bruises, were manacled in heavy irons. The thick links in the chains were attached to spikes embedded in the ground. When she lifted her face, Lucas shuddered with rage. One eye was swollen shut, the other black and blue, and blood trickled from the side of her mouth. Lucas let go of Lily's hand and ran to his mother.

"Mom!"

"No! Don't come any closer."

Blue flames ignited in front of him, encircling the space around Mia. Daniel and Rafe pulled him back. Fuming, he jerked away from his friends.

"Let me go!"

"This is not the way," Daniel said tersely. "Keep it together."

He breathed deeply and shook it off. Daniel was right. He needed to keep his wits about him.

"Mom, we're gonna get you out of here. I promise."

"Lucas, Lily, you shouldn't have come. Cain is too powerful."

His eyes never wavering on his mom, he shouted, "Wei!"

"Here," she said, moving to stand beside him. "I'm here."

"I need you to find a way through these flames."

"You can't be serious!"

"Just like before. Focus on what you need."

"Okay, here goes nothing," she said, extending her hands toward the flames.

Nothing happened. If anything, they grew higher and more intense. The frigid heat emanating from the flames made him shiver.

"It's not working," Wei shouted.

"Keep trying, Wei." Daniel urged, coming up behind Wei. "I've got her, Lucas."

He knew Daniel was the best person to help Wei. His friend had placed his hands on Wei's shoulders and started to pray.

"Hang on, Mom. I will not leave this place without you," he vowed.

Suddenly, he struggled to keep his balance. His senses exploded with sensations. His stomach clenched, and he struggled to catch his breath. The temperature in the arena dropped drastically. He gagged and fought the urge to vomit. He remembered feeling like this only once before.

"Cain is here," he warned, battling to get himself back under control.

The sound of thunder rumbled low and angry. Silver-white lightning cracked, and a cloaked figure emerged from the smoke. He was accompanied by three others, wingless and clad in black leather. Dark green tattoos writhed around their exposed arms. Their eyes were glowing blue orbs, and their palms were crackling with blue flames. Lucas didn't have to wonder about them; he already knew. They were Mescáths!

Lucas recognized one immediately, unmistakable, with that black braid hanging down her back. It was his father's murderer. He forced himself to look away from the assassin and trained his gaze on Cain instead. The demon commander's leathery wings dragged the ground as he advanced. His crimson hair hung straight down his back. He wore the same silver faceplate and ornate ring of obsidian black as he had that day in the clearing. Cain moved through the fiery circle around Mia and stopped in front of Lucas. Only the flames were between them.

"What a touching family reunion," Cain remarked casually. "It almost brings me to tears."

To Lucas, the demon's voice felt like a dagger plunging into his ears. Knowing he must not panic, understanding he must now live out everything Nolan had taught him and all he believed to be truth, Lucas steeled himself and responded bravely.

"We don't fear you."

"Many before you have made the same mistake." Cain smiled. "So much like your father, quick to defend and protect. Will you die with as much bravado as your father did?"

"You forget you are standing in the presence of the Sorcha. Light obliterates darkness."

"Arrogance is the folly of youth, Lucas. I count only five in your number. Without the twelve, your power is no match for mine."

Cain waved his hand, and the flames dissipated. No barrier separated them now. Lucas felt the other Sorcha close ranks beside him.

"I have a little secret I've been keeping about the day Eli died. Would you like to hear it?" Cain teased. "No? Aren't you just a little bit curious?"

"I was there. I saw it all," Lucas gritted through his teeth. "She was the one who murdered him, but you were pulling all the strings! Hiding behind your minions just like you're doing now."

"Not hiding," Cain admonished. "Just waiting for the perfect time. Children!"

Cain and his demon assassins slowly removed the silver faceplates they wore. The truth revealed in that moment rocked him to his core.

"It can't be," Lucas whispered painfully.

The entire Talbot family stood before him, defiant and proud. Lucas couldn't help but take a step back. His best friend? Why hadn't he sensed the truth? His gift should have been triggered by the evil in the Talbot family. But he had missed it!

"Shocked? Well, of course you are, young Lucas. Don't blame yourself or your guardian for not knowing the truth about who and what we are. My children have their mothers' light within. It protects them, allowing them to remain hidden from you and your Dìonadain guardians. This is just one of the many reasons I created my children. And I? Well, long ago, my master, Lucifer, trained me in the high art of deception. And over the years, I have gotten very good at it. But, enough conversation, let me introduce you to my brothers and sisters."

Swooping down out of the nothingness above, Scáths landed all around the arena. Their shrieking chants had Lucas and the others covering their ears to muffle the painful sound. Wei pulled Junjie close, trying to shield him from the terrifying demons hissing at them.

"We can't beat them, Luc. There are too many," Lily said desperately.

"You should listen to your sister, Lucas. You cannot win this. Did you really think you could waltz right into my domain and take your mother from me? I am Cain, commander of the demon horde, the deliverer of darkness!"

The Scáths answered their master with frenzied shrieks. Lucas fought to stay focused and not let his riotous senses overwhelm him.

"Let my mother go, or I promise you'll have a fight you won't soon forget."

Cain laughed smugly, "I'll take that as an invitation."

He unhooked the clasp of his cloak, revealing a perfectly muscled physique, amazing in its vitality and strength. Like his children, green tattoos moved across his exposed chest, arms, and even his face. His eyes flamed, and he began a hideous chant.

"I think you riled him up pretty good," Rafe noted, moving to stand beside Lucas.

Lily, Wei, and Daniel joined them, creating a united front. The Sorcha, eyes wide open and hearts full, stood courageously in the face of the enemy.

"Daniel?"

"Right! Great and mighty God, Creator of all things, out of the belly of the beast, we cry. We believe," Daniel cried.

"Prayers are useless," Cain shouted. "You're in my house now!"

When Cain raised his hands, signaling the Scáth attack, Lucas and the others bellowed, "Dìonadain!"

Instantly, hundreds of glowing winged warriors thundered into the arena, surrounding the Sorcha in an orb of golden light. Swords and shields drawn, they took their battle stances, prepared for the onslaught of Scáths. Darkness met light, exploding in thousands of white-hot sparks. Scáths, tumbling and flying, fired their flaming darts. The Dìonadain, perfectly in sync, deflected their advances, using their weapons like warriors of old. The crash of Scáth on Dìonadain was deafening.

Nolan appeared within the impregnable fortress the Dìonadain had secured around the Sorcha, followed by Yona, Ira, and Jude. Another warrior blasted through the shimmering orb as Nolan commanded, "Agatha!"

Lucas couldn't help but be amazed. She was extraordinary, frightfully intimidating, and flawlessly beautiful at the same time. When the angel moved to protect Wei, he understood that this warrior was his new friend's guardian.

Drawing their gleaming swords, the five guardians drove them simultaneously into the ground, widening the golden orb of protection. The flaming circle surrounding Mia was snuffed out. Lucas and Lily ran to Mia. Weak and injured, she could barely stand.

Nolan rushed to Lucas' side, "We will lead you from the fray. Andreas and his warriors will remain in the battle."

"Got it," he answered, anxious to leave the frenzied mob of Scáths behind.

The Dìonadain retrieved their weapons, ready to defend the Sorcha. "Follow me!" Nolan ordered.

He and Lily, supporting Mia, followed Nolan and Jude. Daniel, carrying Junjie on his back, Rafe, Wei, and their guardians were right behind them. Three massive Dìonadain warriors outside the golden orb cut a path through the hissing Scáths barreling toward them. He marveled at their precision and skill. Four other warriors acted as the rear guard keeping the demons at bay. Once clear of the arena, the golden orb dissipated, and the warriors returned to the fray. The Sorcha and their guardians found their way back through the torchlit tunnel to the elevator.

"Scarlett," Mia said weakly.

His aunt had been waiting for their return.

"I'm here, Sister," Scarlet answered. "I'll take her."

The look in Scarlett's eye left no room for argument. He and Lily passed their mother into her sister's care.

"We made it," Lily whispered.

"We're not out of this yet," Lucas warned.

When the elevator doors slid open, another threat even more deadly than a room full of bloodthirsty Scáths was revealed.

Chapter 34

"I've been dreaming of this day, Sorcha scum," Lysha taunted.

The Dìonadain moved instantly to protect. Lysha stepped out of the elevator and began to circle the group slowly.

"I've waited so patiently for you, Lucas. Since the day I killed your pathetic Daddy in the snow. The beasts feasted on his flesh, but I was the one who took his life. He was my first." Caressing the crystal vial hanging around her neck, she continued, "I wear his blood as a reminder of my power and your destruction."

Cold rage coursed through Lucas.

"I'll kill you myself, demon," he spat and sprang toward Lysha.

Nolan restrained him and warned, "Not yet."

"Did you know, Lucas, that a Dìonadain cannot attack unless he is provoked? I would have to hurt you before Nolan would even move to protect you," Lysha scorned. "Isn't that right, commander? I wonder, is it control or fear keeping you silent? Your race doesn't deserve to be called warriors!"

"My sweet girl, please, stop this!" Scarlett implored. "Your father has blinded you with his lies."

"Don't beg, Mother," she said with contempt, not sparing a glance for Scarlett.

"Mother?" Lucas whispered under his breath.

The noise of the ongoing battle in the arena stormed closer. The Scáths were drawn to the Sorcha like moths to a flame. Lucas knew they were running out of time. Desperately, he looked at Aiden standing silently outside the elevator. He was the one he had trusted above all others, the one who had unlocked his sister's heart. All he received was a malicious glare.

"Lysha, let us pass," Scarlet cried.

"Silence!" Lysha shouted. "That is not my name. I am the darkness before midnight. I am Keket!"

"There is good in you. You are a part of me. Find the light within you," Scarlett continued to plead. "You don't have to do this."

Lucas watched as Keket's countenance changed. Maybe her mother's plea had placed a small bit of doubt in her daughter's heart. Her body shuddered.

"Forgive me," Lysha sobbed.

Scarlett went to her daughter. His aunt's relieved and grateful smile beamed on her tear-stained face as she embraced Lysha.

"I love you, dearest mother," Lysha said softly.

The crack of Scarlett's neck snapping in two echoed throughout the tunnel. Horrified, Lucas watched his aunt's limp body slip to the floor. The look of pure and unadulterated satisfaction on Lysha's face rocked him to his very core. She was pure evil.

Mia screamed in disbelief. Lucas turned to comfort her, but Daniel was already there. His friend held his mother, soothing

Mia with soft words while she continued to sob. Lucas turned to Lysha's demon brother. For just a moment, Aiden's expression showed his confusion and disbelief. A tiny chink in his armor of evil was all Lucas needed.

"Come on, brother. This isn't you. Let us pass."

"Please, Aiden, do it for me," Lily begged, tears flowing freely down her face. "You're breaking my heart."

"Remember who we are, brother," Keket warned.

Lucas watched his friend meet his sister's challenging gaze. When Aiden's eyes flamed intensely, he realized his friend was gone, leaving a vile demon left in his place. Then it was chaos!

Jude thrust his sword deep into the stone floor, creating a glowing barricade around the Sorcha. Sister and brother, both burning fiercely, began a violent spin around the group, which created an ear-piercing hum. Lucas' agony was so excruciating that he felt his brain cells start to implode as he grabbed his ears. Desperately, he cried out, "God, help me."

Suddenly, the pain disappeared, and the debilitating hum became a dull echo. When he opened his eyes, everything was happening in slow motion. Like viewing a movie frame by frame, he watched the Talbots spin and the Dìonadain track their movements. When Aiden and Keket stopped suddenly and flung their fiery darts, Lucas was instantly jarred back into real time. Outside the protective barrier, Tov, Yona, Ira, and Agatha deflected the fast and furious shots of the Mescáth siblings. Nolan swung his armored shield in an arc over his head, sending bolts of white-hot light toward the Talbots. One nicked Keket's shoulder, causing Aiden to turn toward Nolan's assault.

"You will pay for that, Dìonadain," Aiden threatened.

Aiden's palms roared with purple-blue flames, and he pummeled Nolan's shield with darts, sending the guardian to his knees with the force of his blows. And then a great roar signaled Kayanga's entry into the fight. He crashed into Ira, sending sparks into the air at impact. The Dìonadain guardian had a clear advantage. Ira was quicker, deflecting the Mescáth's blue bolts easily, even gracefully. Swinging his radiant sword, Ira aimed for Kayanga's broad chest. Lucas knew the power of the Light encased in a Dìonadain warrior's sword was the only thing able to bind a Scáth. He hoped it would do the same with a Mescáth. But the Mescáth was quick. He jumped over Ira, landing behind him. Ira whirled around a second too late and was unsuccessful in repelling Kayanga's attack. Struck from behind, Ira crumpled to the ground.

"No!" Daniel shouted.

Daniel broke through the barrier to reach his guardian. Lucas watched as Daniel tried to drag Ira back into the barricade. But the guardian would not budge.

"We have to help him!" Lily yelled, running to Daniel's aid.

Lily and Daniel had no idea how vulnerable they were at that moment. Jude moved to defend them. They could not see the danger, but Lucas could. The other guardians were busy fighting. Aiden and Lysha gave their brother the opportunity to move in for the kill. Lucas roared in anguish as deadly blue flames shot from the Mescáth's eyes. Out of nowhere, Aiden catapulted in front of Lily, receiving the full force of his brother's lethal attack. Aiden lay in a crumpled heap at Lily's feet. Lucas rushed to Lily's side while Jude flung two gleaming daggers toward Kayanga, hitting him square in the chest. Immobile, pinned to the stone wall, the Mescáth screamed in agony. Lucas was sure that Jude's daggers burned hot and deep. Then, Jude and Nolan pulled them back into the protective shield.

Keket roared with rage. One brother was bound, and the other was lying motionless on the stone floor. At that moment, the demon commander appeared in a flash of lightning. He rushed to gather Aiden in his arms.

"Finish them," Cain commanded.

Then, father and son were gone.

Lucas fell back a step when Lysha's entire body was consumed in blue flame, and Kayanga, ripping Jude's daggers from his body, joined his sister to fight. The Dìonadain sheathed their glowing broadswords, exchanging them for weapons designed for fighting in close quarters. They moved to repel what would surely be a vicious onslaught; Yona brandished two golden tomahawks, Tov, a pair of bladed sai, and Jude with his daggers. Agatha moved within the barrier to its center and drew her bow. Nolan circled the barrier reinforcing its power.

"You know what to do," he shouted to Lucas.

Lucas grabbed Wei's hand. "Can you stop her? Even for just a second, so we can get out of here?"

Wei nodded with determination in her dark eyes. "I'll try."

"Rafe, Lily, join hands with me. Focus all your energy on Wei. Daniel, start praying."

Beside Wei, Lucas could feel the electricity pulsing from her small frame. When she stretched her hands toward Lysha, Lucas emptied his mind of all thought and willed the power of the gift within him to strengthen Wei. Instantly, Lysha was incapacitated, bound by the light that was flowing through them and joining with Wei's. Without his sister, Kayanga was easily bound once again by the efforts of the Dìonadain guardians.

"It's working," Lucas encouraged. "You got this, Wei."

Wei moved one of her hands and placed it on the wall beside her. Just like before, wielding her gift, she created an opening big enough for the Sorcha to pass through. When she swayed, Agatha was at her side to steady her.

"Are you okay, little one?"

"I will be when you get me out of this mess," she retorted weakly. "Done," Agatha said, lifting Wei into her arms.

The great warrior moved through the shimmering door her charge had created. Wasting no time, Lucas turned to the others and shouted for them to follow. Before leaving, Lucas turned back toward Lysha, powerless in Wei's net.

"This is not over," he vowed.

"Far from it," she gritted through her teeth. "This is just the beginning, Sorcha!"

As he joined Nolan on the other side of the wall, the opening closed behind him.

"Most of the Scáths are bound," Nolan announced. "Our brothers will keep the rest busy until we are clear of danger. Ira?"

The glowing blue wounds covering Ira's body were slowly dissipating.

"I'll make it," Ira said, then tossed his head toward Daniel. "Especially with this one's faith."

"We must free ourselves from the power of Cain's dominion," Nolan commanded.

"Happy to oblige," Agatha responded.

The warrior drew her bow and notched it with a golden arrow. Aiming above her head, Agatha let her arrow fly. Whizzing through the obsidian darkness above, Agatha's golden arrow created a golden path to the surface and blue sky overhead.

"Wow, just when I think I've seen it all," Lucas mused.

Nolan smiled. "Let's go home, everyone."

The Dìonadain unfurled their wings and wrapped their charges within a cocoon of safety. And they were off! Soaring through the air, Lysha's last words echoed in Lucas' ears. He knew they were true. This was just the beginning.

Glossary

Elohim (el-o-heem)

Creator and Judge; He is the one and only true God; Elohim is the Hebrew word for God that occurs 2,000 times in the Old Testament. It also refers to the plurality within the Godhead (Genesis 1, Deuteronomy 4:39).

Yeshua (yēšūăʻ)

Elohim came to earth in human form in the embodiment of His Son, Jesus Christ. Yeshua is the Hebrew translation of Jesus—the light of the world. Christ chose twelve to follow Him (disciples) and be His light unto the world (John 3:16, John 8:12). Christ is the light.

Dìonadain (di-o-na-dane)

Gaelic word meaning "one who guards;" legion of angels created by Elohim; they act as Watchers, Guardians, Messengers, and Warriors of the light (Psalms 91:11, Matthew 26:53).

Simon the Zealot

One of the twelve disciples (original Sorcha) chosen by Jesus Christ; tradition says he was martyred with a saw in Caistor, Lincolnshire, Britain, around 61 AD (Matthew 10:2–4, Luke 6:16).

Sorcha (sor-sha)

Gaelic word meaning "light" (not dark); twelve human beings, possessing supernatural gifts, created by God and chosen to embody the power of His light in each generation (Genesis 1:26–28, Matthew 5:14–16, Matthew 10:2–4, 2 Peter 1:19–21).

Gifts of the Sorcha

The Dreamer (Daniel 1:17, Acts 2:17)
The Crafter (Exodus 31:1–11, 2 Chronicles 2:12)
The Perceiver (1 Corinthians 12:10, 1 John 4:1–6)
The Believer (1 Corinthians 12:9, Hebrews 11:1)
The Healer (Acts 3:1–10, 1 Corinthians 12:28)
The Wielder (Acts 5:12, 19:11)
The Knower (Psalm 119:66, 1 Corinthians 12:8)
The Leader (2 Chronicles 1:7–12, Romans 12:6–8)
The Speaker (Mark 16:17–18, Acts 2:1–12)
The Warrior (Judges 13:24; 16:28; Philippians 4:13)
The Exiler (Mark 9:29, Luke 10:17)
The Psalter (2 Chronicles 20:21, Psalm 68:25)

Lucifer

Hebrew word meaning "destroyer;" the fallen angel who rebelled against God; the prince of darkness; roams the earth seeking to destroy God's creation, His light, and the Sorcha (Revelation 9:11, Isaiah 14:12–15, 1 Peter 5:8–9).

Scàth (skahth)

Gaelic word meaning "shadow;" fallen angels who rebelled with Lucifer against God; warriors of destruction; demons and malevolent spirits (Ephesians 6:12, Jude 1:6, Revelation 12:9–11).

Mescàth (me-skahth)

Beings produced by the union of Scàth and Sorcha; at war with what lives within them, light and dark (Genesis 6:4).

Printed in the USA
CPSIA information can be obtained
at www.ICGtesting.com
LVHW021120261023
762202LV00015B/673